Those Who S

And Eleven Other Stories

Perceval Gibbon

Alpha Editions

This edition published in 2023

ISBN : 9789357946582

Design and Setting By
Alpha Editions
www.alphaedis.com
Email - info@alphaedis.com

Contents

I

THOSE WHO SMILED

From the great villa, marble-white amid its yews and cedars, in which the invaders had set up their headquarters, the two officers the stout, formidable German captain and the young Austrian lieutenant went together through the mulberry orchards, where the parched grass underfoot was tiger-striped with alternate sun and shadow. The hush of the afternoon and the benign tyranny of the North Italian sun subdued them; they scarcely spoke as they came through the ranks of fruit-laden trees to the low embankment where the last houses of the village tailed out beside the road.

"So ist's gut!" said Captain Hahn then. "We are on time nicely on time!" He climbed the grassy bank to the road and paused, his tall young companion beside him. "Halt here," he directed; "we shall see everything from here."

He suspired exhaustively in the still, strong heat, and took possession of the scene with commanding, intolerant eyes. He was a man in the earliest years of middle life, short, naturally full-bodied, and already plethoric with undisciplined passions and appetites. His large sanguine face had anger and impatience for an habitual expression; he carried a thick bamboo cane, with which he lashed the air about him in vehement gesticulation as he spoke; all his appearance and manner were an incarnate ejaculation. Beside him, and by contrast with the violence of his effect, his companion was eclipsed and insignificant, no more than a shape of a silent young man, slender in his close-fitting grey uniform, with a swart, immobile face intent upon what passed.

It was the hour that should crown recent police activities of Captain Hahn with the arrest of an absconding forced-laborer, who, having escaped from his slave-gang behind the firing-line on the Piave, had been traced to his father's house in the village. An Italian renegade, a discovery of Captain Hahn's, had served in the affair; a whole machinery of espionage and secret treachery had been put in motion; and now Lieutenant Jovannic, of the Austrian Army, was to be shown how the German method ensured the German success. Even as they arrived upon the road they saw the carefully careless group of lounging soldiers, like characters on a stage "discovered" at the rise of the curtain, break into movement and slouch with elaborate purposelessness to surround the cottage. Their corporal remained where he was, leaning against a wall in the shade, eating an onion and ready to give the signal with his whistle; he did not glance towards the two watching officers. To Lieutenant Jovannic, the falsity and unreality of it all were as strident as a brass band; yet in the long vista of the village street, brimful of sun and silence, the few people who moved upon their business went indifferently as shadows upon a wall. An old man trudged in the wake of a laden donkey; a girl bore water-buckets slung from a yoke; a child was sweeping up dung. None turned a head.

"Sieh' 'mal!" chuckled Captain Harm joyously. "Here comes my Judas!"

From the door of the cottage opposite them, whose opening showed dead black against the golden glare without, came the renegade, pausing upon the threshold to speak a last cheery word to those within. Poor Jovannic, it was at this moment that, to the fantastic and absurd character of the whole event, as arranged by Captain Hahn, there was now added a quality of sheer horror. The man upon the threshold was not like a man; vastly pot-bellied, so that the dingy white of his shirt was only narrowly framed by the black of his jacket, swollen in body to the comic point, collarless, with a staircase of unshaven chins crushed under his great, jovial, black-mustached face, the creature yet moved on little feet like a spinning-top on its point, buoyantly, with the gait of a tethered balloon. He had the gestures, the attitude upon the threshold, of a jolly companion; when he turned, his huge, fatuous face was amiable, and creased yet with the dregs of smiles. From the breast of his jacket he exhumed a white handkerchief. "Arrivederci!" he called for the last time to the interior of the house; someone within answered pleasantly; then deliberately, with a suggestion of ceremonial and significance in the gesture, he buried the obscenity of his countenance in the handkerchief and blew his nose as one blows upon a trumpet.

"Tadellos!" applauded Captain Hahn enthusiastically. "He invented that signal himself; he's the only man in the village who carries a handkerchief. Und jetzt geht's los!"

And forthwith it went 'los'; the farce quickened to drama. A couple of idle soldiers, rifle-less and armed only with the bayonets at their belts, had edged near the door; others had disappeared behind the house; Judas, mincing on his feet like a soubrette, moved briskly away; and the corporal, tossing the wreck of his onion from him, blew a single note on his whistle. The thin squeal of it was barely audible thirty yards away, yet it seemed to Jovannic as though the brief jet of sound had screamed the afternoon stillness to rags. The two slack-bodied soldiers were suddenly swift and violent; drawn bayonet in hand, they plunged together into the black of the door and vanished within. Down the long street the old man let the donkey wander on and turned, bludgeon in hand, to stare; the child and girl with the buckets were running, and every door and window showed startled heads. From within the cottage came uproar screams, stamping, and the crash of furniture overset.

"You see?" There was for an instant a school-masterly touch in Captain Hahn. "You see? They've got him; not a hitch anywhere. Organization, method, foresight; I tell you."

From the dark door there spouted forth a tangle of folk to the hot dust of the road that rose like smoke under their shifting feet. The soldiers had the fighting, plunging prisoner; between their bodies, and past those of the men and women who had run out with them, his young, black-avised face surged and raged in an agony of resistance, lifting itself in a maniac effort to be free, then dragged and beaten down. An old woman tottered on the fringes of the struggle, crying feebly; others, young and old, wept or screamed; a soldier, bitten in the hand, cried an oath and gave way. The prisoner tore himself all but loose.

"Verfluchter Schweinhund!" roared Captain Halm suddenly. He had stood till then intent, steeped in the interest of the thing, but aloof as an engineer might watch the action of his machine till the moment at which it fails. Suddenly, a dangerous compact figure of energy, he dashed across the road, shouting. "You'd resist arrest, would you?" he was vociferating. His bamboo cane, thick as a stout thumb, rose and fell twice smashingly; Jovannic saw the second blow go home upon the hair above the prisoner's forehead. The man was down in an instant, and the soldiers were over him and upon him. Captain Hahn, cane in hand, stood like a victorious duelist.

The old woman the prisoner's mother, possibly, had staggered back at the thrash of the stick, and now, one hand against the wall of the house and one to her bosom, she uttered a thin, moaning wail. At that voice of pain Jovannic started; it was then that he realized that the other voices, those that had screamed and those that had cursed, had ceased; even the prisoner, dragged to his feet and held, made no sound. For an instant the disorder of his mind made it appear that the sun-drowned silence had never really been broken, that all that had happened had been no more than a flash of nightmare. Then he perceived.

Captain Hahn, legs astraddle, a-bulge with the sense of achievement, was giving orders.

"Tie the dog's hands," he commanded. "Tie them behind his back! Cord? Get a cord somewhere, you fool! Teach the hound to resist, I will! Hurry now!"

The prisoner's face was clear to see, no longer writhen and crazy. For all the great bruise that darkened his brow, it was composed to a calm as strange as the calm of death. He looked directly at Captain Hahn, seeming to listen and understand; and when that man of wrath ceased to speak, his rather sullen young face, heavy-browed, thick-mouthed, relaxed from its quiet. He smiled!

Beyond him, against the yellow front of the cottage, an old man, bareheaded, with a fleshless skull's face, had passed his arm under that of the old woman and was supporting her. The lieutenant saw that bony mask, too, break into a smile. He looked at the others, the barefoot girls and the women; whatever the understanding was, they shared it; each oval, sun-tinged face, under its crown of jet hair, had the same faint light of laughter of tragic, inscrutable mirth, at once contemptuous and pitiful. Along the street, folk had come forth from their doors and stood watching in silence.

"That's right, Corporal; tie him up," came Captain Harm's thickish voice, rich and fruity with the assurance of power. "He won't desert again when I've done with him and he won't resist either."

It was not for him to see, in those smiles, that the helpless man, bound for the flogging-posts of the "Dolina of Weeping," where so many martyrs to that goddess which is Italy had expiated in torment their crimes of loyalty and courage, had already found a refuge beyond the reach of his spies and torturers that he opposed even now to bonds and blows a resistance that no armed force could overcome. If he saw the smiles at all, he took them for a tribute to his brisk, decisive action with the cane.

"And now, take him along," he commanded, when the prisoner's wrists were tied behind him to his satisfaction. "And stand no nonsense! If he won't walk make him!"

The corporal saluted. "Zu Befehl, Herr Hauptmann," he deferred, and the prisoner was thrust down the bank. The old mother, her head averted, moaned softly. The old man, upholding her, smiled yet his death's-head smile.

The tiger-yellow of the grass between the trees was paler, the black was blacker, as the two officers returned across the fields; to the hush of afternoon had succeeded the briskness of evening. Birds were awake and a breeze rustled in the branches; and Captain Hahn was strongly moved to speech.

"System," he said explosively. "All war all life comes down to system. You get your civil labor by system; you keep it by system. Now, that little arrest."

It was as maddening as the noise of a mouse in a wainscot. Jovannic wanted not so much to think as to dwell in the presence of his impressions. Those strange, quiet smiles!

"Did you see them laughing?" he interrupted. "Smiling, I should say. After you had cut the fellow down they stopped crying out and they smiled."

"Ha! Enough to make 'em," said Captain Hahn. "I laughed myself. All that play-acting before his people, and then, with two smacks kaput! Fellow looked like a fool! It's part of the system, you see."

"That was it, you think?" The explanation explained nothing to Jovannic, least of all his own sensations when the sudden surrender and the sad, pitying mirth had succeeded to the struggle and the violence. He let Captain Hahn preach his German gospel of system on earth and organization to man, and walked beside him in silence, with pensive eyes fixed ahead, where the prisoner and his escort moved in a plodding black group.

He had not that gift of seeing life and its agents in the barren white light of his own purposes which so simplified things for Captain Hahn. He was a son of that mesalliance of nations which was Austria-Hungary Slavs, their slipping grasp clutching at eternity, Transylvanians, with pervert Latin ardors troubling their blood, had blended themselves in him; and he was young. Life for him was a depth not a surface, as for Captain Hahn; facts were but the skeleton of truth; glamour clad them and made them vital. He had been transferred to the Italian front from Russia, where his unripe battalion had lain in reserve throughout his service; his experiences of the rush over the Isonzo, of the Italian debacle and the occupation of the province of Friuli, lay undigested on his mental stomach. It was as though by a single violent gesture he had translated himself from the quiet life in his regiment, which had become normal and familiar, to the hush and mystery of the vast Italian plain, where the crops grew lavishly as weeds and the trees shut out the distances.

The great villa, whither they were bound, had a juncture of antique wall, pierced with grilles of beaten iron; its gate, a delicacy of filigree, let them through to the ordered beauty of the lawns, over which the mansion presided, a pale, fine presence of a house. Hedges of yew, like walls of ebony, bounded the principal walks. The prisoner and the retinue of soldiers that dignified him went ahead; the two officers, acknowledging the crash of arms of the sentry's salute at the gate, followed. The improvised prison was in the long wing of the building that housed the stables. They took the crackling pebble path that led to it.

"Nu!" Captain Hahn slacked his military gait at one of the formal openings in the wall of yews that shut them from the lawns before the great housed serene white front. "The women see?"

But Jovannic had already seen the pair, arms joined, who paced upon the side-lawn near at hand and had now stopped to look towards them. It was the old Contessa, who owned the house and still occupied a part of it, and the Contessina, her daughter. He knew the former as a disconcerting and never disconcerted specter of an aged lady, with lips that trembled and eyes that never faltered, and the latter as a serious, silent, tall girl with the black hair and oval Madonna face of her country and he knew her, too, as a vague and aching disturbance in his mind, a presence that troubled his leisure.

"You make your war here as sadly as a funeral," said Captain Hahn. "A fresh and joyous war—that's what it ought to be! Now, in Flanders, we'd have had that girl in with us at the mess." He laughed his rich, throaty laugh that seemed to lay a smear of himself over the subject of his mirth. "That at the very least!" he added.

Jovannic could only babble protestingly. "She she" he began in a flustered indignation. Captain Hahn laughed again. He had the advantage of the single mind over the mind divided against itself.

At the stables the sergeant of the guard received the prisoner. The redness of the sunset that dyed the world was over and about the scene. The sergeant, turning out upon the summons of the sentry, showed himself as an old Hungarian of the regular army, hairy as a Skye terrier, with the jovial blackguard air of his kind. He turned slow, estimating eyes on the bound prisoner.

"What is it?" he inquired.

"Deserter that's what it is," replied Captain Hahn sharply; he found the Austrian soldiers insufficiently respectful. "Lock him up safely, you understand. He'll go before the military tribunal to-morrow. Jovannic, just see to signing the papers and all that, will you?"

"At your orders, Herr Hauptmann," deferred Jovannic formally.

"Right," said Captain Hahn. "See you later, then." He swung off towards the front of the great mansion. Jovannic turned to his business of consigning the prisoner to safe keeping.

"You can untie his hands now," he said to the men of the escort as the sergeant moved away to fetch the committal book. The sergeant turned at his words.

"Plenty of time for that," he said in his hoarse and too familiar tones. "It's me that's responsible for him, isn't it? Well, then, let them stay tied up till I've had a look at him. I know these fellows I do."

"He can't get away from here," began Jovannic impatiently; but the old sergeant lifted a vast gnarled hand and wagged it at him with a kind of elderly rebuke.

"They're getting away in dozens every day," he rumbled. He put his hands on the silent man and turned him where he stood to face the light. "Yes," he said; "you've been knocking him about, too!"

The man had spoken no word; he showed now to the flush of the evening a face young and strongly molded, from which all passion, all force, seemed to have been drawn in and absorbed. It was calm as the face of a sleeper is calm;

only the mark of Captain Hahn's blow, the great swollen bruise on the brow, touched it with a memory of violence. His eyes traveled beyond Jovannic and paused, looking. Upon the pebble path beside the screen of yews a foot sounded; Jovannic turned.

It was the Contessina; she came hurrying towards them. Jovannic saluted. Only two or three times had he stood as close to her as then; and never before had he seen her swift in movement, or anything but grave and measured in gait, gesture and speech. He stared in surprise at her tall slenderness as it stood in relief against the rose and bronze of the west.

"It is" she was a little breathless. "It is yes! young Luigi!" The prisoner, silent till then, stirred and made some little noise of acquiescence. Behind him, still holding to the cord that bound his wrists, his two stolid guards stared uncomprehendingly; the old sergeant, his face one wrinkled mass of bland knowingness, stood with his thumbs in his belt and his short, fat legs astraddle. She leaned forward she seemed to sway like a wind-blown stalk and stared at the prisoner's quiet face. Jovannic saw her lips part in a movement of pain. Then her face came round to him.

"You, oh!" she gasped at him. "You haven't, you didn't strike him?"

Jovannic stared at her. He understood nothing. Granted that she knew the man, as no doubt she knew every peasant of the village, he still didn't understand the touch of agony in her manner and her voice.

"No, signorina," he answered stiffly. "I have not touched him. In fact, I was ordering him to be unbound."

But Her eyes traveled again to the prisoner's bruised and defaced brow; she was breathing quickly, like a runner. "Who, then? Who has?"

The old sergeant wagged his disreputable head. "German handwriting, that is, my young lady," he croaked. "That's how our German lords and masters curse them! write their Gott mit uns! The noble Captain Hahn I knew as soon as I saw it!"

"Shut up, you!" ordered Jovannic, with the parade-snarl in his voice. "And now, untie that man!"

He flung out a peremptory hand; in the girl's presence he meant to have an end of the sergeant's easy manners. But now it was she who astonished him by intervening.

"No!" she cried. "No!"

She moved a swift step nearer to the bound man, her arms half outspread as though she would guard him from them; her face, with its luminous, soft pallor, was suddenly desperate and strange.

"No!" she cried again. "You mustn't, you mustn't untie him now! You, you don't know. Oh, wait while I speak to him! Luigi!" She turned to the prisoner and began to speak with a quick, low urgency; her face, importunate and fearful, was close to the still mask of his. "Luigi, promise me! If I let them, if they untie your hands, will you promise not to, not to do it? Luigi will you?"

Jovannic could only stare at them, bewildered. He heard her pleading "Will you? Will you promise me, Luigi?" passionately, as though she would woo him to compliance. The peasant answered nothing; his slow eyes rested with a sort of heavy meditation on the eagerness of her face. They seemed to be alone in the midst of the soldiers, like men among statues. Then, beyond them, he caught sight of the old sergeant, watching with a kind of critical sympathy; he, at any rate, understood it all.

But Jovannic began in uncertain protest. None heeded him. The prisoner sighed and moved a shoulder in a half-shrug as of deprecation. "No, signorina," he said at last.

"Oh!" The sound was like a wail. The girl swayed back from him.

The sergeant clapped the man on the shoulder. "Be a good lad now!" he said. "Promise the young lady you'll behave and we'll have the cords off as quick as we can cut them. Promise her, such a nice young lady and all!"

The prisoner shook his head wearily. The girl, watching him, shivered.

"All this" Jovannic roused himself. "I don't understand. What's going on here? Sergeant, what's it all about?"

The old man made a grimace. "She knows," he said, with a nod towards the girl. "That proves it's spreading. It's got so now that if you only clout one of 'em on the side of the head he'll go out and kill himself. Won't let you so much as touch 'em!"

"What!" Jovannic gaped at him. "Kill themselves? You mean if his hands are untied, that man will?"

"Him?" The sergeant snorted. "Tonight if he can; tomorrow if he can't. He's dead, he is. I know 'em, Herr Leutnant. Dozens of 'em already, for a flogging or even for a kick; they call it 'escaping by the back door.' And now she knows. It's spreading, I tell you."

"Good Lord!" said Jovannic slowly. But suddenly, in a blaze of revelation, he understood what had lurked in his mind since the scene in the village; the smiles that mirth of men who triumph by a stratagem, who see their adversary vainglorious, strong and doomed. He remembered Captain Hahn's choleric pomp, his own dignity and aloofness; and it was with a heat of embarrassment that he now perceived how he must appear to the prisoner.

It did not occur to him to doubt the sergeant; for the truth sprang at him.

"You, you knew this, signorina?"

The girl had moved half a dozen paces to where the shadow of the great yews was deepening on the path. There she lingered, a slender presence, the oval of her face shining pale in the shade.

He heard her sigh. "Yes," she answered; "I knew."

Jovannic hesitated; then, gathering himself, he turned to the sergeant. "Now, I'm going to have that man's hands untied," he said. The brisk speech relieved him like an oath in anger. "No!" as the sergeant began to rumble "If you answer me when I give you an order I'll put you in irons. He's to be untied and fed; and if anything happens to him, if you don't deliver him alive in the morning, I'll send you before the tribunal and I'll ask to have you shot. You understand that?"

The old sergeant dropped his hands; he saw that he had to deal with an officer who, for the moment, meant what he said, and he was old in wisdom. He dragged himself to a parody of "attention."

"I understand, Herr Leutnant," he growled. But the habit of years was too strong for him, and he slacked his posture. "It means watching him all night; the men'll get no sleep."

"You can watch yourself, for all I care," snapped Jovannic. "Now bring me the book."

The signing and so forth were completed; the prisoner, unbound, stood between two watchful guards, who attitudinised as though ready to pounce and grapple him upon the least movement. "Now," commanded Jovannic, "take him in and feed him. And for the rest you have your orders."

"March him in," directed the sergeant to the men. The prisoner turned obediently between them and passed towards the open door of the guardhouse. He did not look round, and his passivity, his quiescence, suggested to Jovannic, in a thrill of strange vision, that the world, action, life had ceased for him at the moment when Captain Harm's blow fell on his brow.

He was passing in at the door, a guard at either elbow, when the girl spoke in the shadow.

"Arrivederci, Luigi," she called. "Till we meet again, Luigi."

From the doorway came the prisoner's reply: "Addio, adieu, signorina!" Then the guardhouse received him.

Jovannic turned. The girl was walking away already, going slowly in the direction of the wing of the great house that was left to her and her mother. He joined her, and they came together from the night of the yew-walk to where, upon the open lawn, the air was still aflood with the last light of the dying sun.

For a while he did not speak; her mood of tragedy enveloped them both and hushed him. But never before had he had her thus alone; even to share her silence was a sort of intimacy, and he groped for more.

"It it is really true, signorina what the sergeant said?" he asked at length.

She raised her face but did not look towards him. Her profile was a cameo upon the dusk. "It is true," she answered in a low voice.

"I don't know what to do," said Jovannic. "But you know, signorina, it was not I that struck him. I had nothing to do with it. I, I hope you believe that."

Still she gazed straight ahead of her. "I know who struck him," she said in the same low, level voice.

"Well, then isn't there anything one could do?" pressed Jovannic. "To stop him from killing himself, I mean. You see, he can't be tied or watched continually. You know these people. If you could suggest something, signorina, I'd do what I could."

She seemed to consider. Then "No," she answered; "nothing can be done." She paused, and he was about to speak when she added: "I was wrong to try to persuade him."

"Wrong!" exclaimed Jovannic. "Why?"

"It is your punishment," she said. "They have doomed you. You made them slaves but they make you murderers!" She turned to him at last, with dark eyes wide and a light as of exaltation in her face. Her voice, the strong, restrained contralto of the south, broke once as she went on, but steadied again. "You must not strike an Italian; it is dangerous. It is more than death, it is damnation! A blow and they will strike back at your soul and your salvation, and you cannot escape! Oh, this people and I would have persuaded him to live!"

She shrugged and turned to go on. They had reached the end of the wing in which she lived. The path went round it, and beyond was the little irrigation canal one of those small artificial water courses, deep and full-volumed, which carry the snow water of the Cadore to the farms of the plain. The dregs of the sunset yet faintly stained its surface like the lees of wine in water.

"Signorina," began Jovannic. He was not sure f what he wished to say to her. She paused in her slow walk to hear him. "Signorina," he began again, "after all, in war, a blow, you know, and I have never struck one of them never! I don't want you to think of me as, as just a brute."

"No," she said. "And it is because you ordered Luigi to be untied that I have warned you of your danger."

"Oh!" Jovannic sighed. "I don't think I really understand yet; but you have managed to make it all." He made a vague gesture towards the village and the tree-thronged land. "Well, gruesome! Every man in the place, apparently."

"And every woman," she put in quickly. "Never forget, Signor Tenente, it was the women who began it."

"The women began it?"

"Yes," she answered. "The women! You hadn't heard no, it was before you came of the girl here, in this house of my mother's, who was among the first? No? Listen, Signor Tenente."

"Yes," he said. It was in his mind that he was about to hear the stalest story of all, but it was strange that he should hear it from her.

"I am proud to tell it," she said, as though she answered his thought. "Proud! A little Friulana of these parts, a housemaid, we had masses for her till you took our priest away. One of your officers used to, to persecute her. Oh!" she cried, "why am I afraid even to name what she had to endure? He was always trying to get into her bedroom; you understand? And one day he caught hold of her so that she had to tear herself loose from him. She got free and stood there and smiled at him. She knew what she had to do then."

"I know, I know," half whispered Jovannic. "In the village today I saw them smile."

"He did not catch hold of her again; he misread that smile, and said that he would come that night. 'What hour?' she asked, and he answered that he would come at midnight. She put her hand to her bosom and drew out the little crucifix they wear on a string. 'Swear on this that you will come to me at midnight,' she said, and he took it in his hand and swore. Then it was evening she came out here, to where the canal runs under the road. And there she drowned herself."

She paused. "Duilia, her name was," she added quietly.

"Eh?" said Jovannic.

"Duilia, the same as mine."

"But—the officer?" asked Jovannic. "Was he—did he?"

"No," she said. "He did not keep the oath which he swore upon the crucifix."

From the terrace before the house came the blare of the bugle sounding the officers' mess call. She turned to go to her door.

"But, signorina!" Jovannic moved towards her. The sense of her, of the promise and power of her beauty and womanhood, burned in him. And to the allurement of her youth and her slender grace were added a glamour of strangeness and the quality of the moment. She paused and faced him once more.

"It is good night, Signor Tenente," she said.

He watched her pass round the end of the building, unhurried, sad and unafraid. He stood for some seconds yet after she had disappeared; then, drawing a deep breath, like one relaxing from a strain, he turned and walked back to the front of the house.

The burden of the evening lay upon him through the night at mess, where the grey-clad German and Austrian officers ate and drank below the mild faces of Pordenone's frescoed saints, and afterwards in his room, where he dozed and woke and dozed again through the hot, airless hours. The memory of the girl, the impression of her attitude, of her pale, unsmiling face, of her low, strong voice, tormented him; he felt himself alone with her in a hag-ridden land where all men were murderers or murdered; and she would have none of him. He arose sour and unrefreshed.

In the great dining-room the splendor of the morning was tainted with the staleness of last night's cigars, and, for a further flavor, sitting alone at the table, with his cap on his head and his cane on the tablecloth beside him, was Captain Hahn. The mess waiter, lurking near the door, looked scared and worried. He had slept but little.

"Good morning, Herr Hauptmann," said Jovannic, clicking his heels.

Captain Hahn gave him a furious glance and grunted inarticulately. He made the effect as he sat of emitting fumes, vapors of an overcharged personality; his naturally violent face was clenched like a fist.

"Here, you dog!" he exploded. The mess waiter all but leaped into the air. "Get me another glass of brandy." The man dived through the door. "And now you, Jovannic!"

"At your orders, Herr Hauptmann?" Jovannic looked up in astonishment. The other's face was blazing at him across the table.

"Who," Captain Hahn seemed to have a difficulty in compressing his feelings into words, "who ordered you to untie that prisoner?"

"No one," replied Jovannic. His gaze at the convulsed face opposite him narrowed. He put a hand on the table as though to spring up from his seat. "Is he dead, then?" he demanded.

"Damn it; so you knew he'd do it!" roared the captain. "Don't deny it; you've admitted it. You knew he'd hang himself, and yet."

"But he couldn't," cried Jovannic, as Captain Hahn choked and sputtered. "I ordered him to be watched. I told the sergeant"—Captain Hahn broke in with something like a howl. "I wasn't going to have soldiers kept out of their beds for stuff like that rotten, sentimental Austrian nonsense! I sent 'em off to get their sleep; but you, you knew, you."

"Ah!" said Jovannic. "Then the Herr Hauptmann cancelled my arrangements for the prisoner's safety and substituted his own! I am glad I am not responsible. So he hanged himself?"

Captain Hahn opened his mouth and bit at the air. His hand was on his heavy cane. The creeping mess waiter, tray in hand, came quivering to his elbow; never in his service time or his life was he more welcome to a German officer. The captain grabbed the glass and drank. Then with a sweep of his right arm he slashed the man with his cane.

"You slow-footed hound!" he bellowed.

Jovannic looked at him curiously. He had not doubted that what the girl had told him was true; but many things can be true in the stillness and tangled shadows of the evening that are false in the light of the morning. This, then, was a murderer, whom a whole population, a whole country, believed no, knew to be damned to all eternity this incontinent, stagnant-souled, kept creature of the army! Not even eternal damnation could dignify him or make him seem aught but the absurd and noxious thing that he was; a soul like his would make itself at home in hell like the old sergeant in the conquered province.

Later in the forenoon he saw the body; and that, too, he felt, failed to rise to the quality of its fate. Beyond the orchard of old derelict fruit trees behind the stable two men dug a grave in the sun, while from the shade the old sergeant smoked and watched them; and a little apart lay a stretcher, a tattered and stained blanket outlining the shape upon it. Jovannic was aware of the old man's shrewd eye measuring him and his temper as he stopped by the stretcher.

China-bowled pipe in hand, the sergeant lumbered towards him. "You see, he did it," he said. "Did it at once and got it over. Just hitched his belt to the window-bars and swung himself off. You can't stop 'em nowadays."

"Take the blanket off," ordered Jovannic.

The manner of the man's death had distorted the face that lay in the trough of the stretcher, but it was pitiful and ugly rather than terrible or horrifying. The body, its inertness, the still sprawl of the limbs, were puppet-like, with none of death's pomp and menace. Jovannic stood gazing; the sergeant, with the blanket over his arm, stood by smoking.

"Hey!" cried the sergeant suddenly, and flapped loose the blanket, letting it fall to cover the body again. "See, Herr Leutnant the young lady!"

"Eh?" Jovannic started and turned to look. She was yet a hundred yards off, coming through the wind-wrenched old trees of the orchard towards them. In her hand and lying along the curve of her arm she bore what seemed to be the green bough of a tree. The grass was to her knees, so that she appeared to float towards them rather than to walk, and, for the lieutenant, her approach seemed suddenly to lift all that in the affair was mean or little to the very altitude of tragedy.

He stood away from the body and raised his hand to his cap peak in silence. Very slowly she lowered her head in acknowledgment. At the foot of the stretcher she paused, with bowed head, and stood awhile so; if she prayed, it was with lips that did not move. In the grave the diggers ceased to work, and stood, sunk to their waists, to watch. The great open space was of a sudden reverend and solemn. Then she knelt, and, taking in both hands the bough of laurel which she carried, she bent above the covered shape and laid it upon the blanket.

She rose. It seemed to Jovannic that for an instant she looked him in the face with eyes that questioned; but she did not speak. Turning, she went from them by the way she had come, receding through the fantastic trees between whose leaves the sunlight fell on her in drops like rain.

There was much for Jovannic to do in the days that followed, for Captain Harm's dragnet was out over the villages and every day had its tale of arrests. Jovannic, as one of his assistants, was out early and late, on horseback or motoring, till the daily scenes of violence and pain palled on him like a routine. Once, in the village near headquarters, he saw the Contessina; she was entering the house whence the prisoner had been dragged forth, but though he loitered in the neighborhood for an hour she did not come forth. And twice he saw her walking by the canal with the old Contessa; always he marked in her that same supple poise of body, that steady, level carriage of the head. But it was not for a couple of weeks that chance served to give him any speech with her.

And then, as before, it was evening. He had been out on the affairs of Captain Hahn, and was returning on foot along a path through the maize fields. The ripe crops made a wall to either hand, bronze red and man-high, gleaming like burnished metal in the shine of the sunset; and here, at a turning in the way, he met her face to face.

"Good evening, signorina," he said, stopping.

"Good evening, Signor Tenente," she answered, and would have passed on but that he barred the way as he stood.

There was no fear, no doubt, in the quiet of her face as she stood before him. Her eyes were great and dark, but untroubled, and upon the lips, where he had never seen a smile, was no tremor.

"Signorina!" he burst forth. "I, I have wanted to speak to you ever since that evening. I cannot bear that you should think of me as you do."

"I do not think of you," she answered, with the resonance of bell-music thrilling through the low tones of her voice.

He took a step nearer to her; she did not shrink nor fall back.

"But," he said, "I think of you always!" Her face did not change; its even quiet was a challenge and an exasperation. "Signorina, what can I do? This accursed war if it were not for that you would let me speak and at least you would listen. But now."

He broke off with a gesture of helpless anger. She did not alter the grave character of her regard.

"What is it that you wish to say to me?" she asked. "You see that I am listening."

Her very calm, the slender erectness of her body, her fearless and serious gaze, were a goad to him.

"Listening!" he cried. He choked down an impulse to be noisy. "Well then, listen! Signorina signorina, I, I am not one of those. That man who hanged himself, I would have prevented him and saved him. You heard me give the orders that he was to be watched and fed; fed, signorina! It was another who took the guards away and left him to himself."

"That," she said, "I knew."

"Ah!" He came yet closer. "You knew. Then."

He tried to take her hand. The impulse to touch her was irresistible; it was a famine in his being. Without stepping back, without, a movement of retreat or a change of countenance, she put her hands behind her back.

"Signorina!" He was close to her now; the heat of his face beat upon the ice of hers. "Oh! This I can't! Give me at least your hand. Signorina."

Her voice was as level, as calm, as quiet, and yet as loud with allurement as ever.

"Signor Tenente, no!"

His was the pervert blood, the virtues and the sins born of the promiscuity of races. Hers rigid, empty of invitation were the ripe Italian lips, pure, with the fastidious purity of her high birth and the childlike sweetness of her youth.

"Signorina!" He had meant to plead, but the force of her presence overwhelmed him. He felt himself sucked down in a whirlpool of impulse; doom was ahead; but the current of desire was too strong. A movement and his arms were about her!

"Love!" he gasped. His lips were upon hers, Kissing, kissing! He slaked himself on that dead and unresponsive mouth violently; he felt her frail and slender in the crush of his arms. All her virginal and girlish loveliness was his for a mad moment; then—. He released her. They stood apart. He passed a hand over his brow to clear the fog from his eyes.

"I, I" he stammered. He could see her now. She stood opposite him still, her back to the tall wall of maize that bounded the path. Her Hand was to her bosom; she breathed hard, and presently, while he stared, words misshaping themselves upon his abashed lips she smiled! Her sad, ripe mouth relaxed; all her grave face softened; pity the profound pity of a martyr who prays for "those who know not what they do" was alight in her face; the terrible mild mirth of those who are assured of victory these showed themselves like an ensign. She smiled!

He saw that smile, and at first vision he did not know it. "Signorina," he began again hopefully; then he stopped short. He saw again what he had seen in the village when Captain Hahn had struck his memorable, self-revealing blow. The smile the smile of those who choose death for the better part.

"Signorina!" His hands before his eyes hid her and her smile from him. "Please I beg—." There was no answer. He lowered his hands, and lifted timidly, repentantly, his face to seek pardon. But upon the path was no one. She had parted the stout stalks of maize and disappeared.

"God!" said Jovannic.

An energy possessed him. He charged along the narrow path between the high palisades of the metal-hued maize. Upon the next corner he encountered Captain Hahn, swollen and pompous and perfect.

"Well?" said Captain Hahn, exhaling his words as a pricked bladder exhales air. "Well, you searched those villages, did you?"

Jovannic saluted mechanically. Life his own life clogged his feet; to act was like wading in treacle. He had an impulse of utter wild rebellion, of ferocious self-assertion. Then:

"Zu Befehl, Herr Hauptmann!" he said, and saluted.

II

THE DAGO

Eight bells had sounded, and in the little triangular fo'c'sle of the Anna Maria the men of the port watch were waiting for their dinner. The daylight which entered by the open hatch overhead spread a carpet of light at the foot of the ladder, which slid upon the deck to the heave and fall of the old barque's blunt bows, and left in shadow the double row of bunks and the chests on which the men sat. From his seat nearest the ladder, Bill, the ship's inevitable Cockney, raised his flat voice in complaint.

"That bloomin' Dago takes 'is time over fetchin' the hash," he said. "'E wants wakin' up a bit that's wot 'e wants."

Sprawling on the edge of his bunk forward, Dan, the oldest man in the ship, took his pipe from his lips in the deliberate way in which he did everything. Short in stature and huge in frame, the mass of him, even in that half-darkness of the fo'c'sle, showed somehow majestic and powerful.

"The mate came after 'im about somethin' or other," he said in his deep, slow tones.

"That's right," said another seaman. "It was about spillin' some tar on the deck, an' now the Dago's got to stop up this arternoon an' holystone it clean in his watch below."

"Bloomin' fool," growled the Cockney. But it was the wrong word, and the others were silent.

A man in trouble with an officer, though he be no seaman and a Dago, may always count on the sympathy of the fo'c'sle.

"'E ain't fit to paddle a bumboat," the Cockney went on. "Can't go aloft, can't stand 'is wheel, can't even fetch the hash to time."

"Yes!" Dan shifted slowly, and the younger man stopped short. "You better slip along to the galley, Bill, an' see about that grub."

The Cockney swore, but rose from his seat. Dan was not to be disobeyed in the fo'c'sle. But at that moment the hatch above was darkened.

"'Ere's the Dago," cried Bill. "Where you bin, you bloomin' fool?"

A bare foot came over the combing, feeling vaguely for the steps of the ladder. Dan sat up and laid by his pipe; two seamen went to assist in the safe delivery of their dinner.

"Carn't yer never learn to bring the grub down the ladder backwards?" Bill was demanding of the new-comer. "Want to capsize it all again, like yer done before?"

"Ah, no!"

The Dago stood in the light of the hatch and answered the Cockney with a shrug and a timid, conciliatory smile. He was a little swarthy man, lean and anxious, with quick, apprehensive eyes which flitted now nervously from one to the other of the big sailors whose comrade and servant he was. There was upon him none of that character of the sea which shaped their every gesture and attitude. As the Cockney snarled at him he moved his hands in deprecating gesticulation; a touch of the florid appeared in him, of that easy vivacity which is native to races ripened in the sun.

"Keepin' men waitin' like this," mouthed Bill. "Bloomin' flat-footed, greasy 'anded."

Dan's deliberate voice struck in strongly. "Ain't you goin' to have no dinner, Dago?" he demanded. "Come on an' sit down to it, man!"

The Dago made one final shrug at Bill.

"De mate," he said, smiling with raised eyebrows, as though in pitying reference to that officer's infirmities of temper, "'e call me. So I cannot go to de galley for fetch de dinner more quick. Please escuse."

Bill snarled. "Come on with ye," called Dan again.

"Ah, yais!" And now his smile and his start to obey apologized to Dan for not having come at the first summons.

Dan pushed the "kid" of food towards him. "Dig in," he bade him. "You've had better grub than this in yer time, but it's all there is. So go at it."

"Better dan dis!" The Dago paused to answer in the act of helping himself. "Ah, mooch, mooch better, yais. I tell you." He began to gesticulate as he talked, trying to make these callous, careless men see with him the images that his words called up.

"Joost before de hot of de day I sit-a down in a balcao, where it is shade, yais, an' look at-a de water an' de trees, an' hear de bells, all slow an' gentle, in de church. An' when it is time dey bring me de leetle fish like-a de gold, all fresh, an' de leetle bread-cakes, yais, an' de wine."

"That's the style," approved a seaman. Though they did not cease to eat, they were all listening.

Tales of food and drink are always sure of a hearing in the fo'c'sle.

"On a table of de black wood, shining, an' a leetle cloth like snow," the Dago went on; "an' de black woman dat brings it smiles wiz big white teeth."

He paused, seeing it all the tropic languor and sweetness of the life he had conjured up, so remote, so utterly different from the rough-hewn realities that surrounded him.

"Shove that beef-kid down this way, will yer?" called Bill.

"You wait," answered Dan. He jogged the Dago with his elbow. "Now, lad," he said, "that's talk enough. Get yer grub."

The Dago, recalled from his visions, smiled and sighed and leaned forward to take his food. From his seat by the ladder, Bill the Cockney watched with mean, angry eyes to measure the size of his helping.

It was at Sourabaya, in Java, that he had been shipped to fill, as far as he could, the place of a man lost overboard. The port had been bare of seamen; the choice was between the Dago and nobody; and so one evening he had come alongside in a sampan and joined the crew of the Anna Maria. He brought with him as his kit a bundle of broken clothes and a flat paper parcel containing a single suit of clean white duck, which he cherished under the straw mattress of his bunk and never wore. He made no pretence of being a seaman. He could neither steer nor go aloft, and there fell to him, naturally, all the work of the ship that was ignominious or unpleasant or merely menial. It was the Dago, with his shrug and his feeble, complaisant smile, who scraped the boards of the pigsty and hoisted coal for the cook, and swept out the fo'c'sle while the other men lay and smoked.

"What made ye ship, anyway?" men would ask him angrily, when some instance of his incompetence had added to the work of the others. To this, if they would hear him, he had always an answer. He was a Portuguese, it seemed, of some little town on the coast of East Africa, where a land-locked bay drowsed below the windows of the houses under the day-long sun. When he spoke of it, if no one cut him short, his voice would sink to a hushed tone and he would seem to be describing a scene he saw. His jerking, graphic hands would fall still as he talked of the little streets where no one made a noise, and the sailors stared curiously at his face with the glamour of dreams on it.

From a life tuned to that murmur of basking waters a mishap had dragged him forth. It took the shape of a cruise in a fishing boat, in which he and three companions "t'ree senhores, t'ree gentilmen" had run into weather and been blown out to sea, there to be rescued, after four days of hunger and terror, by a steamship which had carried them to Aden and put them ashore there penniless. It was here that his tale grew vague. For something like three years he had wandered, working on ships and ashore, always hoping that sooner or later a chance would serve him to return to his home. Twice already he had got to Mozambique, but that was still nearly a thousand miles from his goal, and on each occasion his ship had carried him inexorably back. The Anna Maria was bound for Mozambique, and he had offered himself, with new hopes for his third attempt.

"D'ye reckon you'll do it this passage?" the seamen used to ask him over their pipes.

He would shrug and spread his hands. "Ah, who can tell? But some time, yais."

"An' what did ye say the name o' that place o' yours was?"

He would tell them, speaking, its syllables with soft pleasure in their mere sound.

"Never heard of it," they always said. "Ships don't go there, Dago."

"Ah, but yais." The Dago had known ships call. "Not often, but sometimes. There is leetle trade, an' ships come. On de tide, floating up to anchor, so close you hear de men talkin' on de fo'c'sle head, and dey hear de people ashore girl singin', perhaps and smell de trees."

"Do they, though?"

"Yais. Dat night I go out to fish in de boat ah, dat night! a girl was singin', and her voice it float on de bay all round me. An' I stand in de boat an' take off my hat" he rose to show them the gesture "and sing back to her, an' she is quiet to listen in de darkness."

When dinner was over it fell to the Dago to take the "kids" back to the galley and sweep down the deck. So he had barely time to smoke the cigarette he made of shredded ship's tobacco rolled in a strip of newspaper before he had to go on deck again to holystone the spilled tar from the planks. Dan gave him advice about using a hard stone and plenty of sand, to which he listened, smiling, and then he went up the ladder again, with his rags shivering upon him, to the toil of the afternoon.

The seamen were already in their bunks, each smoking ruminatively the pipe that prefaces slumber.

"Queer yarn that feller tells," remarked one of them idly. "How much of it d'you reckon's true, Dan?"

In the for'ard lower bunk Dan opened drowsy eyes. He was lying on his back with his hands under his head, and the sleeves of his shirt rolled back left bare his mighty forearms with their faded tattooings. His big, beardless face was red, like rusty iron, with over thirty years of seafaring; it was simple and strong, a transparent mask of the man's upright and steadfast spirit.

"Eh?" he said, and the other repeated his question. Dan sucked at his pipe and breathed the smoke forth in a thin blue mist.

"It might be true enough," he answered at length, in his deliberate bass. "Things like that does happen; you c'n read 'em in newspapers. Anyhow, true or not, the Dago believes it all."

"Meanin' he's mad?" inquired the other. "Blowed if I didn't think it once or twice myself."

"He's mad right enough," agreed another seaman comfortably, while from Bill's bunk came the usual snarl of "bloomin' fool."

Dan turned over on his side and put his pipe away.

"He don't do any harm, anyhow," he said, pulling up his blanket. "There's worse than him."

"Plenty, poor devil," agreed the first speaker, as he too prepared for the afternoon's sleep.

On his knees upon the deck aft, shoving his holystone to and fro laboriously and unhandily along the planks where the accident with the tar-pot had left its stain, the Dago still broke into little meaningless smiles. For him, at any rate, the narrow scope between the stem and stern of the Anna Maria was not the world. He had but to lift up the eyes of his mind to behold, beyond it and dwarfing it to triviality, the glamours of a life in which it had no part. Those who saw him at his dreary penance had their excuse for thinking him mad, for there were moments when his face glowed like a lover's, his lips moved in soundless speech, and he had the aspect of a man illuminated by some sudden and tender joy.

"Now, then, you Dago there," the officer of the watch shouted at him. "Keep that stone movin', an' none of yer shenanikin'!"

"Yais, sir," answered the Dago, and bowed himself obediently.

It needed the ingenuity of Bill to trouble his tranquility of mind. The old Anna Maria was far on her passage, and already there were birds about her, the far-flying scouts of the land, and the color of the water had changed to a softer and more radiant blue. It was as though sad Africa made herself comely to invite them to her shores. Bill had a piece of gear to serve with spun-yarn, and was at work abreast of the foremast, with the Dago to help him. The rope on which they worked was stretched between the rail and the mast. Bill had the serving-mallet, and as he worked it round the rope the Dago passed the ball of spun-yarn in time with him. The mate was aft, superintending some work upon the mizzen, and Bill took his job easily. The Dago, with his little smile to which his lips shaped themselves unconsciously, passed the ball in silence. The Cockney eyed him unpleasantly.

"Say, Dago," he said presently, "wot was the name o' that there place you said you come from?"

"Eh?" The Dago roused from his smiling reverie. "De name? Ah, yais." He pronounced the name slowly, making its syllables render their music.

"Yus," said Bill, "I thought that was it."

He went on working, steadily, nonchalantly. The Dago stared at him, perplexed.

"Why you want to know dat name?" he asked at length.

"Well," said Bill, "you bin talkin' abaht it a lot, and so, d'yer see, I reckoned I'd find out. An' yesterday I 'ad to go into the cabin to get at the lazareet 'atch, an' the chart was spread out on the table."

"De chart?" The Dago was slow to understand. "Ah, yais. Mapa chart. An' you look at-a 'im, yais?"

"Yus," answered Bill, who, like most men before the mast, had never seen a chart in his life. "I looked at ev'ry name on it, ev'ry bloomin' one. A chart o' Africa it was, givin' the whole lot of 'em. But your place."

"Yais?" cried the Dago. "You see 'im? An' de leetle bay under de hills? You find it?"

"No," said Bill, "I didn't find it. It wasn't there."

"Wasn't there?" The Dago's smile was gone now; his forehead was puckered like a child's in bewilderment, and a darker doubt at the back of his thoughts loomed up in his troubled eyes.

"No," said the Cockney, watching him zestfully. "You got it wrong, Dago, an' there ain't no such place. You dreamt it. Savvy? All wot you bin tell in' us about the town an' the bay an' the way you used to take it easy there all that's just a bloomin' lie. See?"

The Dago's face was white and his lips trembled. He tried to smile.

"Not there," he repeated. "It is de joke, not? You fool me, Bill, yais?"

Bill shook his head. "I wouldn't fool yer abaht a thing like that," he declared sturdily. "There ain't no such place, Dago. It's just one o' yer fancies, yer know."

In those three years of wandering there had been dark hours turbulent with pain, hours when his vision, his hope, his memory had not availed to uplift him, and he had known the terror of a doubt lest the whole of it should, after all, be but a creation of his yearnings, a mirage of his desires. Everywhere men had believed him mad. He had accepted that as he accepted toil, hunger and exile, as things to be redeemed by their end. But if it should be true! If this grossness and harshness should, after all, be his real life! Bill saw the agony that broke loose within his victim, and bent his head above his work to hide a smile.

"Ah!" The quiet exclamation was all that issued from the Dago's lips; the surge of emotion within him sought no vent in words. But Bill was satisfied; he had the instincts of a connoisseur in torment, and the Dago's face was now a mask that looked as if it had never smiled.

It was Dan that spoiled and undid the afternoon's work. During the second dog-watch, when the Dago kept the look out, he carried his pipe to the forecastle head and joined him there. Right ahead of the ship the evening sky was still stained with the afterglow of the sunset; the jib-boom swung gently athwart a heaven in whose darkening arch there was still a ghost of color. Between the anchors, where they lay lashed on their chocks, the Dago stood and gazed west to where, beyond the horizon, the shores of Africa had turned barren and meaningless.

"Well, lad," rumbled Dan, "gettin' near it, eh? Gettin' on towards the little town by the bay, ain't we?"

The Dago swung round towards him. "Dere is no town," he said calmly. "No town, no bay, no anyt'ing. I was mad, but now I know."

He spoke evenly enough, and in the lessening light his face was indistinct. But old Dan, for all his thirty and odd years of hard living, had an ear tuned delicately to the trouble of his voice.

"What's all' this?" he demanded shortly. "Who's been tellin' you there ain't no town or anything? Out with it! Who was it?"

"It don't matter," said the Dago. "It was Bill." And briefly, in the same even tones, like those of a man who talks in his sleep, he told the tale of Bill's afternoon's sport.

"Ah, so it was Bill!" said Dan slowly, when the recital was at an end. "Bill, was it? Ye-es. Well, o' course you know that Bill's the biggest liar ever shipped out o' London, where liars is as common as weevils in bread. So you don't want to take no notice of anything Bill says."

The Dago shook his head. "It is not that," he said. "It is not de first time I 'ave been called mad; and sometimes I have think it myself."

- 24 -

"Oh, go on with ye," urged Dan. "You ain't mad."

"T'ree years," went on the Dago in his mournful, subdued voice. "T'ree years I go about an' work, always poor, dirty work, an' got no name, only 'Dago.' I t'ink all de time 'bout my leetle beautiful town; but sometimes I t'ink, too, when I am tired an' people is hard to me: 'It is a dream. De world has no place so good as dat.' What you t'ink, Dan?"

"Oh, I dunno," grunted Dan awkwardly. "Anyhow, there ain't no harm in it. It don't follow a man's mad because he's got fancies."

"Fancies!" repeated the Dago. "Fancies!" He seemed to laugh a little to himself, laughter with no mirth in it.

Night was sinking on the great solitude of waters. Above them the sails of the foremast stood pale and lofty, and there was the rhythmic jar of a block against a backstay. The Anna Maria lifted her weather bow easily to the even sea, and the two men on the fo'c'sle head swung on their feet unconsciously to the movement of the barque.

"Eef it was only a fancy," said the Dago suddenly, "eef it was only a town in my mind, I don' want it no more." He made a motion with his hand as though he cast something from him. "I t'ink all dis time it is true, dat some day I find it again. It help me; it keep me glad; it save me from misery. But now it is all finish."

"But don't you know," cried Dan, "don't you know for sure whether it's true or not?"

The Dago shook his head. "I am no more sure," he said. "For t'ree years I have had bad times, hard times. So now I am not sure. Dat is why I t'ink I am a little mad, like Bill said."

"Never mind Bill," said Dan. "I'll settle with Bill."

He put his heavy hand on the other's arm.

"Lad," he said, "I'm sorry for your trouble. I ain't settin' up to know much about fellers' minds, but it seems to me as if you was better off without them fancies, if they ain't true. An' that town o' yours! It sounded fine, as good a place as ever I heard of; but it was mighty like them ports worn-out sailormen is always figurin' to themselves, where they'll go ashore and take it easy for the rest o' their lives. It was too good, mate, too good to be true."

There was a pause. "Yes," said the Dago at last. "It was too good, Dan."

Dan gave his arm a grip, and left him to his look out over a sea whose shores were now as desolate as itself, a man henceforth to be counted sane, since he knew life as bare of beauty, sordid and difficult.

Dan put his pipe in his pocket and walked aft to the main hatch, where the men were gathered for the leisure of the dog-watch. He went at his usual deliberate gait, a notable figure of seamanlike respectability and efficiency. Upon his big, shaven face a rather stolid tranquility reigned. Bill, leaning against a corner of the galley, looked up at him carelessly.

"'Ullo, Dan," he greeted him.

"Hullo, Bill," responded Dan. "I bin talkin' to the Dago."

"Oh, 'ave yer?" said Bill.

"Yes," said Dan, in the same conversational tone. "I have. An' now I'm goin' to have a word with you. Stand clear of that deckhouse!"

"Eh?" cried Bill. "Say, Dan—"

That was all. Dan's fist, the right one, of the hue and hardness of teak, with Dan's arm behind it, arrived just under his eye, and the rest of the conversation was yelps. No one attempted to interrupt; even the captain and mate, who watched from the poop, made no motion to interfere; Dan's reputation for uprightness stood him in good stead.

"There, now," he said, when it was over, and he allowed the gasping, bleeding Cockney to fall back on the hatch. "See what comes of not takin' hints?"

They made Mozambique upon the morning of a day when the sun poured from the heavens and the light wind came warm off the land. The old Anna Maria, furling sail by sail, floated up to her anchorage and let go her anchors just as a shore-boat, manned by big nearly naked negroes, with a white man sitting in the stern, raced up alongside. In less than an hour the hands were lifting the anchors again and getting ready to go to sea once more. The cook, who had served the captain and his visitor with breakfast, was able to explain the mystery. He stood at his galley door, with his cloth cap cocked sportively over one eye, and gave the facts to the inquisitive sailors.

"That feller in the boat was th' agent," he said. "A Porchuguee, he was. Wanted wine f'r 'is breakfus'. An' the orders is, we're to go down the coast to a place called le'me see, now. What was it called? Some Dago name that I can't call to mind."

Dan was among his hearers, and by some freak of memory the name of the town of which the Dago had been used to speak, the town which was now a dream to be forgotten, came to his lips. He spoke it aloud.

"It wasn't that, I s'pose?" he suggested.

"You've got it," cried the cook. "That was it, Dan; the very place. Fancy you knowin' it. Well, we got to go down there and get in across a sort of bar what's there an' discharge into lighters. Seems it's a bit out o' the way o' shippin'. The skipper said that the charterers seemed to think the old boat ran on wheels."

"Queer!" said Dan. To himself he said: "He must ha' heard the name somewhere and hitched his dream to it."

The name, as it chanced, was one of many syllables, and the sailors managed them badly. Men who speak of the islands of Diego Ramirez as the "Daggarammarines" are not likely to deal faithfully with a narrie that rings delicately like guitar strings, and Dan observed that their mention of the barque's destination had no effect upon the Dago. For him all ports had become indifferent; one was not nearer than another to any place of his desire. He spoke no more of his town; when the men, trying to draw him, spoke about food, or women, or other roads to luxury, he answered without smiling.

"I t'ink no more 'bout dat," he said. "T'ree year work an' have bad times. Before, I don' remember o more."

"He was better when he was crazy," agreed the seamen. It was as though the gaiety, the spring of gladness, within the little man had been dried up; there was left only the incompetent and despised Dago. He faced the routine of his toil now with no smile of preoccupation for a sweeter vision; he shuffled about decks, futile as ever, with the dreariness of a man in prison.

Only to Dan he spoke more freely. It was while the watch was washing down decks in the morning. The two were side by side, plying their brooms along the wet planks, while about them the dawn broadened towards the tropic day.

"I am no more mad," said the Dago. "Now I know I am not mad. Dat name of de place where we go de men don' know how to speak it, but it is de name of my town, de town I t'ink about once so much. Yais I know! At last, after all dis time, I come dere, but I am not glad. I am never glad no more 'bout not'ing."

Dan worked on. He could think of no answer to make.

"Only 'bout one t'ing I am glad," went on the Dago. "'Bout a friend I make on dis ship; 'bout you, Dan."

"Oh, hell!" grunted Dan awkwardly.

"But 'bout de town, I am no more glad. I know now it is more better to be sad an' poor an' weak dan to be mad an' glad about fancies. Yais I know now!"

"You'll be all right," said Dan. "Cheer up, lad. There's fellers worse off than you!" An inspiration lit up his honest and downright brain for a moment. "Why," he said, "it's better to be you than be a feller like Bill that never had a fancy in his life. You've lost a lot, maybe; but you can't lose a thing you never had."

The Dago half-smiled. "Yais," he said. "You are mos' wise, Dan. But, Dan! Dan!"

"Yes. What?"

"If it had been true, Dan dat beautiful town an' all my dream! If it had been true!"

"Shove along wi' that broom," advised Dan. "The mate's lookin'."

They came abreast of their port about midday, and Dan, at the wheel, heard the captain swear as they stood in through a maze of broken water, where coral reefs sprouted like weeds in a neglected garden, towards the hills that stood low above the horizon. He had been furnished, it seemed, with a chart concerning whose trustworthiness he entertained the bitterest doubts. There was some discussion with the mate about anchoring and sending in a boat to bring off a pilot, but presently they picked up a line of poles sticking up above the water like a ruined fence, and these seemed to comfort the captain. Bits of trees swam alongside; a flight of small birds, with flashes of green and red in their plumage, swung about them; the water, as they went, changed color. Little by little the hills lifted from the level of the water and took on color and variety, till from the deck one could make out the swell of their contours and distinguish the hues of the wild vegetation that clothed them. The yellow of a beach and a snowy gleam of surf showed at their feet, and then, dead ahead and still far away, they opened, and in the gap there was visible the still shining blue of water that ran inland and lay quiet under their shelter.

"Stand by your to'gallant halyards!" came the order. "Lower away there!"

It was evening already when the old Anna Maria, floating slowly under a couple of jibs and a foretopsail, rounded the point and opened the town. The bay, with its fringe of palms, lay clear before her; beyond its farthest edge, the sun had just set, leaving his glories to burn out behind him, and astern of them in the east the swift tropic night was racing up the sky. The little town a church-tower and a cluster of painted, flat-roofed houses, lay behind the point at the water's edge. There was a music of bells in the still air; all the scene breathed that joyous languor, that easy beauty which only the sun can ripen, which the windy north never knows. With the night at her heels, the old Anna Maria moved almost imperceptibly towards the town.

"Stand by to anchor!" came the order from aft, and the mate, calling three men with him, went up the ladder to the fo'c'sle head.

Dan was one of the three. He was at the rail, looking at the little town as it unfolded itself, house after house, with the narrow streets between, when he first noticed the white figure at his side. He turned in surprise; it was the Dago, in the cherished suit of duck which he had guarded for so long under his mattress. Heretofore, Dan had known him only in his rags of working-clothes, a mildly pathetic and ridiculous figure; now he was seemly, unfamiliar, a little surprising.

"What's all this?" demanded Dan.

The Dago was looking with all his eyes at the town, already growing dim.

"Dis?" he repeated. "Dese clo'se, I keep dem for my town, Dan. To come back wis yais! For not be like a mendigo a beggar. Now, no need to keep dem no more; and dis place oh, Dan, it is so like, so like! I dream it all yais de church, de praca all of it!"

"Steady!" growled Dan. "Don't get dreamin' it again."

"No," said the Dago; "I never dream no more. Never no more!"

He did not take his eyes from it; he stood at the rail gazing, intent, absorbed. He did not hear the mate's brief order that summoned him and the others across the deck.

"When I go out on de fishin' boat," he said aloud, thinking Dan was still at his side, "a girl was singin' an'—"

"Here, you!" cried the mate. "What's the matter with you? Why don't you?"

He stopped in amazement, for the Dago turned and spat a brief word at him, making a gesture with his hand as though to command silence.

In the moment that followed they all heard it a voice that sang, a strong and sweet contralto that strewed its tones forth like a scent, to add itself to the other scents of earth and leaves that traveled across the waters and reached them on their deck. They heard it lift itself as on wings to a high exaltation of melody and fail thence, hushing and drooping deliciously, down diminishing slopes of song.

"What the-" began the mate, and moved to cross the deck.

His surprises were not yet at an end, for Dan Dan, the ideal seaman, the precise in his duty, the dependable, the prosaically perfect Dan caught him by the arm with a grip in which there was no deference for the authority of a chief officer.

"Leave him be, sir," urged Dan. "I, I know what's the matter with him. Leave him be!"

The voice ashore soared again, sure and buoyant; the mate dragged his arm free from Dan's hold and turned to swear; on the main deck the horse-laugh of Bill answered the singer. The Dago heard nothing. Bending forward over the rail, he stretched both arms forth, and in a voice that none recognized, broken and passionate, he took up the song. It was but for a minute, while the mate recovered his outraged senses, but it was enough. The voice ashore had ceased.

"What the blank blank!" roared the mate, as he dragged the Dago across the deck. "What d'ye mean by it, eh? Get hold o' that rope, or I'll—."

"Yais, sir."

A moment later he turned to Dan, and in the already deepening gloom his smile gleamed white in his face.

"Ah, my frien'!" he said. "Dere was no dream. T'ree years, all bad, all hard, all sad dat was de dream. Now I wake up. Only one t'ing true in all de t'ree years de friend I make yais."

"Hark!" said Dan. "Hear it? There's boats comin' off to us."

"Yais!" The smile gleamed again. "For me. It is no dream. Dey hear my voice when I sing. By'm by you hear dem callin', 'Felipe!' Dat's my name."

"Listen, then," said Dan in a whisper.

The water trickled alongside; they were coming up to their berth. The bells from the church ashore were still. Across the bay there came the clack of oars in rowlocks, pulled briskly, and voices.

"Felipe!" they called. "Felipe!"

The Dago's hand found Dan's.

III

WOOD-LADIES

The pine trees of the wood joined their branches into a dome of intricate groinings over the floor of ferns where the children sat sunk to the neck in a foam of tender green. The sunbeams that slanted in made shivering patches of gold about them. Joyce, the elder of the pair, was trying to explain why she had wished to come here from the glooms of the lesser wood beyond.

"I wasn't 'zactly frightened," she said. "I knew there wasn't any lions or robbers, or anything like that. But—"

"Tramps?" suggested Joan.

"No! You know I don't mind tramps, Joan. But as we was going along under all those dark bushes where it was so quiet, I kept feeling as if there was something behind me. I looked round and there wasn't anything, but well, it felt as if there was."

Joyce's small face was knit and intent with the effort to convey her meaning. She was a slim, erect child, as near seven years of age as made no matter, with eyes that were going to be grey but had not yet ceased to be blue. Joan, who was a bare five, a mere huge baby, was trying to root up a fern that grew between her feet.

"I know," she said, tugging mightily. The fern gave suddenly, and Joan fell over on her back, with her stout legs sticking up stiffly. In this posture she continued the conversation undisturbed. "I know, Joy. It was wood-ladies!"

"Wood-ladies!" Joyce frowned in faint perplexity as Joan rolled right side up again. Wood-ladies were dim inhabitants of the woods, beings of the order of fairies and angels and even vaguer, for there was nothing about them in the story-books. Joyce, who felt that she was getting on in years, was willing to be skeptical about them, but could not always manage it. In the nursery, with the hard, clean linoleum underfoot and the barred window looking out on the lawn and the road, it was easy; she occasionally shocked Joan, and sometimes herself, by the license of her speech on such matters; but it was a different affair when one came to the gate at the end of the garden, and passed as through a dream portal from the sunshine and frank sky to the cathedral shadows and great whispering aisles of the wood. There, the dimness was like the shadow of a presence; as babies they had been aware of it, and answered their own questions by inventing wood-ladies to float among the trunks and people the still, green chambers. Now, neither of them could remember how they had first learned of wood-ladies.

"Wood-ladies," repeated Joyce, and turned with a little shiver to look across the ferns to where the pines ended and the lesser wood, dense with undergrowth, broke at their edge like a wave on a steep beach. It was there, in a tunnel of a path that writhed beneath over-arching bushes, that she had been troubled with the sense of unseen companions. Joan, her fat hands struggling with another fern, followed her glance.

"That's where they are," she said casually. "They like being in the dark."

"Joan!" Joyce spoke earnestly. "Say truly truly, mind! do you think there is wood-ladies at all?"

"'Course there is," replied Joan, cheerfully. "Fairies in fields and angels in heaven and dragons in caves and wood-ladies in woods."

"But," objected Joyce, "nobody ever sees them."

Joan lifted her round baby face, plump, serene, bright with innocence, and gazed across at the tangled trees beyond the ferns. She wore the countenance with which she was wont to win games, and Joyce thrilled nervously at her certainty. Her eyes, which were brown, seemed to seek expertly; then she nodded.

"There's one now," she said, and fell to work with her fern again.

Joyce, crouching among the broad green leaves, looked tensely, dread and curiosity the child's avid curiosity for the supernatural alight in her face. In the wood a breath of wind stirred the leaves; the shadows and the fretted lights shifted and swung; all was vague movement and change. Was it a bough that bent and sprang back or a flicker of draperies, dim and green, shrouding a tenuous form that passed like a smoke-wreath? She stared with wide eyes, and it seemed to her that for an instant she saw the figure turn and the pallor of a face, with a mist of hair about it, sway towards her. There was an impression of eyes, large and tender, of an infinite grace and fragility, of a coloring that merged into the greens and browns of the wood; and as she drew her breath, it was all no more. The trees, the lights and shades, the stir of branches were as before, but something was gone from them.

"Joan!" she cried, hesitating.

"Yes," said Joan, without looking up. "What?"

The sound of words had broken a spell. Joyce was no longer sure that she had seen anything.

"I thought, just now, I could see something," she said. "But I s'pose I didn't."

"I did," remarked Joan.

Joyce crawled through the crisp ferns till she was close to Joan, sitting solid and untroubled and busy upon the ground, with broken stems and leaves all round her.

"Joan," she begged. "Be nice. You're trying to frighten me, aren't you?"

"I'm not," protested Joan. "I did see a wood-lady. Wood-ladies doesn't hurt you; wood-ladies are nice. You're a coward, Joyce."

"I can't help it," said Joyce, sighing. "But I won't go into the dark spots of the wood any more."

"Coward," repeated Joan absently, but with a certain relish.

"You wouldn't like to go there by yourself!" cried Joyce. "If I wasn't with you, you'd be a coward, too. You know you would."

She stopped, for Joan had swept her lap free of debris and was rising to her feet. Joan, for all her plumpness and infantile softness, had a certain deliberate dignity when she was put upon her mettle. She eyed her sister with a calm and very galling superiority.

"I'm going there now," she answered; "all by mineself."

"Go, then!" retorted Joyce, angrily.

Without a further word Joan turned her back and began to plough her way across the ferns towards the dark wood. Joyce, watching her, saw her go at first with wrath, for she had been stung, and then with compunction. The plump baby was so small in the brooding solemnity of the pines, thrusting indefatigably along, buried to the waist in ferns. Her sleek, brown head had a devoted look; the whole of her seemed to go with so sturdy an innocence towards those peopled and uncanny glooms. Joyce rose to her knees to call her back.

"Joan!" she cried. The baby turned. "Joan! Come back; come back an' be friends!"

Joan, maintaining her offing, replied with a gesture. It was a gesture they had learned from the boot-and-knife boy, and they had once been spanked for practicing it on the piano-tuner. The boot-and-knife boy called it "cocking a snook," and it consisted in raising a thumb to one's nose and spreading the fingers out. It was defiance and insult in tabloid form. Then she turned and plodded on. The opaque wall of the wood was before her and over her, but she knew its breach. She ducked her head under a droop of branches, squirmed through, was visible still for some seconds as a gleam of blue frock, and then the ghostly shadows received her and she was gone. The wood closed behind her like a lid.

Joyce, squatting in her place, blinked a little breathlessly to shift from her senses an oppression of alarm, and settled down to wait for her. At least it was true that nothing ever happened to Joan; even when she fell into a water-butt she suffered no damage; and the wood was a place to which they came every day.

"Besides," she considered, enumerating her resources of comfort; "besides, there can't be such things as wood-ladies, really."

But Joan was a long time gone. The dome of pines took on an uncanny stillness; the moving patches of sun seemed furtive and unnatural; the ferns swayed without noise. In the midst of it, patient and nervous, sat Joyce, watching always that spot in the bushes where a blue overall and a brown head had disappeared. The under-note of alarm which stirred her senses died down; a child finds it hard to spin out a mood; she simply sat, half-dreaming in the peace of the morning, half-watching the wood. Time slipped by her, and presently there came Mother, smiling and seeking through the trees for her babies.

"Isn't there a clock inside you that tells you when it's lunch time?" asked Mother. "You're ever so late. Where's Joan?"

Joyce rose among the ferns, delicate and elfin, with a shy perplexity on her face. It was difficult to speak even to Mother about wood-ladies without a pretence of skepticism.

"I forgot about lunch," she said, taking the slim, cool hand which Mother held out to her. "Joan's in there." She nodded at the bushes.

"Is she?" said Mother, and called aloud in her singing voice that was so clear to hear in the spaces of the wood. "Joan! Joan!"

A cheeky bird answered with a whistle, and Mother called again.

"She said," explained Joyce; "she said she saw a wood-lady, and then she went in there to show me she wasn't afraid."

"What's a wood-lady, chick?" asked Mother. "The rascal!" she said, smiling, when Joyce had explained as best she could. "We'll have to go and look for her."

They went hand in hand, and Mother showed herself clever in parting a path among the bushes. She managed so that no bough sprang back to strike Joyce, and without tearing or soiling her own soft, white dress; one could guess that when she had been a little girl she, too, had had a wood to play in. They cut down by the Secret Pond, where the old rhododendrons were, and out to the edge of the fields; and when they paused Mother would lift her head and call again, and her voice rang in the wood like a bell. By the pond, which was a black water with steep banks, she paused and showed a serious face; but there were no marks of shoes on its clay slopes, and she shook her head and went on. But to all the calling there was no answer, no distant cheery bellow to guide them to Joan.

"I wish she wouldn't play these tricks," said Mother. "I don't like them a bit."

"I expect she's hiding," said Joyce. "There aren't wood-ladies really, are there, Mother?"

"There's nothing worse in these woods than a rather naughty baby," Mother replied. "We'll go back by the path and call her again."

Joyce knew that the hand which held hers tightened as they went, and there was still no answer to Mother's calling. She could not have told what it was that made her suddenly breathless; the wood about her turned desolate; an oppression of distress and bewilderment burdened them both. "Joan! Joan!" called Mother in her strong beautiful contralto, swelling the word forth in powerful music, and when she ceased the silence was like a taunt. It was not as if Joan were there and failed to answer; it was as if there were no longer any Joan anywhere. They came at last to the space of sparse trees which bordered their garden.

"We mustn't be silly about this," said Mother, speaking as much to herself as to Joyce. "Nothing can have happened to her. And you must have lunch, chick."

"Without waiting for Joan?" asked Joyce.

"Yes. The gardener and the boot-boy must look for Joan," said Mother, opening the gate.

The dining-room looked very secure and homelike, with its big window and its cheerful table spread for lunch. Joyce's place faced the window, so that she could see the lawn and the hedge bounding the kitchen garden; and when Mother had served her with food, she was left alone to eat it. Presently the gardener and the boot-boy passed the window, each carrying a hedge-stake and looking war-like. There reached her a murmur of voices; the gardener was mumbling something about tramps.

"Oh, I don't think so," replied Mother's voice.

Mother came in presently and sat down, but did not eat anything. Joyce asked her why.

"Oh, I shall have some lunch when Joan comes," answered Mother. "I shan't be hungry till then. Will you have some more, my pet?"

When Joyce had finished, they went out again to the wood to meet Joan when she was brought back in custody. Mother walked quite slowly, looking all the time as if she would like to run. Joyce held her hand and sometimes glanced up at her face, so full of wonder and a sort of resentful doubt, as though circumstances were playing an unmannerly trick on her. At the gate they came across the boot-boy.

"I bin all acrost that way," said the boot-boy, pointing with his stumpy black forefinger, "and then acrost that way, an' Mister Jenks" Jenks was the gardener "'e've gone about in rings, 'e 'ave. And there ain't no sign nor token, mum, not a sign there ain't."

From behind him sounded the voice of the gardener, thrashing among the trees. "Miss Joan!" he roared. "Hi! Miss Jo-an! You're a-frightin' your Ma proper. Where are ye, then?"

"She must be hiding," said Mother. "You must go on looking, Walter. You must go on looking till you find her."

"Yes'm," said Walter. "If's she's in there us'll find her, soon or late."

He ran off, and presently his voice was joined to Jenks's, calling Joan calling, calling, and getting no answer.

Mother took Joyce's hand again.

"Come," she said. "We'll walk round by the path, and you must tell me again how it all happened. Did you really see something when Joan told you to look?"

"I expect I didn't," replied Joyce, dolefully. "But Joan's always saying there's a fairy or something in the shadows, and I always think I see them for a moment."

"It couldn't have been a live woman or a man that you saw?"

"Oh, no!" Joyce was positive of that. Mother's hand tightened on hers understandingly, and they went on in silence till they met Jenks.

Jenks was an oldish man with bushy grey whiskers, who never wore a coat, and now he was wet to the loins with mud and water.

"That there ol' pond," he explained. "I've been an' took a look at her. Tromped through her proper, I did, an' I'll go bail there ain't so much as a dead cat in all the mud of her. Thish yer's a mistry, mum, an' no mistake."

Mother stared at him. "I can't bear this," she said suddenly. "You must go on searching, Jenks, and Walter must go on his bicycle to the police station at once. Call him, please!"

"Walter!" roared Jenks obediently.

"Comin'!" answered the boot-boy, and burst forth from the bushes. In swift, clear words, which no stupidity could mistake or forget, Mother gave him his orders, spoken in a tone that meant urgency. Walter went flying to execute them.

"Oh, Mother, where do you think Joan can be?" begged Joyce when Jenks had gone off to resume his search:

"I don't know," said Mother. "It's all so absurd."

"If there was wood-ladies, they wouldn't hurt a baby like Joan," suggested Joyce.

"Oh, who could hurt her!" cried Mother, and fell to calling again. Her voice, of which each accent was music, alternated with the harsh roars of Jenks.

Walter on his bicycle must have hurried, in spite of his permanently punctured front tire, for it was a very short time before bells rang in the steep lane from the road and Superintendent Farrow himself wheeled his machine in at the gate, massive and self-possessed, a blue-clad minister of comfort. He heard Mother's tale, which embodied that of Joyce, with a half-smile lurking in his moustache and his big chin creased back against his collar. Then he nodded, exactly as if he saw through the whole business and could find Joan in a minute or two, and propped his bicycle against the fence.

"I understand, then," he said, "that the little girl's been missing for rather more than an hour. In that case, she can't have got far. I sent a couple o' constables round the roads be'ind the wood before I started, an' now I'll just 'ave a look through the wood myself."

"Thank you," said Mother. "I don't know why I'm so nervous, but—."

"Very natural, ma'am," said the big superintendent, comfortingly, and went with them to the wood.

It was rather thrilling to go with him and watch him. Joyce and Mother had to show him the place from which Joan had started and the spot at which she had disappeared. He looked at them hard, frowning a little and nodding to himself, and went stalking mightily among the ferns. "It was 'ere she went?" he inquired, as he reached the dark path, and being assured that it was, he thrust in and commenced his search. The pond seemed to give him ideas, which old Jenks disposed of, and he marched on till he came out to the edge of the fields, where the hay was yet uncut. Joan could not have crossed them without leaving a track in the tall grass as clear as a cart-rut.

"We 'ave to consider the possibilities of the matter," said the superintendent. "Assumin' that the wood 'as been thoroughly searched, where did she get out of it?"

"Searched!" growled old Jenks. "There ain't a inch as I 'aven't searched an' seen, not a inch."

"The kidnappin' the'ry," went on the superintendent, ignoring him and turning to Mother, "I don't incline to. 'Owever, we must go to work in order, an' I'll 'ave my men up 'ere and make sure of the wood. All gypsies an' tramps will be stopped and interrogated. I don't think there's no cause for you to feel anxious, ma'am. I 'ope to 'ave some news for you in the course of the afternoon."

They watched him free-wheel down the lane and shoot round the corner.

"Oh, dear," said Mother, then: "Why doesn't the baby come? I wish Daddy weren't away."

Now that the police had entered the affair Joyce felt that there remained nothing to be done. Uniformed authority was in charge of events; it could not fail to find Joan. She had a vision of the police at work, stopping straggling families of tramps on distant by-roads, looking into the contents of their dreadful bundles, flashing the official bull's eye lantern into the mysterious interior of gypsy caravans, and making ragged men and slatternly women give an account of their wanderings. No limits to which they would not go; how could they fail? She wished their success seemed as inevitable to her mother as it did to her.

"They're sure to bring her back, Mother," she repeated.

"Oh, chick," said Mother, "I keep telling myself so. But I wish I wish."

"What, Mother?"

"I wish," said Mother in a sudden burst of speech, as if she were confessing something that troubled her; "I wish you hadn't seen that wood-lady."

The tall young constables and the plump fatherly sergeant annoyed old Jenks by searching the wood as though he had done nothing. It was a real search this time. Each of them took a part of the ground and went over it as though he were looking for a needle which had been lost, and no fewer than three of them trod every inch of the bottom of the Secret Pond. They took shovels and opened up an old fox's earth; and a sad-looking man in shabby plain clothes arrived and walked about smoking a pipe a detective! Up from the village, too, came the big young curate and the squire's two sons, civil and sympathetic and eager to be helpful; they all thought it natural that Mother should be anxious, but refused to credit for an instant that anything could have happened to Joyce.

"That baby!" urged the curate. "Why, my dear lady, Joan is better known hereabouts than King George himself. No one could take her a mile without having to answer questions. I don't know what's keeping her, but you may be sure she's all right."

"Course she is," chorused the others, swinging their sticks lightheartedly. "'Course she's all right."

"Get her for me, then," said Mother. "I don't want to be silly, and you're awfully good. But I must have her; I must have her. I, I want her."

The squire's sons turned as if on an order and went towards the wood. The curate lingered a moment. He was a huge youth, an athlete and a gentleman, and his hard clean-shaven face could be kind and serious.

"We're sure to get her," he said in lower tones. "And you must help us with your faith and courage. Can you?"

Mother's hand tightened on that of Joyce.

"We are doing our best," she said, and smiled she smiled. The curate nodded and went his way to the wood.

A little later in the afternoon came Colonel Warden, the lord and master of all the police in the county, a gay trim soldier whom the children knew and liked. With him, in his big automobile, were more policemen and a pair of queer liver-colored dogs, all baggy skin and bleary eyes bloodhounds! Joyce felt that this really must settle it. Actual living bloodhounds would be more than a match for Joan. Colonel Warden was sure of it too.

"Saves time," he was telling Mother in his high snappy voice. "Shows us which way she's gone, you know. Best hounds in the country, these two; never known 'em fail yet."

The dogs were limp and quiet as he led them through the wood, strange ungainly mechanisms which a whiff of a scent could set in motion. A pinafore, which Joan had worn at breakfast, was served to them for an indication of the work they had to do; they snuffed at it languidly for some seconds. Then the colonel unleashed them.

They smelled round and about like any other dogs for a while, till one of them lifted his great head and uttered a long moaning cry. Then, noses down, the men running behind them, they set off across the ferns. Mother, still holding Joyce's hand, followed. The hounds made a straight line for the wood at the point at which Joan had entered it, slid in like frogs into water, while the men dodged and crashed after them. Joyce and Mother came up with them at a place where the bushes stood back, enclosing a little quiet space of turf that lay open to the sky. The hounds were here, one lying down and scratching himself, the other nosing casually and clearly without interest about him.

"Dash it all," the colonel was saying; "she can't she simply can't have been kidnapped in a balloon."

They tried the hounds again and again, always with the same result. They ran their line to the same spot unhesitatingly, and then gave up as though the scent went no farther. Nothing could induce them to hunt beyond it.

"I can't understand this," said Colonel Warden, dragging at his moustache. "This is queer." He stood glancing, around him as though the shrubs and trees had suddenly become enemies.

The search was still going on when the time came for Joyce to go to bed. It had spread from the wood across the fields, reinforced by scores of sturdy volunteers, and automobiles had puffed away to thread the mesh of little lanes that covered the countryside. Joyce found it all terribly exciting. Fear for Joan she felt not at all.

"I know inside myself," she told Mother, "right down deep in the middle of me, that Joan's all right."

"Bless you, my chick," said poor Mother. "I wish I could feel like that. Go to bed now, like a good girl."

There was discomfort in the sight of Joan's railed cot standing empty in the night nursery, but Joyce was tired and had scarcely begun to be touched by it before she was asleep. She had a notion that during the night Mother came in more than once, and she had a vague dream, too, all about Joan and wood-ladies, of which she could not remember much when she woke up. Joan was always dressed first in the morning, being the younger of the pair, but now there was no Joan, and Nurse was very gentle with Joyce and looked tired and as if she had been crying.

Mother was not to be seen that morning; she had been up all night, "till she broke down, poor thing," said Nurse, and Joyce was bidden to amuse herself quietly in the nursery. But Mother was about again at lunch time when Joyce went down to the dining room. She was very pale and her eyes looked black and deep, and somehow t she seemed suddenly smaller and younger, more nearly Joyce's age, than ever before. They kissed each other, and the child would have tried to comfort.

"No," said Mother, shaking her head. "No dear. Don't let's be sorry for each other yet. It would be like giving up hope. And we haven't done that, have we?"

"I haven't," said Joyce. "I know it's all right."

After lunch again Mother said she wouldn't be hungry till Joan came home they went out together. There were no searchers now in the wood and the garden was empty; the police had left no inch unscanned and they were away, combing the countryside and spreading terror among the tramps. The sun was strong upon the lawn, and the smell of the roses was heavy on the air; across the hedge, the land rolled away to clear perspectives of peace and beauty.

"Let's walk up and down," suggested Mother. "Anything's better than sitting still. And don't talk, chick not just now."

They paced the length of the lawn, from the cedar to the gate which led to the wood, perhaps a dozen times, hand in hand and in silence. It was while their backs were turned to the wood that they heard the gate click, and faced about to see who was coming. A blue-sleeved arm thrust the gate open, and there advanced into the sunlight, coming forth from the shadow as from a doorway Joan! Her round baby face, with the sleek brown hair over it, the massive infantile body, the sturdy bare legs, confronted them serenely. Mother uttered a deep sigh it sounded like that and in a moment she was kneeling on the ground with her arms round the baby.

"Joan, Joan," she said over and over again. "My little, little baby!"

Joan struggled in her embrace till she got an arm free, and then rubbed her eyes drowsily.

"Hallo!" she said.

"But where have you been?" cried Mother. "Baby-girl, where have you been all this time?"

Joan made a motion of her head and her free arm towards the wood, the wood which had been searched a dozen times over like a pocket. "In there," she answered carelessly. "Wiv the wood-ladies. I'm hungry!"

"My darling!" said Mother, and picked her up and carried her into the house.

In the dining-room, with Mother at her side and Joyce opposite to her, Joan fell to her food in her customary workmanlike fashion, and between helpings answered questions in a fashion which only served to darken the mystery of her absence.

"But there aren't any wood-ladies really, darling," remonstrated
Mother.

"There is," said Joan. "There's lots. They wanted to keep me but I wouldn't stay. So I comed home, 'cause I was hungry."

"But," began Mother. "Where did they take you to?" she asked.

"I don't know," said Joan. "The one what I went to speak to gave me her hand and tooked me to where there was more of them. It was a place in the wood wiv grass to sit on and bushes all round, and they gave me dead flowers to play wiv. Howwid old dead flowers!"

"Yes," said Mother. "What else?"

"There was anuvver little girl there," went on Joan. "Not a wood-lady but a girl like me, what they'd tooked from somewhere. She was wearing a greeny sort of dress like they was, and they wanted me to put one on too. But I wouldn't."

"Why wouldn't you?" asked Joyce.

"'Cause I didn't want to be a wood-lady," replied Joan.

"Listen to me, darling," said Mother. "Didn't these people whom you call wood-ladies take you away out of the wood? We searched the whole wood, you know, and you weren't there at all."

"I was," said Joan. "I was there all the time, an' I heard Walter an' Jenks calling. I cocked a snook at them an' the wood-ladies laughed like leaves rustling."

"But where did you sleep last night?"

"I didn't sleep," said Joan, grasping her spoon anew. "I'se very sleepy now."

She was asleep as soon as they laid her in bed, and Mother and Joyce looked at each other across her cot, above her rosy and unconscious face.

"God help us," said Mother in a whisper. "What is the truth of this?"

There was never any answer, any hint of a solution, save Joan's. And she, as soon as she discovered that her experiences amounted to an adventure, began to embroider them, and now she does not even know herself. She has reached the age of seven, and it is long since she has believed in anything so childish as wood-ladies.

IV

A MAN BEFORE THE MAST

In Tom Mowbray's boarding-house, the sailors who sat upon the narrow benches round the big room ceased their talk as the door opened and Tom Mowbray himself entered from the street. The men in the room, for all the dreary stiffness of their shore-clothes, carried upon their faces, in their hands shaped to the rasp of ropes, in every attitude of their bodies, the ineradicable hall-mark of the sea which was the arena of their lives; they salted the barren place with its vigor and pungency. Pausing within the door, Tom Mowbray sent his pale inexpressive glance flickering along the faces they turned towards him.

"Well, boys," he said; "takin' it easy fer a spell?"

There was a murmur of reply from the men; they watched him warily, knowing that he was not genial for nothing. He was a man of fifty or more, bloated in body, with an immobile grey face and a gay white moustache that masked his gross and ruthless mouth. He was dressed like any other successful merchant, bulging waistcoat, showy linen and all; the commodity in which he dealt was the flesh and blood of seamen, and his house was eminent among those which helped the water-front of San Francisco "the Barbary Coast," as sailors call it to its unholy fame. He stood among the sunburnt, steady-eyed seamen like a fungus in fresh grass.

"An' now, who's for a good ship?" he inquired. There was a sort of mirth in his voice as he spoke. "Good wages, good grub, an' a soft job. Don't all of ye speak at once."

The sailors eyed him warily. From the end of the room a white-haired American looked up wryly.

"What's her name?" he asked.

"Name?" Tom Mowbray kept his countenance, though the name was the cream of the joke. He paused, watching the faces of those who had been ashore a week and were due to ship again when he should give the word. "Oh, you don't want to be scared of her name; her name's all right. She's the Etna."

Somebody laughed, and Tom Mowbray gave him an approving glance; the others interchanged looks. The Etna had a reputation familiar to seamen and a nickname too; they called her the "Hell-packet." Of all the tall and beautiful ships which maintained their smartness and their beauty upon the agony of wronged and driven seamen, the Etna was the most terrible, a blue-water penitentiary, a floating place of torment. To enhance the strange terror of her, the bitter devil who was her captain carried his wife on board; the daily brutalities that made her infamous went on under the eyes and within the hearing of a woman; it added a touch of the grotesque to what was otherwise fearful enough.

Tom Mowbray stood enjoying the dumb consternation of his victims.

"Well, who's for it?" he inquired. "Ain't there none of you that wants a good ship like that Noo York an' back here, an' eighteen dollars a month? Well, I s'pose I'll have to take my pick of yer."

They knew he had proposed the matter to them only in mockery of their helplessness; they were at his mercy, and those he selected would have to go. He would secure an advance of three months of their wages as payment for their week or so of board; and they would desert penniless in New York to escape the return voyage. There was no remedy; it was almost a commonplace risk of their weary lives so commonplace a risk that of all those men, accustomed to peril and violence, there was none to rise and drive a fist into his sleek face. But, from the back of the room, one, nursing a crossed knee, with his pipe in his mouth, spoke with assurance.

"I'm not goin' aboard of her," he said.

Tom Mowbray's heavy brows lowered a little; he surveyed the speaker. It was a young man, sitting remote from the windows, whose face, in the shadows of the big, bare room, showed yet a briskness of coloring. His name Tom remembered it with an effort was Goodwin, Daniel Goodwin; he had been paid off from a "limejuicer" little more than a week before.

"Oh, you're not goin' aboard of her?" he queried slowly.

"No," answered the young man calmly. "I'm not."

It was defiance, it was insult; but Tom Mowbray could stand that. He smoothed out his countenance, watching while the young man's neighbor on the bench nudged him warningly.

"Well, I gotta find a crowd for her," he said in tones of resignation. "I dunno how I'm goin' to do it, though."

He sighed, the burlesque sigh of a fat man pitying himself, and passed through the room to the door at the far end. Not till it had closed behind him did talk resume. A man who had been three weeks ashore leant back against the wall and let his breath escape in a sigh, which was not burlesque. For him there was no hope; he was as much doomed as if a judge had pronounced sentence on him.

"Oh, hell!" he said. "Wonder if he'll let me have a dollar to get a drink 'fore I go aboard of her?"

The others turned their eyes on him curiously; whatever happened to them, he was a man who would sail in the Etna; already he was isolated and tragic.

The neighbor who had nudged young Goodwin nudged him again.

"Come out," he breathed into the ear that the young man bent towards him. "Come out; I want to speak t' ye."

In the street, the mean cobbled street of the Barbary Coast, the man who nudged took Goodwin by the arm and spoke urgently.

"Say, ain't ye got no sense?" he demanded. "Talkin' like that to Tom Mowbray! Don't ye know that's the way to fix him to ship ye aboard the 'Hell-packet?'"

"He can't ship me aboard any 'Hell-packet,'" answered Goodwin serenely. "When I ship, I ship myself, an' I pay my board in cash. There ain't any advance note to be got out o' me."

The other halted and drew Goodwin to halt, facing him at the edge of the sidewalk, where a beetle-browed saloon projected its awning above them. Like Goodwin, he was young and brown; but unlike Goodwin there was a touch of sophistication, of daunting experience, in the seriousness of his face. The two had met and chummed after the fashion of sailors, who make and lose their friends as the hazard of the hour directs.

"You don't know Tom Mowbray," he said in a kind of affectionate contempt. "He's, he's a swine an' he's cute! Didn't you hear about him shippin' a corpse aboard o' the Susquehanna, an' drawin' three months' advance for it? Why, you ain't got a show with him if he's got a down on ye."

Goodwin smiled. "Maybe I don't know Tom Mowbray," he said; "but it's a sure thing Tom Mowbray don't know me. Come on an' have a drink, Jim. This thing of the Etna it's settled. Come on!"

He led the way into the saloon beside them; Jim, growling warningly, followed him.

At twenty-six, it was Goodwin's age, one should be very much a man. One's moustache is confirmed in its place; one has the stature and muscle of a man, a man's tenacity and resistance, while the heart of boyishness still pulses in one's body. It is the age at which capacity is the ally of impulse, when heart and hand go paired in a perfect fraternity. One is as sure of oneself as a woman of thirty, and with as much and as little reason. Goodwin, when he announced that he, at any rate, would not be one of the crew of the Etna, spoke out of a serene confidence in himself. He knew himself for a fine seaman and a reasonably fine human being; he had not squandered his wages, and he did not mean to be robbed of his earnings when he shipped himself again. It was his first visit to San Francisco; the ports he knew were not dangerous to a man who took care of himself, who was not a drunkard, and would fight at need. He showed as something under six feet tall, long in the limb and moving handily, with eyes of an angry blue in a face tanned russet by wind and sun.

In the saloon he laughed down Jim's instances of Tom Mowbray's treachery and cunning, lounging with an elbow on the bar, careless and confident under the skeptical eyes of the white-jacketed barman.

"I reckon Tom Mowbray knows when he's safe," he said. "Why, if he was to do any o' them things to me I'd get him if I had to dig for him. Yes, sir!"

From thence the course of events ran as anyone familiar with the Barbary Coast might have prophesied. They returned to the boarding-house for supper and joined their fellows at the long table in the back room, and were waited on by Tom Mowbray's "runners." Mowbray himself, with his scared, lean wife and his wife's crippled brother, had a table apart from the men; as he ate he entertained himself by baiting the unhappy cripple, till the broken man stammered tearfully across the table at him, shaking and grimacing in a nervous frenzy, which Tom Mowbray always found comical. The woman between them sat with her eyes downcast and her face bitter and still; they made a picture of domesticity at which the sailors stared in a fascination of perplexity, while the hard-faced "runners" in their shirt-sleeves carried the plates to and from the kitchen, and the ritual of the evening meal proceeded to its finish.

If there was in Goodwin a quality more salient than his youthful force and his trust in his own capacity, it was the manner he had of seeing absorbedly the men and things that presented themselves to his eyes, so that even in dull and trivial matters he gathered strong impressions and vivid memories. The three people at the little table made a group from which, while he ate, he could not withdraw his eyes. The suffering passivity of the woman, the sly, sinister humor in Tom Mowbray's heavy, grey face, the livid and impotent hate that frothed in the crippled man, and his strange jerky gestures, the atmosphere of nightmare cruelty and suffering that enveloped them like a miasma these bit themselves into his imagination and left it sore. He saw and tasted nothing of what he ate and drank; he was lost in watching the three at the other table; the man who refilled his cup with coffee winked across his head to one of the others as though in mirth at his abstraction.

In the ordinary way he would have gone for a walk up-town with his friend after supper; but he was not in a mood for company that evening and found himself sleepy besides. He went upstairs to the bedroom he shared with two other men to get some tobacco he had there, and discovered in himself so strong an inclination to slumber that he decided to go to bed forthwith. He lit his pipe and sat down on his bed to take his boots off. He had one boot unlaced but still on his foot when his pipe dropped from his lips. Across his drugged and failing brain there flickered for an instant the blurred shape of a suspicion.

"What's the matter with me?" he half cried; and tried to rise to his feet.

He knew he had failed to stand up and had fallen back on the bed. With his last faculties he resisted the tides of darkness that rushed in upon him; then his grasp upon consciousness loosened and his face, which had been knitted in effort, relaxed. When half an hour later Tom Mowbray and two of his "runners" came to find him, he lay, scarcely breathing, in the appearance of a profound and natural sleep.

It was thirty-six hours later when a vague consciousness of pain, growing upon his poisoned nerves, sharpened to a climax, and he opened his eyes, lying where he found himself without moving. It took him some minutes before he brought his mind into co-ordination with his senses to realize what he saw. Then it was plain to him that he was lying upon the bare slats of a bunk in the narrow forecastle of a ship. Its door, hooked open, made visible a slice of sunlit deck and a wooden rail beyond it, from which the gear of the foremast slanted up. Within the forecastle only three of the bunks contained mattresses and blankets, and there was no heave and sway under him to betoken a ship under sail in a seaway.

Slowly the sailor within him asserted itself. "This hooker's at anchor!"

By degrees he began to account for himself. Recollection returned: he had waked in a bare and bedless bunk, but it was at Tom Mowbray's he had fallen asleep. He remembered going up to his room and the sleepiness that had pressed itself upon him there. And there was a thought, a doubt, that had been with him at the last. It eluded him for a moment; then he remembered and sat up, in an access of vigor and anger as he recalled it.

"Knock-out drops," he said. "Yes, by God! Tom Mowbray's shanghaied me!"

His head ached, his skin and his mouth were parched as if by a fever. Stiffly he swung himself over the edge of his bunk and went on feet that were numb and uncertain through the door to the deck. He was sore all over from lying on the bare slats of the bunk, and the dregs of the drug still clogged his mind and muscles; but like the flame in a foul lantern there burned in him the fires of anger.

"Shanghaied!" he repeated as he reeled to the rail and caught at a backstay to steady himself. "Well, the man that did it wants to hide when I get ashore again."

He cast his eyes aft over the ship on which he found himself, summing her up with an automatic expertness. An American ship, it was plain, and a three-skysail-yarder at that, with a magnificent stature and spread of spars. Abeam of her San Francisco basked along its shore; she was at an anchor well out in the bay. What ship was it that he had viewed from a dock-head lying just there? The answer was on his lips even before his eyes discovered the boat she carried on top of the fo'c'sle, with her name lettered upon it. Tom Mowbray had proved his power by shanghaiing him aboard the Etna!

He said nothing: the situation was beyond mere oaths, but wrath surged in him like a flood.

Around the for'ard house, walking with measured steps, came Mr. Fant, the mate of the Etna, and accosted him.

"Sobered up, have ye?" said Mr. Fant.

"Yes, sir," said Goodwin.

"That's right," said Mr. Fant, smiling, surveying him with an appearance of gentle interest. "Knock-out drops?" he inquired.

"Yes, sir," answered Goodwin again, watching him.

"Ah!" Mr. Fant shook his head. "Well, you're all right now," he said. "Stick yer head in a bucket an' ye'll be ready to turn to."

Mr. Fant had his share in the fame of the Etna; he was a part of her character. Goodwin, though his mind still moved slowly, eyed him intently, gauging the man's strange and masked quality, probing the mildness of his address for the thing it veiled. He saw the mate of the Etna as a spare man of middle-age, who would have been tall but for the stoop of his shoulders. His shaven face was constricted primly; he had the mouth of an old maid, and stood slack-bodied with his hands sunk in the pockets of his jacket. Only the tightness of his clothes across his chest and something sure and restrained in his gait as he walked hinted of the iron thews that governed his lean body; and, while he spoke in the accents of an easy civility, his stony eyes looked on Goodwin with an unblinking and remorseless aloofness. It was not hard to imagine him, when the Etna, with her crew seduced or drugged to man her, should be clear of soundings and the business of the voyage put in shape, when every watch on deck would be a quaking ordeal of fear and pain, and every watch below an interval for mere despair.

The vision of it made Goodwin desperate.

"I haven't signed on, sir," he protested. "I've been shanghaied here. This ain't."

He paused under the daunting compulsion of Mr. Fant's eye.

"You've signed on all right," said Mr. Fant. "Your name's John Smith an' you signed on yesterday. You don't want to make any mistake about that, Smith."

He spoke as mildly as ever and yet was menacing and terrible. But Goodwin was insistent.

"My name's Goodwin," he persisted. "Tom Mowbray drugged me and shoved me on board. I want to go ashore."

Mr. Fant turned to go aft. "You get yer head into a bucket," he counselled. "Hurry up, now. There's work waitin' to be done."

"I won't!" shouted Goodwin.

"Eh!" Mr. Fant's voice was still mild as he uttered the exclamation, but before Goodwin could repeat himself he had moved. As if some spring in him had been released from tension, the mild and prim Mr. Fant whirled on his heel, and a fist took Goodwin on the edge of the jaw and sent him gasping and clucking on to his back; while, with the precision of a movement rehearsed and practiced, Mr. Fant's booted foot swung forward and kicked him into the scuppers. He lay there on his back, looking up in an extremity of terror and astonishment at the unmoved face of the mate.

"Get up, Smith," commanded Mr. Fant. Goodwin obeyed, scarcely conscious of the pain in his face and flank in the urgency of the moment. "Now you get the bucket, same as I told you, and when you've freshened yourself come aft an' I'll start you on a job. See?"

"Aye, aye, sir," responded Goodwin mechanically, and started for-ard. The Etna had absorbed him into her system; he was initiated already to his role of a driven beast; but tenacious as an altar fire there glowed yet within him the warmth of his anger against Tom Mowbray. It was secret, beyond the reach of Mr. Fant's fist; the fist was only another item in Tom Mowbray's debt.

From his place on the crossjack-yard, to which Mr. Fant sent him, Goodwin had presently a view of the captain's wife. She came to the poop from the cabin companion-way and leaned for a while on the taffrail, seeming to gaze at the town undulating over the hills, dwarfed by the distance. It was when she turned to go down again that Goodwin had a full view of her face, bleak and rigid, with greying hair drawn tightly back from the temples, as formal and blank as the face of a clock. It was told of her that she would sit knitting in her chair by the mizzen fife-rail while at the break of the poop a miserable man was being trodden and beaten out of the likeness of humanity and never lift her head nor shift her attitude for all his cries and struggles. It was her presence aboard that touched the man-slaughtering Etna with her quality of the macabre.

"But she won't see me broken up," swore Goodwin to himself as her head vanished in the hood of the companion. "No not if I've got to set the damn ship alight!"

He made the acquaintance, when work was over for the day, of his fellows in ill-fortune, the owners of the three occupied bunks in the forecastle. As if the Etna had laid herself out to starve him of every means of comfort, they proved to be "Dutchmen" that is to say, Teutons of one nationality or another and therefore, by sea-canons, his inferiors, incapable of sharing his feelings and not to be trusted with his purpose. One question, however, they were able to answer satisfactorily. It had occurred to him that since even Tom Mowbray could only get men for the Etna by drugging them, her officers would probably take special precautions to guard against desertion.

"Do they lock us in here at night?" he asked of the three of them when they sat at supper in the port fo'c'sle.

They stared at him uncomprehendingly. For them, helots of the sea, the Etna's terrors were nothing out of the way; all ships used them harshly; life itself was harsh enough. Their bland blond faces were stupid and amiable.

"Log us in!" answered one of them. "No! For what shall they log us in?"

"That's all right, then," said Goodwin and let them continue to stare at him, ruminating his reasons for the question.

There was a fourth "Dutchman" who slumbered through the day in the starboard fo'c'sle and sat all night in the galley, in the exercise of his functions as night-watchman. His lamp shed a path of light from the galley door to the rail when, his fellows in the fo'c'sle being, audibly asleep, Goodwin rose from his bunk and came forth to the deck. Far away, across the level waters of the great bay, the lights of the city made an illumination against the background of the night; overhead there was a sky bold with stars; the Etna floated mute in a rustle of moving waters. There were no ships near her; only now and again a towboat racing up from the Golden Gates went by with the noise of a breaking wave on a steep shore. In the break of the poop there showed the light of Mr. Fant's window, where he lay in his bunk, relaxing his grisly official personality with a book and a cigar.

In deft haste Goodwin stepped to the fore side of the fo'c'sle, where he would be hidden should the watchman take a fancy to look out of his galley. In him a single emotion was constant: he had a need to find Tom Mowbray. It was more than an idea or a passion: it was like the craving of a drug maniac for his poison. The shore that blinked at him across the black waters was not inaccessible under the impulse of that lust of anger; he was at all times a strong swimmer. Under shelter of the deckhouse he stripped his clothes and made of them it was only his shirt and trousers a bundle which the belt that carried his sheath-knife fastened upon his head, descending under his chin like a helmet-strap. With infinite precaution to be unheard he went in this trim across the deck to the rail.

The Etna's chain-plates were broad as a frigate's; he had but to let himself down carefully and he was in the water without a splash. A dozen strokes took him clear of her, and presently he paused, up-ending and treading water, to look back at her. She stood up over her anchors like a piece of architecture, poising like a tower; the sailor in him paid tribute to the builders who had conceived her beauty. They had devised a ship: it needed Mr. Fant and his colleagues to degrade her into a sea-going prophet and give aptness to her by-name of "Hell-packet." He was clear of her now; he might fail to reach the shore and drown, but at least the grey woman aft would never see his humiliation and defeat. He turned over, setting his face to the waterside lights of the city, and struck out.

It was a long swim, and it was fortunate for him that he took the water on the turn of the tide, so that where the tail of the ebb set him down the first of the flood bore him back. The stimulus of the chill and the labor of swimming cleared the poison from his body and brain; he swam steadily, with eyes fixed on the lights beading the waterside and mind clenched on the single purpose to find Tom Mowbray, to deal with him, to satisfy the anger which ached in him like a starved appetite. How he would handle him, what he would do with him, when he found him, did not occupy his thoughts; it was a purpose and not a plan which was taking him ashore. He had the man's pursy large face for ever in his consciousness; the vision of it was a spur, an exasperation; he found himself swimming furiously, wasting strength, in the thought of encountering it.

Good luck and not calculation brought him ashore on the broadside of the Barbary Coast, in a small dock where a Norwegian barque lay slumbering alongside the wharf. Her watchman, if she had one, was not in sight; it was upon her deck that he dressed himself, fumbling hurriedly into the shirt and trousers which he had failed, after all, to keep dry. He jerked his belt tight about him and felt the sheath-knife which it carried pressing against his back. He reached back and slid it round to his right side, where his hand would drop on it easily; it might chance that before the night was over he would need a weapon.

He had no notion of the hour nor of the length of time he had been in the water. As he passed bare-footed from the wharf he was surprised to find the shabby street empty under its sparse lamps. It lay between its mean houses vacant and unfamiliar in its quietude; it seemed to him as though the city waited in a conscious hush till he should have done what he had come to do. His bare feet on the sidewalk slapped and shuffled, and he hurried along close to the walls; the noise he made, for all his caution, appeared to him monstrous, enough to wake the sleepers in the houses and draw them to their windows to see the man who was going to find Tom Mowbray.

An alley between gapped and decrepit board fences brought him to the back of the house he sought; he swung himself into the unsavory back yard of it without delaying to seek for the gate. The house was over him, blank and lightless, its roof a black heap against the night sky. He paused to look up at it. He was still without any plan; not even now did he feel the need of one. To go in to break in, if that were the quickest way to stamp his stormy way up the room where Tom Mowbray was sleeping, to wrench him from his bed and then let loose the maniac fury that burned within him all that was plain to do. He cast a glance at the nearest window, and then it was that the door of the house opened.

He was standing to one side, a dozen paces from it; a single, noiseless step took him to the wall, against which he backed, screened by the darkness, and waited to see who would come forth. A figure appeared and lingered in the doorway, and he caught the sibilance of a whisper, and immediately upon it a dull noise of tapping, as though someone beat gently and slowly against the door with a clenched hand. It was a noise he had heard before; his faculties strained themselves to identify it. Then a second figure appeared, smaller than the first, moving with a strange gait, and he knew. It was the cripple, Mowbray's brother-in-law, and it was his leather-shod crutch which had tapped on the floor of the passage. The two figures moved down the yard together, and presently, as they passed from the shadow of the house and came within the feeble light of a lamp that burned at the mouth of the alley, he saw that the taller of the two was Tom Mowbray's wife. They found the gate in the fence and opened it, manifestly hesitating at the strident creaking it made, and passed through. At no moment were they clear to see, but to Goodwin's eyes their very gait was in some way expressive of a tragic solemnity that clad them.

He remained silent in his place as they went along the alley towards the street, passing him at arm's length on the other side of the fence. Their footsteps were muffled on the unpaved ground of the alley, but there was another noise which he heard the noise of the woman weeping weeping brokenly and openly. Then the cripple's harsh, hopeless voice spoke.

"Anyway, we're alone together again for a bit, Sally," he croaked.

The woman checked her sobs to answer. "Yes, honey," she replied.

Goodwin waited till the tapping of the crutch had receded. "So they've quit him at last," he reflected. "And" he stepped forth from his hiding place briskly "they've left the door open. Now for Tom Mowbray!"

Once within the door he was no longer careful to be silent. The house was dark, and he had to grope his way to the stairs, or he would have run at and up them at the top of his speed. The place seemed full of doors closed upon sleeping people; someone on an upper floor was. snoring with the noise of a man strangling. He moved among them awkwardly, but he knew which was the room that harbored his man. The door of it was before him at last. He fumbled and found the handle.

"Now!" he said aloud, and thrust it open.

His vision of vengeance had shown him the room that was to be its arena, but this room was dark and he could not see it. He had not allowed for that. He swore as the door swung to behind him.

"Mowbray!" he called. "Mowbray, you blasted robber! Wake up an' get what's comin' to you!"

There was no answering stir to tell him the direction in which to spring with hands splayed for the grapple. The room had a strange stillness; in spite of himself he held his breath to listen for Tom Mowbray's breathing. His right arm brushed the hilt of his sheath-knife as he stood, tense and listening. There was no sound of breathing, but there was something.

It was like the slow tick of a very quiet clock, measured and persistent. He could not make it out.

"Mowbray!" he called once more, and the only answer was that pat-a-pat that became audible again when he ceased to call.

"I bet I'll wake you," he said, and stepped forward feeling before him with his hands. They found the surface of a table, struck and knocked over a glass that stood upon it, and found a box of matches. "Ah!" grunted Goodwin triumphantly.

The match-flame languished ere it stood steady and let the room be seen. Goodwin had passed the bed and was standing with his back to it. With the match in his fingers and his eyes dazzled by its light, he turned and approached it. The face of Mowbray showed wide-open eyes at him from the pillow. The bedclothes lay across his chest; one arm hung over the edge of the bed with the hand loose and limp. And above his neck his night-clothes and the linen of the bed were sodden and dreadful with blood that had flowed from a frightful wound in the throat. What had sounded like the ticking of a clock was now the noise of its dripping. "Drip!" it went; "drip-drip!"

The match-flame stung his fingers and went out.

"Hell!" cried Goodwin, and out of the darkness panic swooped on him.

There was a moment when he tried to find the door and could not, alone in the blackness of the room with the murdered man. He caught at himself desperately to save himself from screaming, and found the matchbox was in his hand. He failed to light two matches, standing off the lunatic terror that threatened him.

Somewhere out of sight he knew that Tom Mowbray's eyes were open. The third match fired and he had the door by the handle. It restored him like a grip of a friendly hand.

He was able to pause in the door while the match burned and his mind raced. There leaped to the eye of his imagination the two stricken figures he had seen slinking from the house, the weeping of the woman, the muffled tap of the man's crutch. There followed, in an inevitable sequence, the memory of them in their torment as they sat at meat with Tom Mowbray.

"I wonder which o' them done it?" he thought, and shuddered. Where he stood he could see the still face of the dead man, with its shape of power and pride overcast now by the dreadful meekness of the dead. He could not pursue the thought, for another came up to drive it from his mind.

"Supposin' somebody woke and come out and saw me here!"

To think of it was enough. Drawing the door to behind him he went down the stairs. He had been careless of noise in ascending; now each creak of the warped boards was an agony. The snorer had turned over in bed; the awful house had a graveyard stillness. He held his breath till he was clear of it and again in the hushed and empty street.

"The Etna for mine, if I can make it," he breathed to himself as he went at a run in the shadow of the silent houses. "God! If anyone was to see me!"

And thus it was that the first pallor of dawn beheld the incredible and unprecedented sight of an able seaman, with his clothes strapped upon his head, swimming at peril of his life in San Francisco bay, to get aboard of the "Hell-packet."

V

THE GIRL

The little mission hall showed to the shabby waterside street of Jersey City its humble face of brick and the modest invitation of its open door, from which at intervals there overflowed the sudden music of a harmonium within. Goodwin, ashore for the evening, with the empty hours of his leisure weighing on him like a burden, heard that music rise about him, as he moved along the saloon-dotted sidewalk, with something of the mild surprise of a swimmer who passes out of a cold into a warm current. For lack of anything better to do, he had been upon the point of returning to his ship, where she lay in her dock. He had not spoken to a soul since he had come ashore at sundown, and the simple music was like a friendly prompting. He hesitated a moment for he was not a frequenter of missions then turned in at the entrance of the hall.

The music of the harmonium and of the voices that sang with it seemed to swell at him as he pushed open the swing door and tiptoed in toward a back seat, careful to be noiseless. But there were heads that turned, none the less heads of tame sailors from the ships, for whose service the mission struggled to exist, and a few sleek faces of shore folk; and, on the low platform at the upper end of the hall, the black-coated, whiskered missioner who presided over the gathering craned his neck to look at the new-comer, without ceasing to sing with vigor. It was, in short, such a meeting as an idle sailor might drop in upon in any one of a hundred ports. Goodwin recognized the very atmosphere of it its pervading spirit of a mild and very honest geniality, the peculiar nasal tone of its harmonium, and the timidity of the singing. Standing in his place in the back row of seats, he was going on to identify it at further points, when he felt a touch on his arm.

"Eh?" he demanded under his breath, turning.

A tall girl was offering him a little red, paper-covered hymn-book, open at the hymn that was then being sung, her ungloved finger pointing him the very verse and line. He did not at once take it. She had come upon him surprisingly, and now, while he stared at her, he was finding her surprising in herself. Under the brim of her hat her face showed gentle and soft, with something of a special kindliness; and, because others were watching her, she had a little involuntary smile of embarrassment.

She glanced up at him shyly, and let her eyes fall before his. The finger with which she pointed him the place on the page seemed to Goodwin, whose hands were like hoofs for callousness and size, exquisite and pathetic in its pink slenderness. It was not merely that she was beautiful and feminine in that moment Goodwin could not have been positive that she was beautiful but a dim allurement, a charm made up of the grace of her bowed head, her timid gesture of proffering him the book, her nearness, and her fragile delicacy of texture, enhanced and heightened the surprise of her.

"Gosh!" breathed Goodwin, unthinking; then, "Thank you, miss," as he took the hymn-book from her.

She smiled once more, and went back to her place at the farther end of the row of seats in front of Goodwin's, where he could still see her. He found himself staring at her in a sort of perplexity; she had revealed herself to him with a suddenness that gave her a little the quality of an apparition. The bend of her head above her book brought to view, between the collar of her coat and her soft brown hair, a gleam of white nape that fascinated him; she was remote, ethereal, wondrously delicate and mysterious. He sprawled in his place, when the hymn was over, with an arm over the back of his seat, intent merely to see her and slake the appetite of his eyes.

"She's she's a looker, all right!" He had a need to make some comment upon this uplifting experience of his, and this was the best he could do.

He had come in late sailors' missions are used to late-comers and early-goers and it was not long before the simple service came to a close and the meeting began to break up. Goodwin took his cap and rose, watching the tall girl as she went forward to join a couple of older women. The black-coated man came down from the platform and made his way toward Goodwin, amiable intentions visibly alight in his whiskered face.

"Haven't seen you here before," he said at Goodwin's elbow. "What ship d'you belong to?"

Goodwin, recalled to himself, looked down into the kindly, narrow face of the missioner. He himself was tall, a long-limbed young man, with a serious, darkly tanned face in which the blue of the eyes showed up strongly; and in his bearing and the fashion of his address there was a touch of that arrogance which men acquire who earn their bread at the hourly hazard of their lives.

"Oh, I just dropped in," he said awkwardly. "I belong to th' Etna, lyin' in the dock down yonder."

The missioner smiled and nodded.

"Etna, eh? Ah, yes. Somebody was tellin' me about the Etna. A hard ship that's what you call her, eh?"

Goodwin nodded, and considered the face upturned toward his own innocent, benevolent, middle-aged, worn, too, with hopes and disappointments, yet unscarred by such bitter knowledge as men gained early aboard the Etna.

"We call her the 'Hell-packet,'" he answered seriously.

The missioner nodded, and his smile, though it flickered, survived.

"It's an ugly name," he said; "but maybe she deserves it. An' so you saw our door open and just stepped in? It's always open in the evenin's and on Sundays, an' we'll always be glad to see you. Now, I'd like to make you acquainted with one of our young ladies, so's you won't feel you're a stranger, eh? An' then maybe you'll come again."

"Oh, I dunno" began Goodwin, fidgeting.

But the missioner was already beckoning with a black-sleeved arm. His pale elderly face seemed to shine.

Goodwin turned, looked to see whom he summoned, and forthwith dropped his cap, so that he was bent double to pick it up when the young lady, the tall girl who had offered him the hymn-book, arrived. He came upright again face to face with her, abandoned by his faculties, a mere sop of embarrassment before the softness of her eyes and the smile of her lips.

The missioner's official voice brayed between them benevolently. Goodwin had a momentary sense that there was a sort of indecency in thus trumpeting forth the introduction; it should have been done solemnly, gracefully, like a ceremony.

"Miss James," said the missioner noisily, "here's a friend that's visitin' us for the first time. Now, I want you to persuade him to come again, an' tell him he'll be welcome just as often as he likes to come an' see us. His name's, er."

"Goodwin," replied the sailor awkwardly.

The missioner shook his hand warmly, putting eloquence into the shake. He cut it short to intercept a brace of seamen who were making for the door. Goodwin saw him bustle up and detain them with his greeting: "Haven't seen you here before. What ship d'you belong to?" Then he turned back to the girl.

"Do you belong to a ship?" she asked.

"Yes," he answered. "The Etna."

He had been eager to hear her speak. She had a voice with shadows in it, a violin voice. Goodwin, relishing it like an apt gift, could only tell himself that it fitted and completed that strange effect she had of remoteness and unreality.

"What was your last port?" she asked.

He told her, and she went on with her conventional string of questions to make talk, to carry out the missioner's purpose in summoning her. The danger of seafaring, the strangeness of life in ships, the charm of travel she went through the whole list, getting answers as conventional as her queries. He was watching her, taking pleasure in her quality and aspect; and at last he saw, with a small thrill, that she was watching him likewise.

If he had been a vainer man, he might have been aware that he, in his way, was as well worth looking at as she in hers. He was big and limber, in the full ripeness of his youth, sunburned and level-eyed. His life in ships had marked him as plainly as a branding-iron. There was present in him that air which men have, secret yet visible, who know familiarly the unchanging horizons, the strange dawns, the tempest-pregnant skies of the sea. For the girl he was as unaccountable as she for him.

"Say, Miss James," he asked suddenly, breaking in on her twentieth polite question, "d'you come to this joint, I mean, to this meetin' house every night?"

Her face seemed to shape itself naturally to a smile; she smiled now.

"I can't come every night," she answered; "but I come pretty often. I, I hope you'll come sometimes, now."

Goodwin discounted that; it was no more than the missioner had bidden her to say.

"Are you goin' to be here tomorrow?" he demanded.

Her mild, pretty face flushed faintly; the meaning of his question was palpable.

"Ye-es," she hesitated; "I expect I'll be coming to-morrow."

"That's all right, then," said Goodwin cheerfully. "An' I'll be along, too."

The elderly woman whom she had left at the missioner's summons was hovering patiently. Goodwin held out his hand.

"Good night, Miss James," he said.

She gave him her hand, and he took it within his own, enveloping its pale slenderness in his rope-roughened palm. He held it just long enough to make her raise her eyes and meet his; then he released her, and, avoiding the anti-climax of a further talk with the missioner, passed out of the hall to the dark and sparsely peopled street.

At a small saloon whose lights spilled themselves across his path, he got himself a glass of beer; he was feeling just such a thirst as a man knows after nervous and exacting labor. The blond, white-jacketed barman glanced at him curiously, marking perhaps something distraught and rapt in his demeanor. Goodwin, ignoring him, took his beer and leaned an elbow on the bar, looking round the place.

A couple of Germans were playing a game at a table near the door. A man in the dumb-solemn stage of drunkenness stood regarding his empty glass with owlish fixity. It was all consistent with a certain manner and degree of life; it was commonplace, established in the order of things. In the same order were the dreary street without, and the Etna, loading at her wharf for the return voyage to San Francisco. Their boundaries were the limits of lives; one had but to cross them, to adventure beyond them, and all the world was different. A dozen steps had taken him from the sidewalk into the mission hall and the soft-glowing wonder of the girl; another dozen steps had replaced him on the sidewalk. It almost seemed as if a man might choose what world he would live in.

"Feelin' bad?" queried the barman softly; he could no longer contain his curiosity.

"Me!" exclaimed Goodwin. "No!"

"Well," said the barman apologetically Goodwin was a big and dangerous-looking young man "you're lookin' mighty queer, anyway." And he proceeded to wipe the bar industriously.

The Etna had left San Francisco with a crew of fourteen men before the mast, of whom twelve had been "Dutchmen." On her arrival in New York, these twelve had deserted forthwith, forfeiting the pay due to them rather than face the return voyage under the Etna's officers. There remained in her forecastle now only Goodwin and one other, an old seaman named Noble, a veteran who had followed the sea and shared the uncertain fate of ships since the days of single topsails.

Noble was seated on his battered chest when Goodwin unhooked the fo'c'sle door and entered. A globe-lamp that hung above him shed its light upon his silver head as he bent over his work of patching a pair of dungaree overalls, and he looked up in mild welcome of the other's return. His placidity, his venerable and friendly aspect, gave somehow to the bare forecastle, with its vacant bunks like empty coffin-shelves in a vault, an air of domesticity, the comfortable quality of a home. Save for brief intervals between voyages, in sailors' boarding-houses, such places had been "home" to Noble for fifty years.

Goodwin rehooked the door, and stood outside the globe-lamp's circle of dull light while he took off his coat. Old Noble, sail needle between his fingers, looked up from his work amiably.

"Well?" he queried. "Been havin' a hell of a good time uptown, eh?"

"That's so," retorted Goodwin shortly. "A hell of a time an' all."

The old man nodded and began to sew again, sailor fashion, thrusting the big needle with the leather "palm" which seamen use instead of a thimble. Goodwin, standing by his bunk, began to cut himself a fill for his pipe.

"Ain't been robbed, have ye?" inquired old Noble.

In his view, and according to his experience, a sailor with money on him ran peculiar risks when he went ashore. When Goodwin had been "shanghaied" in San Francisco drugged and carried on board unconscious while another man "signed on" for him and drew three months of his wages in advance those who shipped him had omitted to search him, and his money-belt was intact.

"Robbed? No!" answered Goodwin impatiently.

He lit his pipe, drawing strongly at the pungent ship's tobacco, and seated himself on the edge of the lower bunk, facing old Noble. The old man continued to sew, his hand moving rhythmically to and fro with the needle, his work spread conveniently in his lap. But for the rusty red of his tanned skin, he looked like a handsome and wise old woman.

"Jim," said Goodwin at last.

"Yes?" The old man did not look up.

"There wasn't nothin' doin' ashore there," said Goodwin. "I just went for a walk along the street, and then I well, there wasn't nothin' doin', ye see, so I went into a sort o' mission that there was."

"Eh?" Old Noble raised his head sharply and peered at him. "Ye ain't been an' got religion, Dan?"

"No, I haven't," answered Goodwin. "But say, Jim, I went into the place, and there was a girl there. She come over to loan me a hymn-book first of all, an' afterwards what ye laughin' at, blast ye?"

Old Noble had uttered no sound, but he had bent his head over his sewing and his broad shoulders were shaking. He lifted a face of elderly, cynical mirth.

"It ain't nothin', Dan," he protested. "It's just me thinkin' first ye'd bin robbed and then ye'd got religion; an' all the time it's just a girl ye've seen. Go on, Dan; how much did she get out of ye?"

"Stow that!" warned Goodwin. "She wasn't that kind. This one was say, Jim, if you was to see her just once, you'd know things ashore ain't all as bad as you fancy. Sort of soft, she was all tender and gentle and shining! Gosh, there ain't no words to put her in. I didn't know there was any girls like that."

"Nor me," put in old Noble dryly. He inspected Goodwin with a shrewd and suspicious eye. For him, a citizen of the womanless seas, beauty, grace, femininity were no more than a merchandise. "Then, to put it straight, she didn't get yer money from ye?" he demanded.

"No, she didn't," retorted Goodwin. "Not a cent, is that plain enough? Ain't you ever known no women but the rotten ones, man?"

Noble shook his head.

"Then you don't know what you're talkin' about," said Goodwin. "This one it ain't no use tellin' you, Jim. I seen her, that's all; an' I'm goin' to quit. This sailorizin' game ain't the only game there is, an' I'm done with it."

"Ah!" The old man sat with both gnarled and labor-stained hands lying upon the unfinished work in his lap. The cynical, half-humorous expression faded from his thin, strong face. He frowned at the younger man consideringly, seriously.

"Then she did get something out o' ye," he said harshly. "You're talkin' like a fool, Dan. This old ship ain't no soft berth, I know; but then, you ain't no quitter, either. This girl's got ye goin'; ye want to watch out."

"Quitter!" Goodwin took him up hotly. They faced each other across the narrow fo'c'sle vehemently; their shadows sprawled on deck and bulkhead as they bent forward and drew back in the stress of talk. "When a man's shanghaied aboard a blasted hooker like this, with three months of his wages stolen before he gets the knockout drops out o' his head, is he a quitter when he takes his chance to leave her an' look for a white man's job?"

"Yes, he is," answered Noble. "You're a sailor, ain't you? Then stick by your ship."

"Oh, it ain't no use talkin' to you!" Goodwin rose to his feet. "You'd make out that a man 'u'd go to heaven for stickin' to his ship, even if he done forty murders. I'm goin' to quit, an' that's all there is to it."

Old Noble looked up at him where he stood. The old face, that had been mild and indulgent, was hardened to an angry contempt. He was old and strong, dexterous in all seamanlike arts, a being shaped for good and evil both by half a century of seafaring, of wrong and hardship, or danger and toil, of scant food and poor pay. Never in his life had he held back from a task because it was dangerous or difficult, nor sided with an officer against a man before the mast, nor deserted a ship. His code was simple and brief, but it was of iron.

"Well, quit, then," he said. "Quit like the Dutchmen! There's no one will stop ye."

"They better not," menaced Goodwin angrily.

He had been shanghaied, of course, without chest or bag, without even bedding, so that he had worked his way around the Horn in shoddy clothes and flimsy oilskins obtained from the ship's slop-chest. There was little that he had a mind to take ashore with him; it went quickly into a small enough bundle. While he turned out his bunk, old Noble sat watching him without moving, with judgment in his face, and sorrow. He was looking on at the death of a good seaman.

"Say, Jim!" Goodwin was ready; he stood with his bundle in his hand, his cap on his head. "You don't want to be a fool, now. I reckon we can shake hands, anyhow."

He felt himself loath to leave the old man in anger; he had for him both liking and respect. But Noble did not answer only continued for some moments to look him in the face, unsoftened, stern and grieved, then bent again above his sewing.

Goodwin withdrew the hand he had held out.

"Have it your own way," he said, and went forth from the forecastle, leaving the old man, with the lamplight silvering his sparse hair, at work upon the patched overalls. And, in that moment, not even the vision of the girl and his hope of the future could save him from a pang of sadness. It was as if he had, by his going, darkened a home.

Outside upon the deck he stayed to cast a glance about him. The big ship, beautiful as a work of art in her lines and proportions, showed vacant of life. A light glimmered from the galley door, where the decrepit watchman slumbered at his ease. There was nothing to detain him. The great yards, upon which he had fought down the sodden and frozen canvas in gales off the Horn, spread over him. She was fine, she was potent, with a claim upon a man's heart; and she was notorious for a floating, hell upon the seas. It was her character; she was famous for brutality to seamen, so that they deserted at the first opportunity and forfeited their wages. And Noble would have him loyal to her!

He swore at her shortly, and forced himself to cross the deck and climb over the rail to the wharf. The conduct of Noble was sore in his mind. But, as the earth of the shore gritted under his boots, that trouble departed from him. The world, after all, was wider than the decks of the Etna; and in it, an item in its wonder and complexity, there lived and smiled the girl.

Miss James, who smiled so indescribably and asked so many questions about seafaring in the way of civil conversation, would probably have shown small interest in the adventures of a seaman in search of a lodging ashore. She would have smiled, of course, with her own little lift and fall of shy eyes, and been as intangible and desirable as ever; but one could never tell her of carrying a small bundle of underclothes from one obdurate door to another, unable to show money in any convincing amount because one's capital was in a belt under one's shirt. Othello told Desdemona of "antres vast and deserts idle," not of skeptical landladies. Goodwin felt all this intensely when, in the evening of the following day, having finally established himself in a room, he beheld her again in the mission. He beheld her first, indeed, as she entered the hall, he watching from the opposite side of the street. He had no intention of going in if she were not present. As it was, a swoop across the street and a little brisk maneuvering secured him a place next to her.

He had been a little at a loss all day; it was years since he had lived altogether apart from sailors and he had found himself lonely and depressed; but the sight of her sufficed to restore him. She gave him the welcome of a look, and a slow flush mounted on her face. The missioner was already preparing to open the service, and conversation was impossible. Nevertheless, as she turned over the pages of her hymn-book, Goodwin bent toward her.

"Didn't I say I'd be along?" he whispered, and saw her cheek move with her smile.

To be close to her, knowing her to be conscious of him, was in itself a gladness; but Goodwin was impatient for the end of the service. It was not his way to stand off and on before a thing he meant to do, and he wanted more talk with her, to get within her guard, to touch the girl who was screened behind the smile and dim sweetness and the polite questions of Miss James. He sat frowning through the latter part of the service, till the missioner, standing upright with tight-shut eyes, gave the closing benediction. Then, compellingly, he turned upon the girl.

"Say," he said, "let's get out o' this. I'd like to walk along with you and talk. Come on!"

Miss James looked at him with startled eyes. He was insistent.

"Aw, come on," he pressed. "That preacher'll be here in a minute if you don't, and we've had enough of him for one time. I tell you, I want to talk to you."

He rose, and by sheer force of urgency made her rise likewise. He got her as far as the door. "But" she began, hesitating there.

"Steady as ye go," bade Goodwin, and took her down the shallow steps to the sidewalk. "Now, which way is it to be?" he demanded suddenly.

She did not reply for a couple of moments. The light that issued from the hall showed her face as she stood and considered him doubtfully, a little uncertain of what was happening. Even in that half-obscurity of the long street, where she was seen as an attitude, a shape, she made her effect of a quiet, tender beauty. Then, at last, she smiled and turned and began to walk. Goodwin fell into step beside her, and the confusion of voices within the hall died down behind them.

"I had to make you come," said Goodwin presently. "I just had to. An' you don't want to be scared."

She glanced sideways at him, but said nothing.

"You ain't scared, are ye?" he asked.

"No," she replied.

The answer even the brevity of it fulfilled his understanding of her. He nodded to himself.

"I said I wanted to talk to ye," he went on; "an' I do. I want to talk to you a whole lot. But there ain't much I got to say. 'Ceptin', maybe, one thing. I'd like to know what your first name is. Oh, I ain't goin' to get fresh an' call you by it I reckon you know that. But thinkin' of you all day an' half the night, like I do, 'Miss James' don't come handy, ye see."

"Oh!" murmured the girl. It was plain that he had startled her a little.

"My first name is Mary," she answered.

"Ah!" said Goodwin, and repeated it again and again under his breath. "I might 'most ha' guessed it," he said. "It's well, it's a name that fits ye like a coat o' paint, Miss James, A clean, straight name, that is. Mary b'gosh, it was my mother's name."

"I'm glad you like it," said the girl, in her deep-toned, pleasant voice. "You know, Mr. Goodwin, it was a bit queer the way you made me come away from the hall."

"Ah, but that's not troublin' you," replied Goodwin quickly. "I reckon you know what's wrong wi' me, Miss James. I'm not askin' you for much yet; only to let me see you, when you go to that mission-joint, and talk to ye sometimes."

They were at an intersection of streets, where a few shops yet shone and surface-cars went by like blazing ships. There was a movement of folk about them; yet, by reason of what had passed between them, it seemed that they stood in a solitude of queer, strained feeling. The girl halted in the light of a shop-window.

"I get my car here," she said.

Goodwin stopped, facing her. She looked up at the tense seriousness of his young, set face, hard and strong, with the wind-tan coloring it. She was kindly, eager to handle him tactfully, and possibly a little warmed by his sincerity and admiration. To him she seemed the sum of all that was desirable, pathetic, and stirring in womanhood.

"No," she said; "that's not much to ask. I'll be glad to meet you at the mission, Mr. Goodwin, and maybe we can talk, too, sometimes. And when you go away again, when your ship sails."

"Eh?" Goodwin's exclamation interrupted her. "Goin' away? Why, Miss James, I ain't goin' away. That was all fixed up last night. I've quit goin' to sea."

She stared at him, with parted lips.

"You don't understand," said Goodwin gently. "I knew, just as soon as I seen you, that I wasn't going away no more. I went down an' fetched my dunnage ashore right off."

She continued to stare. "Not going away?" she repeated.

Goodwin shook his head, smiling. He did not in the least understand the embarrassment of a young woman who finds herself unexpectedly the object of a romantic and undesired sacrifice.

A street-car jarred to a halt beside them. The girl made a queer little gesture, as if in fear.

"My car!" she flustered indistinctly, and, turning suddenly, ran from him towards it, taking refuge in its ordinariness against Goodwin and all the strangeness with which he seemed to assail her.

He, smiling fatuously on the curb, saw it carry her off, swaying and grinding. "Mary," he repeated. "Mary!"

Following his purpose, within the next few days he found himself employment as one of a gang of riggers at work on a great German four-masted barque which had been dismasted in a squall off Fire Island. In the daytime he dealt with spars and gear, such stuff as he knew familiarly, in the company of men like himself. Each evening found him, washed and appareled, at the mission, furnishing a decorous bass undertone to the hymns, looked on with approval by the missioner and his helpers. Commonly he got himself a seat next to Miss James; but he could not again contrive a walk with her along the still street to the lighted corner where she ran to catch her car. There seemed always to be a pair of voluminous elderly matrons in attendance upon her, to daunt and chill him. She herself was unchanged; her soft, beneficent radiance, her elusive, coy charm, all her maddening quality of delicacy and shrinking beauty, uplifted him still.

"Say," he always whispered, as he let himself down beside her, "are we goin' to have a talk tonight?"

And she would shake her averted head hurriedly, and afterwards the iron-clad matrons would close in on her and make her inaccessible. And, in the end, he would go off to get a drink in a saloon before going back to his room, baffled and discontented.

There were three evenings running on which she did not come to the mission at all. On the fourth Goodwin was there before her. He looked at her steadily as she came to her place.

"I want to talk to you to-night," he said, varying his formula, as she sat down.

She gave him a swift, uncertain glance.

"Got to," he added gravely. "It's a case, an' I just got to."

"What about?" she asked, with a touch of resentment that was new in her.

"I guess you know," he answered quietly, and hitched nearer to her along the bench to make room for a new-comer who was thrusting in beside him. He turned perfunctorily to see who it might be. It was old Noble.

"Friends!" grated the voice of the missioner. "Let us begin by singing hymn number seventy-nine: 'Pull for the shore, sailor; pull for the shore!'"

The noise of the harmonium drowned the rustling of hymn-book pages. Noble's elbow drove against Goodwin's.

"Found ye!" rumbled the old man. "Say, come on out where I can talk to ye. We're sailin' in the mornin'."

"Hush!" whispered Goodwin. "I can't come out. What d'you want?"

The little congregation rose to its feet for the singing of the hymn. Old Noble, rising with them, leaned forward and peered past Goodwin at the girl. His keen old face inspected her inscrutably for a while.

"That's her, I reckon," he said to Goodwin in a windy whisper. "Well, I'm not sayin' nothin'. Come on out."

"I can't, I tell ye," breathed Goodwin. "Don't you go startin' anything here, now! Say what ye got to say, an' be done with it."

Old Noble scowled. About him the simple hymn rose and fell in its measured cadences. Among the honest folk who sang it there was none more venerable and seemly than he. His head was white with the sober snow of years; by contrast with his elderly gravity, the young vividness and force of Goodwin seemed violent and crude.

"I won't start nothin'," whispered Noble harshly. "Don't be afeared. I bin lookin' for ye, Dan; I want ye to have a chanst. We're sailin' in the mornin', an', Dan, we're short-handed three hands short, we are!"

His words came and went under cover of the hymn.

"Men won't ship aboard of her; she's got a bad name," the whisper continued. "She's full o' Dutchmen an' Dagoes again. It's goin' to be the hell of a passage an' the Horn in August, too. Come on an' stand yer share of it, Dan."

Goodwin glared down indignantly at the old rusty-red face beside him.

"You're crazy," he said shortly.

"Ye ain't comin'?"

For answer Goodwin only shrugged. It sufficed. With no further word Noble turned away and walked forth on heavy feet from the hall. There followed him to the street, as if in derision, the refrain of that landsman's hymn: "Leave the poor old stranded wreck, and pull for the shore!"

"Now!" said Goodwin, when at last the missioner had closed the service with his blessing.

The girl was nervous; plainly, she would have been glad to refuse. But Goodwin was in earnest, and, unwillingly enough, she surrendered to the compulsion of his will and went out with him. Outside upon the sidewalk she spoke angrily.

"I don't like the way you act," she said, and her voice had tears in it. "You think a person's got."

Goodwin interrupted. "I don't think nothin'," he said. "I got to find out. An' I can't find out while we're hustlin' to the corner. Come down towards the docks. You're all right with me; an' I got to find out."

He did not even touch her arm, but she went with him.

"Find out what?" she asked uncertainly, as they crossed the street.

"Come on," he answered. "We'll talk by an' by."

He took her down a dark side way which led them to the water-front. Wharves where work was going on roared and shone. The masts and spars of ships rose stark against the sky. Beyond, the river was dotted with lights against the luminous horizon of Manhattan. He slackened his pace. At his side the silent girl trembled and sulked.

"Kid," said Goodwin, "there's one of us two that hasn't made good. Which is it?"

A jib-boom slanted across a wall over their heads. They were alone among sleeping ships.

"I don't know what you mean," answered the girl. "You say you've got to talk to me, and you act—." She stopped.

"You don't know what I mean?" repeated Goodwin. "I'll have to tell you, then."

They had come to a pause under the jib-boom of the silent ship. She waited for him to go on, servile to the still mastery of his mien.

"That night the night I come to the mission for the first time," went on Goodwin, "when you loaned me the book, I quit my ship to keep close to you. That ain't nothin'; the ship was a terror, anyway. But I seen you, and, girl, I couldn't get you out o' my head. You was all right the next night, when I went along with you to your car; it wasn't just because the missionary feller set you at me, neither. What's gone wrong with me since?"

He asked the question mildly, with a tone of gentle and reasonable inquiry.

"I haven't said anything was wrong with you," Answered the girl sullenly. "I don't have to answer your questions, anyway."

"I reckon you do these questions," said Goodwin. "What is it, now? Am I different to what you reckoned I was, or what? I never set up to be anythin' but just plain man. Tell me what I'm shy of. Are you scared you'll have to to marry me?"

"Oh!" The girl shrank away from him.

"That's it, is it? Well, you don't need to be." His voice was bitter. "I'd never ha' dared to ask you before, an' now I wouldn't, anyway. See? But I know, all the same, if I wasn't just a blasted sailor if I was a storekeeper or a rich man I c'd have ye. Why, damme, I c'd have ye anyway!"

She had backed before him; and now she was against the wall, uttering a small moan of protest.

"I could," he repeated. "You know it. I'd only to go chasin' you, an' in the end you'd give in. You're pretty; you got a shine on you that fools a man. But you're a quitter a quitter! See? An' now you can come away from that wall an' I'll see you back on the street."

He was very lofty and erect in the meager light, rather a superb figure, if the girl had had eyes for it. But she, to all seeming, was dazed. He went in silence at her side till they reached the street and saw that the open door of the mission still showed lights.

"There ye are," said Goodwin, halting.

The girl hesitated, looking back and forth. It was wonderful how her suggestion of soft beauty persisted. She was abashed, stricken, humiliated upon the dark street; and still she was lovely. She moved away and paused.

"Good night!" said her faintly ringing voice, and she passed towards the mission.

"Yes, it's me!" said Goodwin, answering the dumb surprise of old Noble as he entered the fo'c'sle of the Etna. "An' you want to shut your head. See?"

VI

THE BREADWINNER

The noonday bivouac was in a shady place nigh-hand the road, where a group of solemn trees made a shadow on the dusty grass. It was a day of robust heat; the sky arched cloudless over Sussex, and the road was soft with white dust that rose like smoke under the feet. Trotter no sooner saw the place than he called a halt and dropped his bundle. The Signor smiled lividly and followed suit; Bill, the dog, lay down forthwith and panted.

"Look at 'im!" said Trotter. "Just look at 'im, will yer! 'E ain't carried no bundle; 'e ain't got to unpack no grub. And there 'e lies, for us to wait on 'im."

"Where ees da beer?" demanded the Signor, who had the immediate mind.

The word drew Trotter from his wrongs, and together the men untied the shabby bundles and set forth their food.

They made a queer picture in that quiet place of English green. Trotter still wore tights, with hobnailed boots to walk in and a rusty billycock hat for shelter to his head. He somewhat clung to this garb, though his tumbling days were over. One had only to look at his bloated, pouchy face to see how drink and sloth had fouled his joints and slacked his muscles. Never again could he spread the drugget in a rustic village street and strut about it on his hands for the edification of a rustic audience. But the uniform he still wore; he seemed to think it gave him some claim to indulgent notice. The Signor, in his own way, was not less in contrast with his background. His lean, predatory face and capacious smile went fitly with the shabby frock coat and slouched hat he affected. He carried a fiddle under his arm, but the most he could do was strum on it with his thumb. Together, they made a couple that anyone would look twice at, and no one care to meet in a lonely place.

Bill, the dog, shared none of their picturesque quality. An uglier dog never went footsore. A dozen breeds cropped out here and there on his hardy body; his coat was distantly suggestive of a collie; his tail of a terrier. But something of width between the patient eyes and bluntness in the scarred muzzle spoke to a tough and hardy ancestor in his discreditable pedigree, as though a lady of his house had once gone away with a bulldog. His part in the company was to do tricks outside beerhouses. When the Signor's strumming had gathered a little crowd, Trotter would introduce Bill.

"Lydies and gents all," he would say, "with yore kind permission, I will now introduce to yer the world-famous wolf 'ound Boris, late of the Barnum menagerie in New York. 'E will commence 'is exhibition of animal intelligence by waltzin' to the strines of Yankee Doodle on the vi'lin."

Then the Signor would strum on two strings of the fiddle, smiling the while a smile that no woman should see, and Bill would waltz laboriously on his hind legs. After that he would walk on his front legs, throw somersaults, find a hidden handkerchief, and so on. And between each piece of clowning, he would go round with Trotter's hat to collect coppers. Bill was an honest dog, and a fairly big one as well, and when a man tried to ignore the hat, he had a way of drawing back his lips from his splendid teeth which by itself was frequently worth as much to the treasury as all his other tricks put together. But the truth of it was, it was a feeble show, a scanty, pitiful show; and only the gross truculence of Trotter and the venomous litheness of the Signor withheld the average yokel from saying so flatly.

But it gave them enough to live on and drink on. At any rate, Trotter grew fat and the Signor grew thinner. Bill depended on what they had left when they were satisfied; it was little enough. He begged at cottages on his own account, sometimes; sitting up in the attitude of mendicancy till something was thrown to him. Occasionally, too, he stole fowls or raided a butcher's shop. Then Trotter and the Signor would disown him vociferously to the bereaved one, and hasten on to come up with him before he had eaten it all. He preferred being beaten to going hungry, so they never caught him till he had fed full. But what troubled him most was the tramping, the long dusty stages afoot in country where the unsociable villages lay remote from each other, and the roads were hot and long. A man can outwalk any other animal. After thirty miles, a horse is nowhere and the man is still going, but even fifteen miles leaves the ordinary dog limp and sorry. And then, when every bone in him was aching, a wretched village might poke up at an elbow of the way, and there would be dancing to do and his whole fatuous repertoire to accomplish, while his legs were soft under him with weariness.

Trotter took his heavy boots off; he threw one at Bill.

It was a pleasant spot. Where they sat, in a bay of shade, they could see a far reach of rich land, bright in the sunshine and dotted with wood, stretching back to where the high shoulder of the downs shut out the sea.

The two men ate in much contentment, passing the bottle to and fro.

Bill waited for them to have done and fling him his share. In common with all Bohemians, he liked regular meals.

"That dog's goin' silly," said Trotter, looking at him where he lay.

"Oh, him!" said the Signor.

"He's bin loafin' a furlong be'ind all the mornin'," said Trotter. "Yer know if he was to get lazy, it 'ud be a poor lookout for us. He's bin spoilt, that dog 'as spoilt with indulgence. Soon as we stop for a spell oh, he plops down on 'is belly and 'angs on for us to chuck 'im a bit of grub. Might be a man by the ways of 'im, 'stead of a dog. Now I don't 'old with spoilin' dogs."

"Pass da beer," requested the Signor.

Bill looked up with concern, for Trotter was filling his pipe; the meal was at an end.

"Yus, yer can look," snarled Trotter. "You'll wait, you will."

He began to pack up the bread and meat again in the towel where it belonged.

"Think you've got yer rights, don't yer?" he growled, as he swept the fragments together. "No dog comes them games on me. Hey, get out, ye brute!"

Bill had walked over and was now helping himself to the food that lay between Trotter's very hands.

Trotter clenched a bulging red fist and hauled off to knock him away. But Bill had some remainder of the skill, as well as the ferocity, of the fighting dog in him. He snapped sideways in a purposeful silence, met the swinging fist adroitly, and sank his fine teeth cruelly in the fat wrist.

"Hey! Signor, Signor!" howled Trotter. "Kick 'im orf, can't yer! Ow, o-o-ow!"

Bill let him go as the Signor approached, but the kick that was meant for him spent itself in the air. Again he snapped, with that sideways striking action of the big bony head, and the Signor shrieked like a woman and sprang away.

Bill watched the pair of them for half a minute, as they took refuge among the trees, and both saw the glint of his strong teeth as he stared after them. Then he finished the food at his ease, while they cursed and whimpered from a distance.

"'E's mad," moaned Trotter. "'Es 'ad a stroke. An' we'll get hydrophobia from 'im as like as not."

He nursed his bitten wrist tenderly.

"Look at my laig!" babbled the Signor. "It is a sacred bite, an' all-a da trouser tore. What da hell you fool wid da dog for, you big fool?"

"'E was pinchin' the grub," growled Trotter. "'E's mad. Look at 'im, lyin' down on my coat. 'Ere, Bill! Goo' dog, then. Good ole feller!"

Bill took no notice of the blandishments of Trotter, but presently he rose and strolled off to where a little pond stood in the corner of a field.

"'E's drinkin'," reported Trotter, who had stolen from cover to make observations. "So 'e can't be mad. Mad dogs won't look at water. Go into fits if they sees it. 'Ere, Signor, let's make a grab for those bundles before 'e gets back."

Bill rejoined them while they were yet stuffing their shabby possessions together.

The Signor moved behind Trotter and Trotter picked up a boot. But Bill was calm and peaceful again. He lay down in the grass and wagged his tail cheerfully.

"Bill, ole feller," said Trotter, in tones of conciliation, and Bill wagged again.

"'Ell, I can't make nothing of it," confessed Trotter blankly. "Must have gone sort o' temp'ry insane, like the sooicides. But well, we'll be even with 'im before all's over."

And the lean Signor's sidelong look at the dog was full of menace.

They reached another village before dark, a village with a good prosperous alehouse, and here Bill showed quite his old form. He waltzed, he threw somersaults, he found handkerchiefs, he carried the hat; his docility was all that Trotter and the Signor could have asked. They cleared one and sevenpence out of his tricks, and would have stayed to drink it; but Bill walked calmly on up the road and barely gave them time enough to buy food.

They cursed him lavishly; the Signor raved in a hot frenzy; but they dared not lose him. The dog led them at an easy pace and they labored after him furiously, while a great pale moon mounted in the sky and the soft night deepened over the fields.

He let them down at last at an end of grass where a few of last year's straw ricks afforded lodging for the night. Both the men were tired enough to be glad of the respite and they sank down in the shadow of a rick with little talk.

"It gets me," Trotter said. "The dog's a danger. 'E ought to be drownded."

The Signor snarled. "An' us?" he demanded. "We go to work, eh? You pick da grass-a to make-a da hay and me I drive-a da cart, eh? Oh, Trottair, you fool!"

"'Ere, let's 'ave some grub and stow the jaw for a bit," said Trotter.

He had bread and meat, bought in a hurry at the tail of the village while Bill receded down the road.

As soon as he laid it bare, Bill growled.

"T'row heem some, queeck," cried the Signor.

Bill caught the loaf and settled down to it with an appetite. Trotter stared at him with a gape.

"Well, blow me!" he said. "'Ave we come to feedin' the bloomin' dog before we feeds ourselves? 'As the beggar struck for that? I s'pose 'e'll be wantin' wages next."

"Oh, shutta da gab!" snapped the Signor.

"That's all very well," retorted Trotter. "But I'm an Englishman, I am. You're only a furriner; you're used to bein' put upon. But I'm—."

Bill growled again and rose to his feet. Trotter tossed him a piece of meat.

All that was long ago. Now if you stray through the South of England during the months between May and October, you may yet meet Bill and his companions. Trotter still wears tights, but he is thinner and much more wholesome to see; but the Signor has added a kind of shiny servility to his courtly Italian manner.

Bill is sleek and fat.

And now, when they come to rest at noonday, you will see, if you watch them, that before Trotter takes his boots off he feeds the dog. And the Signor fetches him water.

VII

"PLAIN GERMAN"

Beyond the arcaded side-walks, whose square-pillared arches stand before the house-fronts like cloisters, the streets of Thun were channels 'of standing sunlight, radiating heat from every cobblestone. Herr Haase, black-coated and white-waistcoated as for a festival, his large blond face damp and distressful, came panting into the hotel with the manner of an exhausted swimmer climbing ashore. In one tightly-gloved hand he bore a large and bulging linen envelope.

"Pfui!" He puffed, and tucked the envelope under one arm in order to take off his green felt hat and mop himself. "Aber what a heat, what a heat!"

The brass-buttoned hotel porter, a-sprawl in a wicker chair in the hall, lowered his newspaper and looked up over his silver spectacles. He was comfortably unbuttoned here and there, and had omitted to shave that morning, for this was July, 1916, and since the war had turned Switzerland's tourists into Europe's cannon-fodder, he had run somewhat to seed.

"Yes, it is warm," he agreed, without interest, and yawned. "You have come to see" he jerked his head towards the white staircase and its strip of red carpet "to see him not? He is up there. But what do you think of the news this morning?"

Herr Haase was running, his handkerchief round the inside of his collar. "To see him! I have come to see the Herr Baron von Steinlach," he retorted, crossly. "And what news are you talking about now?" He continued to pant and wipe while the porter read from his copy of the Bund, the German official communique of the previous day's fighting on the Somme.

"I don't like it," said the porter, when he had finished. "It looks as if we were losing ground. Those English."

Herr Haase pocketed his handkerchief and took the large envelope in his hand again. He was a bulky, middle-aged man, one of whose professional qualifications it was that he looked and sounded commonplace, the type of citizen who is the patron of beer-gardens, wars of aggression, and the easily remembered catchwords which are the whole political creed of his kind. His appearance was the bushel under which his secret light burned profitably; it had indicated him for his employment as a naturalized citizen of Switzerland and the tenant of the pretty villa on the hill above Thun, whence he drove his discreet and complicated traffic in those intangible wares whose market is the Foreign Office in Berlin.

He interrupted curtly. "Don't talk to me about the English!" he puffed. "Gott strafe England!" He stopped. The porter was paid by the same hand as himself. The hall was empty save for themselves, and there was no need to waste good acting on a mere stage-hand in the piece.

"The English," he said, "are going to have a surprise."

"Eh?" The slovenly man in the chair gaped up at him stupidly. Herr Haase added to his words the emphasis of a nod and walked on to the stairs.

In the corridor above, a row of white-painted bedroom doors had each its number. Beside one of them a tall young man was sunk spinelessly in a chair, relaxed to the still warmth of the day. He made to rise as Herr Haase approached, swelling for an instant to a drilled and soldierly stature, but, recognizing him, sank back again.

"He's in there," he said languidly. "Knock for yourself."

"Schlapschwanz!" remarked Herr Haase indignantly, and rapped upon the door. A voice within answered indistinctly. Herr Haase, removing his hat, opened the door and entered.

The room was a large one, an hotel bedroom converted into a sitting-room, with tall French windows opening to a little veranda, and a view across the lime-trees of the garden to the blinding silver of the lake of Thun and the eternal snow-fields of the Bernese Oberland. Beside the window and before a little spindle-legged writing-table a man sat. He turned his head as Herr Haase entered.

"Ach, der gute Haase," he exclaimed.

Herr Haase brought his patent leather heels together with a click and bowed like a T-square.

"Excellenz!" he said, in a strange, loud voice, rather like a man in a trance. "Your Excellency's papers, received by the train arriving from Bern at eleven-thirty-five."

The other smiled, raising to him a pink and elderly face, with a clipped white moustache and heavy tufted brows under which the faint blue eyes were steady and ironic. He was a large man, great in the frame and massive; his movements had a sure, unhurried deliberation; and authority, the custom and habit of power, clad him like a garment. Years and the moving forces of life had polished him as running water polishes a stone. The Baron von Steinlach showed to Herr Haase a countenance supple as a hand and formidable as a fist.

"Thank you, my good Haase," he said, in his strong deliberate German. "You look hot. This sun, eh? Poor fellow!"

But he did not bid him sit down. Instead, he turned to the linen envelope, opened it, and shook out upon the table its freight of lesser envelopes, typed papers, and newspaper-clippings. Deliberately, but yet with a certain discrimination and efficiency, he began to read them. Herr Haase, whose new patent leather boots felt red-hot to his feet, whose shirt was sticking to his back, whose collar was melting, watched him expressionlessly.

"There is a cloud of dust coming along the lake road," said the Baron presently, glancing through the window. "That should be Captain von Wetten in his automobile. We will see what he has to tell us, Haase."

"At your orders, Excellency," deferred Herr Haase.

"Because" he touched one of the papers before him "this news, Haase, is not good. It is not good. And this discovery here, if it be all that is claimed for it, should work miracles."

He glanced up at Herr Haase and smiled again. "Not that I think miracles can ever be worked by machinery," he added.

It was ten minutes after this that the column of dust on the lake road delivered its core and cause in the shape of a tall man, who knocked once at the door and strode in without waiting for an answer.

"Ah, my dear Von Wetten," said the Baron pleasantly. "It is hot, eh?"

"An oven," replied Von Wetten curtly. "This place is an oven. And the dust, ach!"

The elder man made a gesture of sympathy. "Poor fellow!" he said. "Sit down; sit down. Haase, that chair!"

And Herr Haase, who controlled a hundred and twelve subordinates, who was a Swiss citizen and a trusted secret agent, brought the chair and placed it civilly, neither expecting nor receiving thanks.

The new-comer was perhaps twenty-eight years of age, tall, large in the chest and little in the loins, with a narrow, neatly-chiseled face which fell naturally to a chill and glassy composure. "Officer" was written on him as clear as a brand; his very quiet clothes sat on his drilled and ingrained formality of posture and bearing as noticeably as a mask and domino; he needed a uniform to make him inconspicuous. He picked up his dangling monocle, screwed it into his eye, and sat back.

"And now?" inquired the Baron agreeably, "and now, my dear Von Wetten, what have you to tell us?"

"Well, Excellenz" Captain von Wetten hesitated. "As a matter of fact, I've arranged for you to see the thing yourself this afternoon."

The Baron said nothing merely waited, large and still against the light of the window which shone on the faces of the other two.

Captain von Wetten shifted in his chair awkwardly. "At five, Excellenz," he added; "it'll be cooler then. You see, Herr Baron, it's not the matter of the machine I've seen that all right; it's the man."

"So!" The explanation, which explained nothing to Herr Haase, seemed to satisfy the Baron. "The man, eh? But you say you have seen the machine. It works?"

"It worked all right this morning," replied Von Wetten. "I took my own explosives with me, as you know some French and English rifle-cartridges and an assortment of samples from gun charges and marine mines. I planted some in the garden; the place was all pitted already with little craters from his experiments; and some, especially the mine stuff, I threw into the lake. The garden's on the edge of the lake, you know. Well, he got out his machine thing like a photographic camera, rather, on a tripod turned it this way and that until it pointed to my explosives, and pop! off they went like a lot of fireworks. Pretty neat, I thought."

"Ah!" The Baron's elbow was on his desk and his head rested in his hand. "Then it is what that Italian fellow said he had discovered in 1914. 'Ultra-red rays,' he called them. What was his name, now?"

"Never heard of him," said Von Wetten.

From the background where Herr Haase stood among the other furniture came a cough. "Oliver," suggested Herr Haase mildly.

The Baron jerked a look at him. "No, not Oliver," he said. "Ulivi that was it; Ulivi! I remember at the time we were interested, because, if the fellow could do what he claimed." He broke off. "Tell me," he demanded of Von Wetten. "You are a soldier; I am only a diplomat. What would this machine mean in war in this war, for instance? Supposing you were in command upon a sector of the front; that in the trenches opposite you were the English; and you had this machine? What would be the result?"

"Well!" Von Wetten deliberated. "Pretty bad for the English, I should think," he decided.

"But how, man how?" persisted the Baron. "In what way would it be bad for them?"

Von Wetten made an effort; he was not employed for his imagination. "Why," he hesitated, "because I suppose the cartridges would blow up in the men's pouches and in the machine-gun belts; and then the trench-mortar ammunition and the hand grenades; well, everything explosive would simply explode! And then we'd go over to what was left of them, and it would be finished."

He stopped abruptly as the vision grew clearer. "Aber," he began excitedly.

The old Baron lifted a hand and quelled him.

"The machine you saw this morning, which you tested, will do all this?" he insisted.

Von Wetten was staring at the Baron. Upon the question he let his monocle fall and seemed to consider. "I, I don't see why not," he replied.

The Baron nodded thrice, very slowly. Then he glanced up at Herr Haase. "Then miracles are worked by machinery, after all," he said. Then he turned again to Von Wetten.

"Well?" he said. "And the man? We are forgetting the man; I think we generally do, we Germans. What is the difficulty about the man?"

Von Wetten shrugged. "The difficulty is that he won't name his price," he answered. "Don't understand him! Queer, shambling sort of fellow, all hair and eyes, with the scar of an old cut, or something, across one side of his face. Keeps looking at you as if he hated you! Showed me the machine readily enough; consented to every test even offered to let me take my stuff to the other side of the lake, three miles away, and explode it at that distance. But when it came to terms, all he'd do was to look the other way and mumble."

"What did you offer him?" demanded the Baron.

"My orders, Your Excellency," answered Captain von Wetten formally, "were to agree to his price, but not to attempt negotiations in the event of difficulty over the terms. That was reserved for Your Excellency."

"H'm!" The Baron nodded. "Quite right," he approved. "Quite right; there is something in this. Men have their price, but sometimes they have to be paid in a curious currency. By the way, how much money have we?"

Herr Haase, a mere living ache inhabiting the background, replied.

"I am instructed, Excellency, that my cheque will be honored at sight here for a million marks," he answered, in the loud hypnotized voice of the drill-ground. "But there is, of course, no limit."

The Baron gave him an approving nod. "No limit," he said. "That is the only way to do things no limit, in money or anything else! Well, Haase can bring the car round at what time, Von Wetten?"

"Twenty minutes to five!" Von Wetten threw the words over his shoulder.

"And I shall lunch up here; it's cooler. You'd better lunch with me, and we can talk. Send up a waiter as you go, my good Haase."

Herr Haase bowed, but clicked only faintly. "Zu Befehl, Excellenz," he replied, and withdrew.

In the hall below he sank into a chair, groaned and fumbled at the buttons of his boots. He was wearing them for the first time, and they fitted him as though they had been shrunk on to him. The porter, his waistcoat gaping, came shambling over to him.

"You were saying," began the porter, "that the English."

Herr Haase boiled over. "Zum Teufel mit den Englandern und mit Dir, Schafskopf!" he roared, tearing at the buttons. "Send up a waiter to the Herr Baron and call me a cab to go home in!"

It was in a sunlight tempered as by a foreboding of sunset, when the surface of the lake was ribbed like sea sand with the first breathings of the evening breeze, that Herr Haase, riding proudly in the back seat of honor, brought the motor-car to the hotel. He had changed his garb of ceremony and servitude; he wore grey now, one of those stomach-exposing, large-tailed coats which lend even to the straightest man the appearance of being bandy-legged; and upon his feet were a pair of tried and proven cloth boots.

The porter, his waistcoat buttoned for the occasion, carried out a leather suit-case and placed it in the car, then stood aside, holding open the door, as the Baron and Von Wetten appeared from the hall. Von Wetten, true to his manner, saw neither Herr Haase's bow nor the porter's lifted cap; to him, salutations and civilities came like the air he breathed, and were as little acknowledged. The Baron gave to Herr Haase the compliment of a glance that took in the grey coat and the cloth boots, and the ghost of an ironic, not unkindly smile.

"Der gute Haase," he murmured, and then, as though in absence of mind, "Poor fellow, poor fellow!"

His foot was upon the step of the car when he saw the leather suit-case within. He paused in the act of entering.

"What is this baggage?" he inquired.

Von Wetten craned forward to look. "Oh, that! I wanted you to see the machine at work, Excellenz, so I'm bringing a few cartridges and things."

His Excellency withdrew his foot and stepped back. "Explosives, eh?" He made a half-humorous grimace of distaste. "Haase, lift that bag out carefully, man! and carry it in front with you. And tell the chauffeur to drive cautiously!"

Their destination was to the eastward of the little town, where the gardens of the villas trail their willow-fringes in the water. Among them, a varnished yellow chalet lifted its tiers of glassed-in galleries among the heavy green of fir-trees; its door, close beside the road, was guarded by a gate of iron bars. The big car slid to a standstill beside it with a scrape of tires in the dust.

"A moment," said the old baron, as Herr Haase lifted his hand to the iron bell-pull that hung beside the gate. "Who are we? What names have you given, Von Wetten? Schmidt and Meyer or something more fanciful?"

"Much more fanciful, Excellenz." Von Wetten allowed himself a smile. "I am Herr Wetten; Your Excellency is Herr Steinlach. It could not be simpler."

The Baron laughed quietly. "Very good, indeed," he agreed. "And Haase? You did not think of him? Well, the good Haase, for the time being, shall be the Herr von Haase. Eh, Haase?"

"Zu Befehl, Excellenz," deferred Herr Haase.

The iron bell-pull squealed in its dry guides; somewhere within the recesses of the house a sleeping bell woke and jangled. Silence followed. The three of them waited upon the road in the slant of the sunshine, aware of the odor of hot dust, trees, and water. Herr Haase stood, in the contented torpor of service and obedience, holding the heavy suit-case to one side of the gate; to the other, the Baron and Von Wetten stood together. Von Wetten, with something of rigidity even in his ease and insouciance, stared idly at the windows through which, as through stagnant eyes, the silent house seemed to be inspecting them; the Baron, with his hands joined behind him, was gazing through the gate at the unresponsive yellow door. His pink, strong face had fallen vague and mild; he seemed to dream in the sunlight upon the threshold of his enterprise. All of him that was formidable and potent was withdrawn from the surface, sucked in, and concentrated in the inner centers of his mind and spirit.

There sounded within the door the noise of footsteps; a bolt clashed, and there came out to the gate a young woman with a key in her hand. The Baron lifted his head and looked at her, and she stopped, as though brought up short by the impact of his gaze. She was a small creature, not more than twenty-two or twenty-three years of age, as fresh and pretty as apple-blossom. But it was more than shyness that narrowed her German-blue eyes as she stood behind the bars, looking at the three men.

Von Wetten, tall, comely, stepped forward.

"Good afternoon, gnadige Frau. We have an appointment with your husband for this hour. Let me present Herr Steinlach Herr von Haase."

The two bowed at her; she inspected each in turn, still with that narrow-eyed reserve.

"Yes," she said then, in a small tinkle of a voice. "My husband is expecting you."

She unlocked the gate; the key resisted her, and she had to take both hands to it, flushing with the effort of wrenching it over. They followed her into the house, along an echoing corridor, to a front room whose windows framed a dazzling great panorama of wide water, steep blue mountain, and shining snow-slopes. Herr Haase, coming last with the suitcase, saw around the Baron's large shoulders how she flitted across and called into the balcony: "Egon, the Herren are here!" Then, without glancing at them again, she passed them and disappeared.

Herr Haase's wrist was aching with his burden. Gently, and with precaution against noise, he stooped, and let the suit-case down upon the floor. So that he did not see the entry at that moment of the man who came from the balcony, walking noiselessly upon rubber-soled tennis-shoes. He heard Von Wetten's "Good afternoon, Herr Bettermann," and straightened up quickly to be introduced.

He found himself taking the hand it lay in his an instant as lifelessly as a glove of a young man whose eyes, over-large in a tragically thin face and under a chrysanthemum shock of hair, were at once timid and angry. He was coatless, as though he had come fresh from some work, and under his blue shirt his shoulders showed angular. But what was most noticeable about him, when he lifted his face to the light, was the scar of which Von Wetten had spoken a red and jagged trace of some ugly wound, running from the inner corner of the right eye to the edge of the jaw. He murmured some inaudible acknowledgment of Herr Haase's scrupulously correct greeting.

Then, as actually as though an arm of flesh and blood had thrust him back. Herr Haase was brushed aside. It was as if the Baron von Steinlach, choosing his moment, released his power of personality upon the scene as a man lets go his held breath. "A wonderful view you have here, Herr Bettermann," was all he said. The young man turned to him to reply; it was as though their opposite purposes and wills crossed and clashed like engaged swords. Herr Haase, and even the salient and insistent presence of Von Wetten, thinned and became vague ghostly, ineffectual natives of the background in the stark light of the reality of that encounter.

There were some sentences, mere feigning, upon that radiant perspective which the wide windows framed.

Then: "My friend and associate, Herr Wetten here, has asked me to look into this matter," said the Baron. His voice was silk, the silk "that holds fast where a steel chain snaps."

"First, to confirm his impressions of the the apparatus; second" the subtle faint-blue eyes of the old man and the dark suspicious eyes of the young man met and held each other "and second, the question, the minor question, of the price. However" his lips, under the clipped, white moustache, widened in a smile without mirth "that need not take us long, since the price, you see, is not really a question at all."

The haggard young man heard him with no change in that painful intensity of his.

"Isn't it?" he said shortly. "We'll see! But first, I suppose, you want to see the thing at work. I have here cordite, gelignite, trinitrotoluol," but his hare's eyes fell on the suit-case, "perhaps you have brought your own stuff?"

"Yes," said the Baron; "I have brought my own stuff."

The garden of the villa was a plot of land reaching down to a parapet lapped by the still stone-blue waters of the lake. Wooden steps led down to it from the balcony; Herr Haase, descending them last with the suit-case, paused an instant to shift his burden from one hand to the other, and had time to survey the place the ruins of a lawn, pitted like the face of a small-pox patient with small holes, where the raw clay showed through the unkempt grass the "craters" of which Captain von Wetten had spoken. Tall fir-trees, the weed of Switzerland, bounded the garden on either hand, shutting it in as effectually as a wall. Out upon the blue-and-silver floor of the lake a male human being rowed a female of his species in a skiff; and near the parapet something was hooded under a black cloth, such as photographers use, beneath whose skirts there showed the feet of a tripod.

Herr Bettermann, the young man with the scar, walked across to it. At first glimpse, it had drawn all their eyes; each felt that here, properly and decently screened, was the core of the affair. It was right that it should be covered up and revealed only at the due moment; yet Bettermann went to it and jerked the black cloth off, raping the mystery of the thing as crudely as a Prussian in Belgium.

"Here it is," he said curtly. "Put your stuff where you like."

The cloth removed disclosed a contrivance like two roughly cubical boxes, fitted one above the other, the upper projecting a little beyond the lower, and mounted on the apex of the tripod. A third box, evidently, by the terminals which projected from its cover, the container of a storage battery, lay between the feet of the tripod, and wires linked it with the apparatus above. Beside the tripod lay a small black bag such as doctors are wont to carry.

Von Wetten took a key from his pocket and threw it on the ground. "Unlock that bag," he said to Herr Haase, and turned towards the Baron and his host.

Herr Haase picked up the key, unlocked the suitcase, and stood ready for further orders. The Baron was standing with Bettermann by the tripod; the latter was talking and detaching some piece of mechanism within the apparatus. His voice came clearly across to Herr Haase.

"Two blades," he was saying, "and one varies their angle with this. The sharper the angle, the greater the range of the ray and the shorter the effective arc. But, of course, this machine is only a model."

"Quite so," acquiesced the Baron.

"These" his hand emerged from the upper box "are the blades."

He withdrew from the apparatus a contrivance like a pair of brief tongs, of which the shanks were stout wires and the spatulates were oblongs of thin, whitish metal like aluminum, some three inches long by two wide.

"The essence of the whole thing," he said. "You see, they are hinged; one sets them wider or closer according to the range and the arc one requires. These plates they are removable. I paint the compound on them, and switch the current on through this battery."

"Ah, yes," agreed the Baron dreamily. "The compound that has to be painted on."

The thin face of the inventor turned upon him; the great eyes smoldered. "Yes," was the answer; "yes. I, I paint it on enough for three or four demonstrations, and then I throw the rest into the lake. So my secret is safe, you see."

The Baron met his eyes with the profound ironic calm of his own. "Safe, I am sure," he replied. "The safer the better. And now, where would you prefer us to arrange our explosives?"

The other shrugged his shoulders. "Where you like," he said, bending to the little black hand-bag. "Lay them on the ground or bury them, or throw them into the lake, if they're waterproof. Only don't put them too near the house. I don't want any more of my windows broken."

There was a tone of aggression in his voice, and his eyes seemed to affront them, then strayed in a moment's glance towards the house. Herr Haase, following his look, had a glimpse of the little wife upon the upper balcony looking down upon the scene. The young man with the scar it glowed at whiles, red and angry seemed to make her some sign, for she drew back out of sight at once.

Herr Haase would have liked to watch the further intercourse of the Baron and the lean young man; but Von Wetten, indicating to him a small iron spade, such as children dig with on the sea-beach, and a pointed iron rod, set him to work at making graves for the little paper-wrapped packages which he took from the suit-case. The captain stood over him while he did it, directing him with orders curt as oaths and wounding as blows, looking down upon his sweating, unremonstrant obedience as from a very mountain-top of superiority. The clay was dry as flour, and puffed into dust under the spade; the slanting sun had yet a vigor of heat; and Herr Haase, in his tail-coat and his cloth boots, floundered among the little craters and earth-heaps, and dug and perspired submissively.

As he completed each hole to Von Wetten's satisfaction, that demigod dropped one or more of his small packages into it, and arranged them snugly with the iron rod. While he did so, Herr Haase eased himself upright, wiped the sweat from his brow, and gazed across at the other two. He saw the young man dipping a brush in a bottle, which he had taken from the black bag, and painting with it upon the metal plates, intent and careful; while beside him the old baron, with his hands clasped behind his back, watched him with just that air of blended patronage and admiration with which a connoisseur, visiting a studio, watches an artist at work.

Von Wetten spoke at his elbow. "Fill this in!" he said, in those tones of his that would have roused rebellion in a beast of burden. "And tread the earth down on it firmly!"

"Zu Befehl, Herr Hauptmann," answered Herr Haase hastily. But he was slow enough in obeying to see the young man, his painting finished, take the bottle in his hand, and toss it over the parapet into the lake and turn, the great jagged scar suddenly red and vivid on the pallor of his thin face, to challenge the Baron with his angry eyes.

The Baron met them with his small indomitable smile. "The machine is ready now?" he inquired smoothly.

"Ready when you are," snapped the other.

Herr Haase had to return to his labors then and lose the rest of that battle of purposes, of offence offered and refused, which went on over the head of the waiting machine. Von Wetten left him for a while and was busy throwing things that looked like glass jars into the lake. When at last the fifth and final hole was filled and trodden down under the sore heels in the cloth boots, the others were standing around the apparatus. They looked up at him as he cast down the spade and clapped a hand to the main stiffness in the small of his back.

"All finished?" called the Baron. "Then come over here, my good friend, or you will be blown up. Eh, Herr Bettermann?"

Herr Bettermann shrugged those sharp shoulders of his; he was shifting the tripod legs of his machine. "Blow him up if you like," he said. "He's your man."

Von Wetten and the Baron laughed at that, the Baron civilly and perfunctorily, as one laughs at the minor jests of one's host, and Von Wetten as though the joke were a good one. Herr Haase smiled deferentially, and eased himself into the background by the parapet.

"And now," said the Baron, "to our fireworks!"

Herr Bettermann answered with the scowl-like contraction of the brows which he used in place of a nod.

"All right," he said. "Stand away from the front of the thing, will you? You know yourselves the kind of stuff you've buried yes? Also, los!"

The old baron had stepped back to Herr Haase's side; as the young man put his hands to the apparatus, he crisped himself with a sharp intake of breath for the explosion. A switch clicked under the young man's thumb, and he began to move the machine upon its pivot mounting, traversing it like a telescope on a stand. It came round towards the fresh yellow mounds of earth which marked Herr Haase's excavations; they had an instant in which to note, faint as the whirring of a fly upon a pane, the buzz of some small mechanism within the thing. Then, not louder than a heavy stroke upon a drum, came the detonation of the buried cartridges in the first hole, and the earth above them suddenly ballooned and burst like an over-inflated paper-bag and let through a spit of brief fire and a jet of smoke.

"Ach, du lieber" began the Baron, and had the words chopped off short by the second explosion. A stone the size of a tennis-ball soared slowly over them and plopped into the water a score of yards away. The Baron raised an arm as if to guard his face, and kept it raised; Von Wetten let his eyeglass fall, lifted it in his hand and held it there; only Herr Haase, preserving his formal attitude of obedient waiting, his large bland face inert, stood unmoved, passively watching this incident of his trade.

The rest of the holes blew up nobly; the last was applauded by a crash of glass as one of the upper windows of the house broke and came raining down in splinters. The lean young man swore tersely. "Another window!" he snarled. The Baron lowered his arm and let his breath go in a sigh of relief.

"That is all, is it not?" he demanded. "Gott sei Dank I hate things that explode. But I am glad that I saw it, now that it is over, very glad indeed!"

There was a touch of added color in the even pink of his face, and something of restlessness, a shine of excitement, in his eyes. Even his voice had a new tone of unfamiliar urgency. He glanced to and fro from Herr Wetten to Herr Haase as though seeking someone to share his emotion.

Bettermann's thin voice broke in curtly. "It isn't over," he said. "There's the stuff he" with a glance like a stab at Von Wetten "threw into the lake. Ready?"

"Ach!" The Baron stepped hastily aside. "Yes; I had forgotten that. Quite ready, my dear sir quite ready. Haase, my good friend, I think I'll stand behind you this time."

"Zu Befehl, Excellenz," acquiesced Herr Haase, and made of his solidity and stolidity a screen and a shield for the master-mind in its master-body. Herr Bettermann, bending behind his machine, took in the grouping with an eye that sneered and exulted, jerked his angular blue-clad shoulders contemptuously, and turned again to his business.

The eye of the machine roamed over the face of the water, seeming to peer searchingly into the depths of shining blue; the small interior whir started again upon the click of the switch, and forthwith three explosions, following upon each other rapidly, tore that tranquil water-mirror, spouting three geyser-jets into the sun-soaked evening air. The waves they raised slapped loudly at the wall below the parapet, and there were suddenly dead fish floating pale-bellied on the surface.

"Mines!" It was a whisper behind Herr Haase's large shoulder. "English mines!"

Herr Bettermann straightened himself upright behind the tripod. "There's a fine for killing fish like that," he remarked bitterly. "And the window besides, curse it!"

The Baron looked round at him absently. "Too bad!" he agreed. "Too bad!" He moved Herr Haase out of his way with a touch of his hand and walked to the parapet. He stood there, seeming for some moments to be absorbed in watching the dead fish as they rocked in the diminishing eddies. Herr Bettermann picked up the black cloth and draped it again over his apparatus. There was a space of silence.

Presently, with a shrug as though he withdrew himself unwillingly from some train of thought, the Baron turned. "Yes," he said, slowly, half to himself. "Y-es!" He lifted his eyes to the inventor.

"Well, we have only three things to do," he said. "They should not take us long. But it is pleasant here in your garden, Herr Bettermann, and we might sit down while we do them."

He sat as he spoke, letting himself down upon the low parapet with an elderly deliberation; at his gesture Von Wetten sat likewise, a few yards away; Herr Haase moved a pace, hesitated, and remained standing.

"I'll stand," said Bettermann shortly. "And what are the three things that you have got to do?"

"Why," replied the Baron, evenly, "the obvious three, surely to pay for your broken window nicht wahr? to pay the fine for killing the fish, and to pay your price for the machine. There is nothing else to pay for, is there?"

"Oh!" The young man stared at him.

"So, if you will tell us the figure that will content you, we can dispatch the matter," continued the Baron. "That is your part to name a figure. Supposing always" his voice slowed; the words dropped one by one "supposing always that there is a figure!"

The other continued to stare, gaunt as a naked tree in the evening flush, his face white under his tumbled hair, the jagged scar showing, upon it like a new wound.

"You don't suppose you'll get the thing for nothing, do you?" he broke out suddenly.

The Baron shook his head. "No," he said, "I don't think that. But it has struck me I may not need my cheque-book. You see, for all I can tell, Herr Bettermann, the window may be insured; and the police may not hear of the fish; and as for the machine well, the machine may be for sale; but you have less the manner of a salesman, Herr Bettermann, than any man I have ever seen."

The gaunt youth glowered uncertainly. "I'm not a salesman," he retorted resentfully.

The Baron nodded. "I was sure of it," he said. "Well, if you will let me, I'll be your salesman for you; I have sold things in my time, and for great prices too. Now, I can see that you are in a difficulty. You are a patriotic Swiss citizen and you have scruples about letting your invention go out of your own country; is that it? Because, if so, it can be arranged."

He stopped; the lean youth had uttered a spurt of laughter, bitter and contemptuous.

"Swiss!" he cried. "No more Swiss than yourself, Herr Baron!"

"Eh?" To Herr Haase, watching through his mask of respectful aloofness, it was as though the Baron's mind and countenance together snapped almost audibly into a narrowed and intensified alertness. The deep, white-fringed brows gathered over the shrewd pale eyes. "Not a Swiss?" he queried. "What are you, then?"

"Huh!" the other jeered, openly. "I knew you the moment I saw you. Old Herr Steinlach, eh? Why, man, I've been expecting you and getting ready for you ever since your blundering, swaggering spy there" with a jerk of a rigid thumb towards Von Wetten "and this fat slave" Herr Haase was indicated here "first came sniffing round my premises. I knew they'd be sending you along, with your blank cheques and your tongue; and here you are!"

He mouthed his words in an extravagance of offence and ridicule; his gaunt body and his thin arms jerked in a violence of gesticulation, and the jagged scar that striped his face pulsed from red to white. The old baron, solid and unmoving on his seat, watched him with still attention.

"Not a Swiss?" he persisted, when the young man had ceased to shout and shrug.

For answer, suddenly as an attacker, the young man strode across to him and bent, thrusting his feverish and passion-eaten face close to the other man's. His forefinger, long, large-knuckled, jerked up; he traced with it upon his face the course of the great disfiguring scar that flamed diagonally from the inner corner of the right eye to the rim of the sharp jaw.

"Did you ever see a Swiss that carried a mark like that?" he cried, his voice breaking to a screech. "Or an Englishman, or a Frenchman? Or anybody but but" he choked breathlessly on his words "or anybody but a German? Man, it's my passport!"

He remained yet an instant, bent forward, rigid finger to face, then rose and stepped back, breathing hard. The three of them stuck, staring at him.

Von Wetten broke the silence. "German?" he said, in that infuriating tone of peremptory incredulity which his kind in all countries commands. "You, a German?"

The lean youth turned on him with a movement like a swoop. "Yes me!" he spat. "And a deserter from my military service, too! Make the best of that, you Prussian Schweinhund!"

"Was!" Von Wetten started as though under a blow; his monocle fell; he made a curious gesture, bringing his right hand across to his left hip as though in search of something; and gathered himself as though about to spring to his feet. The Baron lifted a quiet hand and subdued him.

"Yes," he said, in his even, compelling tones. "Make the best of that, Von Wetten."

Von Wetten stared, arrested in the very act of rising. "Zu Befehl, Herr Baron," he said, in a strained voice, and continued staring. The Baron watched him frowningly an instant, to make sure of his submission, and turned again to Herr Bettermann where he stood, lean and glowering, before them.

"Now," he said, "I am beginning to see my way dimly, dimly. A deserter a German and that scar is your passport! Ye-es! Well, will you tell me, Herr Bettermann, in plain German, how you came by that scar?"

"Yes," said Bettermann, fiercely, "I will!"

Behind him, where the house windows shone rosy in the sunset, Herr Haase could see upon the lower balcony the shimmer of a white frock and a face that peeped and drew back. The little wife was listening.

"It was the captain of my company," said Bettermann, with a glare at Von Wetten. "Another Prussian swine-dog like this brute here." He waited. Von Wetten regarded him with stony calm and did not move. Bettermann flushed. "He sent me for his whip, and when I brought it, he called me to attention and cut me over the face with it."

"Eh?" The old baron sat up. "Aber-"

"Just one cut across the face, me with my heels glued together and my hands nailed to my sides," went on Bettermann. "Then 'Dismiss!' he ordered, and I saluted and turned about and marched away with my smashed face. And then you ask me if I am a Swiss!" He laughed again.

"But," demanded the Baron, "what had you done? Why did he do that to you?"

"Didn't I tell you he was a Prussian swine?" cried Bettermann. "Isn't that reason enough? But, if you will know, he'd seen me speak to a lady in the street. Afterwards me standing to attention, of course! he made a foul comment on her, and asked me for her name and address."

"And you wouldn't tell him?"

"Tell him!" cried Bettermann. "No!"

Herr Haase saw the girl on the balcony lean forward as though to hear the word, its pride and its bitterness, and draw back again as though to hear it had been all that she desired.

"Von Wetten!" The Baron spoke briskly. "You hear what Herr Bettermann tells me? Such things happen in the army do they?"

Von Wetten shrugged. "They are strictly illegal, sir," he replied, formally. "There are severe penalties prescribed for such actions. But, in the army, in the daily give-and-take of the life of a regiment, of course, they do happen. Herr Bettermann," very stiffly, "was unfortunate."

Betterman was staring at him, but said nothing. The Baron glanced from Von Wetten to the lean young man and shook his head.

"I am beginning I think I am beginning to see," he said. "And it seems to me that I shall not need that cheque-book. Herr Bettermann, I am very sure you have not forgotten the name of that officer."

"Forgotten!" said the other. "No, I've not forgotten. And, so that you shan't forget, I've got it written down for you!"

He fished a card from the breast-pocket of his blue shirt. The Baron received it, and held it up to the light.

"Captain Graf von Specht, the Kaiserjaeger," he read aloud. "Ever hear of him, Von Wetten?"

Von Wetten nodded. "Neighbor of mine in the country, Excellenz," he replied. "We were at the cadet-school together. Colonel now; promoted during the war. He would regret, I am sure."

"He will regret, I am sure," interrupted the Baron, pocketing the card. "And he will have good cause. Well, Herr Bettermann, I think I know your terms now. You want to see the Graf von Specht again here? I am right, am I not?"

Bettermann's eyes narrowed at him. "Yes," he said. "You're right. Only this time it is he that must bring the whip!"

Herr Haase's intelligence, following like a shorthand-writer's pencil, ten words behind the speaker, gave a leap at this. Till now, the matter had been for him a play without a plot; suddenly understanding, he cast a startled glance at Von Wetten.

The captain sat up alert.

"Certainly!" The old baron was replying to young Bettermann. "And stand to attention! And salute! I told you that I would agree to your terms, and I agree accordingly. Captain that is, Colonel von Specht shall be here, with the whip, as soon as the telegraph and the train can bring him. And then, I assume, the machine."

"Pardon!" Captain von Wetten had risen. "I have not understood." He came forward between the two, very erect and military, and rather splendid with his high-held head and drilled comeliness of body. "There has been much elegance of talk and I am stupid, no doubt; but, in plain German, what is it that Colonel von Specht is to do?"

Bettermann swooped at him again, choking with words; the captain stood like a monument callous to his white and stammering rage, the personification and symbol of his caste and its privilege.

It was the Baron who answered from his seat on the parapet, not varying his tone and measured delivery.

"Colonel von Specht," he said, "is to bring a whip here and stand to attention while Herr Bettermann cuts him over the face with it. That is all. Now sit down and be silent."

Captain von Wetten did not move. "This is impossible," he said. "There are limits. As a German officer, I resent the mere suggestion of this insult to the corps of officers. Your Excellency."

The Baron lifted that quiet hand of his. "I order you to sit down and be silent," he said.

Captain von Wetten hesitated. It seemed to Herr Haase, for a flattering instant, that the captain's eyes sought his own, as though in recognition of a familiar and favorable spirit. He tried to look respectfully sympathetic.

"Very good, your Excellency," said Von Wetten, at length. "The Emperor, of course, will be informed."

He turned and stalked away to his former place. The Baron, watching him, smiled briefly.

"Well, Herr Bettermann," said the Baron, rising stiffly, "it will not help us to have this arrangement of ours in writing. I think we'll have to trust one another. Our chemists, then, can come to you for the formula as soon as you have finished with Colonel von Specht? That is agreed yes? Good! And you see, I was right from the beginning; I did not need my cheque-book after all."

He began to move towards the house, beckoning Captain von Wetten and Herr Haase to follow him. Herr Haase picked up the empty suit-case, stood aside to let Von Wetten pass, and brought up the rear of the procession.

At the foot of the wooden steps that led up to the veranda, the Baron halted and turned to Bettermann.

"One thing makes me curious," he said. "Suppose we had not accepted your terms, what would you have done? Sold your machine to our enemies?"

Bettermann was upon the second step, gauntly silhouetted against the yellow wood of the house. He looked down into the elder man's strong and subtle face.

"No," he answered. "I meant to at first, but I haven't purged the German out of me yet and I couldn't. But I'd let your army of slaves and slave-drivers be beaten by its own slavery as it would be and you know it. I wouldn't take a hand in it; only, if anything happened to me; if, for instance, I disappeared some night, well, you'd find the machine and the formula in the hands of the English, that's all!"

He turned and led the way up the wooden steps. It seemed to tired Herr Haase, lugging the suit-case, that Captain von Wetten was swearing under his breath.

He was not imaginative, our Herr Haase; facts were his livelihood and the nurture of his mind. But in the starved wastes of his fancy something had struck a root, and as he rode Thun-wards in the front seat of the car, with the suit-case in his lap and the setting sun in his eyes, he brooded upon it. It was the glimpse of the little wife in the balcony the girl who had lived with the scar upon her husband's face and in his soul, and had leaned forward to eavesdrop upon his cruel triumph. Behind him, the two demi-gods talked together; snatches of their conversation tempted him to listen; but Herr Haase was engrossed with another matter. When the Prussian colonel, one living agony of crucified pride, stood for the blow, and the whip whistled through the air to thud on the flesh of his upturned face would she be watching then?

He was still thinking of it when the car drew up at the hotel door.

"Upstairs at once," directed the Baron, as he stepped hastily to the sidewalk. "You too, my good Haase; we shall want you."

In the Baron's upper room, where that morning he had suffered the torture of the boot, Herr Haase was given a seat at the little writing-table. The Baron himself cleared it for him, wiping its piles of papers to the floor with a single sweep of his hand.

"Get ready to write the telegrams which we shall dictate," he commanded. "But first will you be able to get them through in code?"

"Code is forbidden, your Excellency," replied Herr Haase, in his parade voice. "But we have also a phrase-code, a short phrase for every word of the message which passes. It makes the telegram very long."

"Also gut!" approved the Baron. "Now, Von Wetten, first we will wire the Staff. You know how to talk to them; so dictate a clear message to Haase here."

Von Wetten was standing by the door, hat and cane in hand. His face, with its vacant comeliness, wore a formality that was almost austere.

"Zu Befehl, Excellenz," he replied. "But has your Excellency considered that, after all, there may be other means? I beg your Excellency's pardon, but it occurs to me that we have not tried alternative offers. For instance, we are not limited as to money."

The Baron made a little gesture of impatience, indulgent and paternal. He leaned a hand on the table and looked over Herr Haase's head to the tall young officer.

"We are not limited as to colonels, either," he answered. "We must think ourselves lucky, I suppose, that he went no higher than a colonel. There was a moment when I thought he was going very much higher to the very top, Von Wetten. For, make no mistake, that young man knows his value."

Von Wetten frowned undecidedly. "The top," he repeated. "There is only one top. You can't mean?"

The Baron took the word from his mouth. "Yes," he said, "the Emperor. I thought for a while he was going to demand that. And do you know what I should have answered?"

Von Wetten threw up his head and his face cleared. "Of course I know," he said. "You'd have cut the dirty traitor down where he stood!"

The Baron did not move. "No," he said. "I should have accepted those terms also, Von Wetten."

The Baron's hand rested on the edge of the table in front of Herr Haase; he sat, staring at it, a piece of human furniture on the stage of a tragedy. The other two confronted each other above his patient and useful head. He would have liked to look from one to the other, to watch their faces, but he was too deeply drilled for that. He heard Von Wetten's voice with a quaver in it.

"Then things are going as badly as all that?"

"Yes," answered the Baron. "Badly! It is not just this battle that is going on now in France; it strikes deeper than that. The plan that was to give us victory has failed us; we find ourselves, with a strength which must diminish, fighting an enemy whose strength increases. We must not stop at anything now; what is at stake is too tremendous."

"But—."

The Baron hushed him. "Listen, Von Wetten," he said. "I will be patient with you. I do not speak to you of of the Idea of which Germany and Prussia are the body and the weapon. No; but have you ever realized that you, yes, you! belong to the most ridiculed, most despised nation on earth? That your countrywomen furnish about eighty per cent. of the world's prostitutes; that a German almost anywhere is a waiter, or a sausage-manufacturer, or a beer-seller, the butt of comic papers in a score of languages? All that has not occurred to you, eh?

"Well, think of it, and think, too, of what this machine may do for us. Think of a Germany armed in a weaponless world, and, if empire and mastery convey nothing to you, think of oh! American women walking the streets in Berlin, comic English waiters in German cafe's, slavish French laborers in German sweat-shops. And all this boxed into a machine on a tripod by a monomaniac whose price we can pay!"

He paused and walked towards the window. "Dictate the telegram to the Staff, Von Wetten," he said, over his shoulder.

Von Wetten laid his hat and cane on a chair and crossed the room. "I feel as if I were stabbing a fellow-officer in the back," he said, drearily. Then, to Herr Haase: "Take this, you!"

"Zu Befehl, Herr Hauptmann," said Herr Haase, and picked up his pen.

There were twelve long telegrams in all, of which many had to be amended, pruned, sub-edited, and rewritten; each was directed to a plain private address in Berlin, and each was to be answered to the address of Herr Haase. One, which gave more trouble than any of the others, was to Siegfried Meyer, Number One, Unter den Linden; it was long before the Baron and Von Wetten could smooth its phrases to a suavity and deference which satisfied them. Coffee was brought them to lubricate their labors, but none to Herr Haase; his part was to write down, scratch out, rewrite, while beyond the windows the night marched up from the east and the lake grew bleak and vague.

"Now, my good Haase," said the Baron, when the last word-fabric was decided upon and confirmed, "you will take those home with you, put them into code, and dispatch them. You should have the last of them off by midnight. And to-morrow, when the answers begin to come, you will report here as quickly as possible."

"Zu befehl, Excellenz," said Herr Haase, his hands full of papers.

"Then good night, my good Haase," said the Baron.

"Good night to your Excellency," returned Herr Haase, from the doorway. "Good night, Herr Hauptmann!" to Von Wetten's back.

"Shut the door," replied Von Wetten.

There was a moon at midnight, a great dull disc of soft light touching the antique gables and cloistered streets of the little city to glamour, blackening the shadows under the arches, and streaking the many channels of the swift river with long reflections. Herr Haase, returning from the telegraph office, walked noiseless as a ghost through those ancient streets, for he had soft bedroom slippers on his feet. His work was done for the day; he had put off business as one lays aside a garment. From his lips ascended the mild incense of one of those moist yellow cigars they make at Vevey. He paused upon the first bridge to gaze down upon the smooth, hurrying water, and his soul that soul which served the general purpose of a monkey-wrench in adjusting the machine of history spoke aloud.

"A rum-punch," it confided to the night and the moon. "Yes, two glasses; and a belegtes Brodchen; and a warm foot-bath. And then, bed!"

Not for him, at any rate, were the doubts and hopes that tangled in the Baron von Steinlach's massive head. A man with sore feet is prone to feel that the ground he stands on is at least solid. In his pleasant veranda next morning, with his coffee fragrant before him on the chequered tablecloth, he read in the Bund: the British communiqué of the battle of the Somme, new villages taken, fortified woods stormed, prisoners multiplying, the whole monstrous structure of the German war-machine cracking and failing. While he read he ate and drank tranquilly; no thoughts of yesterday's business intruded upon his breakfast peace. He finished the communique.

Then: "Liars!" he commented, comfortably, reaching for his cup. "Those English are always liars!"

It was a good and easy day that thus opened. The answers to his telegrams did not begin to arrive till noon, and then they were only formulae acknowledging receipt, which he did not need his code-book to decipher. With his black umbrella opened against the drive of the sun, he carried them at his leisure to the Baron, where he sat alone in his cool upper chamber working deliberately among his papers, received the customary ghost of a smile and the murmur, "Der gute Haase," and got away. The slovenly porter, always with his look of having slept in his clothes, tried to engage him in talk upon the day's news. "You," said Herr Haase, stepping round him, "are one of those who believe anything; schamen Sie sich!" And so back to the comfortable villa on the hillside with its flaming geraniums and its atmosphere of that comfort and enduring respectability which stood to Herr Haase for the very inwardness of Germany. Yes, a good day!

It lasted as long as the daylight; the end of it found Herr Haase, his lamp alight, his back turned to the Alpine-glow on the mountains, largely at ease in his chair, awaiting the arrival of his Dienstmadchen with the culminating coffee of the day. His yellow cigar was alight; he was fed and torpid; digestion and civilization were doing their best for him. As from an ambush there arrived the fat, yellow telegraph envelope.

"Ach, was!" protested Herr Haase. "And I thought it was the coffee you were bringing."

"'S Kaffee kommt gleich," the stout, tow-haired girl assured him; but already he had torn open the envelope and was surveying its half-dozen sheets of code. Two hours of work with the key, at least; he groaned, and hoisted himself from his chair.

"Bring the coffee to the office," he bade, and went to telephone a warning to the Baron.

The code was a cumbersome one; its single good quality was that it passed unsuspected at a time when nervous telegraph departments were refusing all ciphers. It consisted of brief phrases and single words alternately; the single words the codebook offered a selection of a couple of hundred of them were meaningless, and employed solely to separate the phrases; and for half an hour Herr Haase's task was to separate this ballast from the cargo of the message and jettison it. There lay before him then a string of honest-looking mercantile phrases "market unsettled," "collections difficult," and the like which each signified a particular word. He sat back in his chair and took a preliminary glance at the thing.

It was a code he used frequently himself, and there were phrases in the message, two or three, which he knew by heart. As he scanned it it struck him that all of these were of the same character; they were words of deprecation or demur. "Existing rate of exchange" meant "regret"; "active selling" meant "impossible"; and "usual discount" was the code-form of "unfortunate." Herr Haase frowned and reached for his key.

Midnight was close at hand when he reached the Baron's room, with the telegram and his neatly-written interpretation in an envelope. He had changed his coat and shoes for the visit; it was the usual Herr Haase, softish of substance, solemn of attire, official of demeanor, who clicked and bowed to the Baron and Von Wetten in turn.

"Our good Haase," said the Baron. "At last!"

He wore a brown cloth dressing-gown with a cord about the middle; and somehow the garment, with its long skirts and its tied-in waist, looked like a woman's frock? With the white hair and the contained benevolence and power of his face it gave him the aspect of a distorted femininity, a womanhood unnatural and dire. Even Herr Haase perceived it, for he stared a moment open-mouthed before he recovered himself. Von Wetten, smoking, in an easy chair, was in evening dress.

Herr Haase, with customary clockwork-like military motions, produced his envelope and held it forth.

"The code-telegram of which I telephoned your Excellency and a transcription of it," he announced.

Von Wetten took his cigar from his lips and held it between his fingers. The Baron waved the proffered envelope from him.

"Read it to us, my good Haase," he said.

"Zu befehl, Excellenz!" Herr Haase produced from the envelope the crackling sheet of thin paper, held it up to the light, standing the while with heels together and chest outthrust, and read in the high barrack-square voice:

"Herr Sigismund Haase, Friedrichsruhe, Thunam-See, Switzerland. From Secret Service Administration, Berlin. July 21st, 1916. In reply to your code-message previously acknowledged, regret to report that officer you require was recently severely wounded. Hospital authorities report that it is impossible to move him. Trust this unfortunate event does not stultify your arrangements. Your further instructions awaited."

Herr Haase refolded the paper and returned it to the envelope and stood waiting.

It was Von Wetten who spoke first. "Thank God!" he said loudly.

The old baron, standing near him, hands joined behind his back, had listened to the reading with eyes on the floor. He shook his head now, gently, dissenting rather than contradicting.

"Oh, no," he said slowly. "Don't be in a hurry to do that, Von Wetten."

"But, Excellency," Von Wetten protested, "I meant, of course."

"I know," said the Baron. "I know what you thanked God for; and I tell you don't be in too great a hurry."

He began to walk to and fro in the room. He let his hands fall to his sides; he was more than ever distortedly womanlike, almost visibly possessed and driven by his single purpose. Von Wetten, the extinct cigar still poised in his hand, watched him frowningly.

"Sometimes" the Baron seemed to speak as often a man deep in thought will hum a tune "sometimes I have felt before what I feel now a current in the universe that sets against me, against us. Something pulls the other way. It has all but daunted me once or twice."

He continued to pace to and fro, staring at the varnished floor.

"But, Excellency," urged Von Wetten, "there are still ways and means. If we can decoy this inventor-fellow across the frontier and then, there is his wife!

Pressure could be brought to bear through the woman. If we got hold of her, now!"

The Baron paused in his walk to hear him.

"And find an English army blasting its way through Belgium with that machine to come to her rescue? No," he said; and then, starting from his moody quiet to a sudden loudness: "No! We know his price to lash this Von Specht across the face with a whip and we have agreed to it. Let him lash him as he lies on a stretcher, if he likes! I know that type of scorched brain, simmering on the brink of madness. He'll do it, and he'll keep faith; and it'll be cheap at the price. Haase!"

He wheeled on Herr Haase suddenly.

"Zu befehl, Excellenz," replied Herr Haase.

The Baron stared at him for some moments, at the solid, capable, biddable creature he was, stable and passive in the jar of the overturned world. He pointed to the table.

"Sit there, my good Haase," he ordered. "I will dictate you a telegram. Not code this time, plain German!"

He resumed his to-and-fro walk while Herr Haase established himself.

"Direct it to our private address in the Wilhelmstrasse," he ordered. "Then write: 'You are to carry out orders previously communicated. Send Von Specht forthwith, avoiding all delay. Telegraph hour of his departure and keep me informed of his progress. No objections to this order are to be entertained.'"

"'Entertained,'" murmured Herr Haase, as he wrote the last word.

"Sign it as before," directed the Baron. "You see, Von Wetten, it was too soon!"

Von Wetten had not moved; he sat staring at the Baron. His hand twitched and the dead cigar fell to the floor.

"I don't care," he burst out, "it's wrong; it's not worth it nothing could be. I'd be willing to go a long way, but a Prussian officer! It's, it's sacrilege. And a wounded man at that!"

The Baron did not smile but mirth was in his face. "That was an afterthought, Von Wetten," he said "the wounded man part of it." He turned to Herr Haase impatiently.

"Off with you!" he commanded. "Away, man, and get that message sent! Let me have the replies as they arrive. No, don't wait to bow and say good night; run, will you!"

His long arm, in the wide sleeve of the gown, leaped up, pointing to the door. Herr Haase ran.

Obediently as a machine, trotting flat-footed over the cobbles of the midnight streets, he ran, pulling up at moments to take his breath, then running on again. Panting, sweating, he lumbered up the steps of the telegraph office and thrust the message through the grille to the sleepy clerk.

"What is Von Specht?" grumbled the clerk. "Is this a cipher-message?"

"No," gasped Herr Haase. "Can't you read? This is plain German!"

Herr Haase, one has gathered, was not afflicted with that weakness of the sense which is called imagination. Not his to dream dreams and see visions; nor, while he tenderly undressed himself and put himself into his bed, to dwell in profitless fancy over the message he had sent, bursting like a shell among the departments and administrations which are the body of Germany's official soul. Nor later either, when the spate of replies kept him busy decoding and carrying them down to the Baron, did he read into them more than the bare import of their wording. "Von Specht transferred to hospital coach attached special train, accompanied military doctor and orderlies in civil clothes. Left Base Hospital No. 64 at 3:22 P.M. Condition weak, feverish," said the first of them. It did not suggest to him the hush of the white ward broken by the tread of the stalwart stretcher-bearers, the feeble groaning as they shifted the swathed and bandaged form from the bed to the stretcher, the face thin and haggard with yet remains of sunburn on its bloodlessness, the progress to the railway, the grunt and heave of the men as they hoisted their burden to the waiting hospital-carriage. None of all that for Herr Haase.

Later came another message: "Patient very feverish. Continually inquires whither going and why. Please telegraph some answer to meet train at Bengen with which may quiet him." To that Herr Haase was ordered to reply: "Tell Colonel von Specht that he is serving his Fatherland," and that elicited another message from the train at Colmar: "Gave patient your message, to which he replied, 'That is good enough for me.' Is now less feverish, but very weak."

And finally, from Basle, came the news that the train and its passengers had crossed the frontier; Colonel von Specht was in Switzerland.

"You, my good Haase, will meet the train," said the Baron von Steinlach. "The Embassy has arranged to have it shunted to a siding outside the station.

You will, of course, tell them nothing of what is in contemplation. Just inform whoever is in charge that I will come later. And, Von Wetten, I think we will send the car with a note to bring Herr Bettermann here at the same time."

"Here, Excellency?"

"Yes," said the Baron. "After all, we want to keep the thing as quiet as possible, and that fellow is capable of asking a party of friends to witness the ceremony." There was malicious amusement in the eye he turned on Von Wetten. "And we don't want that, do we?" he suggested.

Von Wetten shuddered.

The siding at which the special train finally came to rest was "outside the station" in the sense that it was a couple of miles short of it, to be reached by a track-side path complicated by piles of sleepers and cinder-heaps. Herr Haase, for the purpose of his mission, had attired himself sympathetically rather than conveniently; he was going to visit a colonel and, in addition to other splendors, he had even risked again the patent leather boots. He was nearly an hour behind time when he reached at length the two wagons-lits carriages standing by themselves in a wilderness of tracks.

Limping, perspiring, purple in the face, he came alongside of them, peering up at their windows. A face showed at one of them, spectacled and bearded, gazing motionlessly through the panes with the effect of a sea-creature in an aquarium. It vanished and reappeared at the end door of the car.

"Hi! You, what do you want here?" called the owner of the face to Herr Haase.

Herr Haase came shuffling towards the steps.

"Ich stelle Mich vor; I introduce myself," he said ceremoniously. "Haase sent by his Excellency, the Herr Baron von Steinlach."

The other gazed down on him, a youngish man, golden-blond as to beard and hair, with wide, friendly eyes magnified by his glasses. He was coatless in the heat, and smoked a china-bowled German pipe like a man whose work is done and whose ease is earned; yet in his face and manner there was a trace of perturbation, an irritation of nervousness.

"Oh!" he said, and spoke his own name. "Civil-doctor Fallwitz. I've been expecting somebody. You'd better come inside, hadn't you?"

Outside was light and heat; inside was shadow and heat. Dr. Fallwitz led the way along the corridor of the car, with its gold-outlined scrollwork and many brass-gadgeted doors, to his own tiny compartment, smelling of hot upholstery and tobacco. Herr Haase removed his hat and sank puffing upon the green velvet cushions.

"You are hot, nicht wahr?" inquired Dr. Fallwitz politely.

"Yes," said Herr Haase. "But, Herr Doktor, since you are so good it is not only that. If it is gross of me to ask it but if I might take off my boots for some moments. You see, they are new."

"Aber ich bitte," cried the doctor.

The doctor stood watching him while he struggled with the buttons, and while he watched he frowned and gnawed at the amber mouthpiece of his pipe.

He waited till Herr Haase, with a loud, luxurious grunt, had drawn off the second boot.

"There will be a row, of course," he remarked then. "These Excellencies and people are only good for making rows. But I told them he couldn't be moved."

Herr Haase shifted his toes inside his socks. "You mean Colonel von Specht? But isn't he here, then?"

The young doctor shook his head. "We obeyed orders," he said. "We had to. Those people think that life and death are subject to orders. I kept him going till we got here, but about an hour ago he had a hemorrhage."

He put his pipe back into his mouth, inhaled and exhaled a cloud of smoke, and spoke again.

"Died before we could do anything," he said. "You see, after all he had been through, he hadn't much blood to spare. What did they want him here for, do you know?"

"No," said Herr Haase. "But I know the Herr Baron was needing him particularly. Was fur eine Geschichte!"

"Want to see him?" asked the young doctor.

It had happened to Herr Haase never to see a dead man before. Therefore, among the incidents of his career, he will not fail to remember that the progress in his socks from the one car to the other, the atmosphere of the second car where the presence of death was heavy on the stagnant air, and the manner in which the thin white sheet outlined the shape beneath. A big young orderly in shabby civilian clothes was on guard; at the doctor's order he drew down the sheet and the dead man's face was bare. He who had slashed a helpless conscript across the face with a whip, for whom yet any service of his Fatherland was "good enough," showed to the shrinking Herr

Haase only a thin, still countenance from whose features the eager passion and purpose had been wiped, leaving it resolute in peace alone.

"I I didn't know they looked like that," whispered Herr Haase.

The two homeward miles of cindery path were difficult; the sun was tyrannical; his boots were a torment; yet Herr Haase went as in a dream. He had seen reality; the veil of his daily preoccupations had been rent for him; and it needed the impertinence of the ticket-collector at the door of the station, who was unwilling to let him out without a ticket, to restore him. That battle won, he found himself a cab, and rattled over the stones of Thun to the hotel door. He prepared no phrases in which to clothe his news; facts are facts and are to be stated as facts. What he murmured to himself as he jolted over the cobbles was quite another matter.

"Ticket, indeed!" he breathed rancorously. "And I tipped him two marks only last Christmas!"

The Baron's car was waiting at the hotel door; the cab drew up behind it. The cabman, of course, wanted more than his due, and didn't get it; but the debate helped to take Herr Haase's mind still further off his feet. He entered the cool hall of the hotel triumphantly and made for the staircase.

"O, mein Herr!"

He turned; he had not seen the lady in the deep basket-chair just within the door, but now, as she rose and came towards him, he recognized her. It was the wife of Bettermann, the inventor, the shape upon the balcony of the chalet who had overlooked their experiments and overheard the bargain they had made.

Herr Haase bowed. "Gnadige Frau?"

He remembered her as little and pleasantly pretty; her presence above them on the balcony had touched his German sentimentalism. She was pretty now, with her softness and blossom-like fragility, but with it was a tensity, a sort of frightened desperation.

She hesitated for words, facing him with lips that trembled, and large, painful eyes of nervousness. "He he is here," she said, at last. "My husband they sent a car to fetch him to them. He is up there now, with them!"

Herr Haase did not understand. "But yes, gracious lady," he answered. "Why not? The Herr Baron wished to speak to him."

She put out a small gloved hand uncertainly and touched his sleeve.

"No," she said. "Tell me! I, I am so afraid. That other, the officer who cut Egon's face my husband's I mean, he has arrived? Tell me, mein Herr! Oh, I thought you would tell me; I saw you the other day, and those others never spoke to you, and you were the only one who looked kind and honest." She gulped and recovered. "He has arrived?"

"Well, now," began Herr Haase paternally. In all his official life he had never "told" anything. Her small face, German to its very coloring, pretty and pleading, tore at him.

"Yes, he has arrived," he said shortly. "I have I have just seen him."

"Oh!" It was almost a cry. "Then then they will do it? Mein Herr, mein Herr, help me! Egon, he has been thinking only of this for years; and now, if he does it, he will think of nothing else all his life. And he mustn't he mustn't! It's it will be madness. I know him. Mein Herr, there is nobody else I can ask; help me!"

The small gloved hand was holding him now, holding by the sleeve of his superlative black coat of ceremony, plucking at it, striving to stir him to sympathy and understanding; the face, hopeful and afraid, strained up at him.

Gently he detached the gloved hand on his sleeve, holding it a second in his own before letting it go.

"Listen," he said. "That bargain is cancelled. Colonel von Specht died to-day."

He turned forthwith and walked to the stairs. He did not look back at her.

"Herein!" called somebody from within the white-painted door of the Baron's room, when he knocked.

Herr Haase, removing his hat, composing his face to a nullity of official expression, entered.

After the shadow of the hall and the staircase, the window blazed at him. The Baron was at his little table, seated sideways in his chair, toying with an ivory paper-knife, large against the light. Von Wetten stood beside him, tall and very stiff, withdrawn into himself behind his mask of Prussian officer and aristocrat; and in a low chair, back to the door and facing the other two, Bettermann sat.

He screwed round awkwardly to see who entered, showing his thin face and its scar, then turned again to the Baron, large and calm and sufficient before him.

"I tell you," he said, resuming some talk that had been going on before Herr Haase's arrival: "I tell you, the letter of the bargain or nothing!"

The Baron had given to Herr Haase his usual welcome of a half smile, satiric and not unkindly. He turned now to Bettermann.

"But certainly," he answered. He slapped the ivory paper-knife against his palm. "I was not withdrawing from the bargain. I was merely endeavoring to point out to you at the instance of my friend here" a jerk of the elbow towards Von Wetten "the advantages of a million marks, or several million marks, plus the cashiering of Colonel von Specht from the army, over the personal satisfaction which you have demanded for yourself. But since you insist."

Bettermann, doubled up in his low chair, broke in abruptly: "Yes, I insist!"

The Baron smiled his elderly, temperate smile. "So be it," he said. "Well, my good Haase, what have you to tell us?"

Herr Haase brought his heels together, dropped his thumbs to the seams of his best trousers, threw up his chin, and barked:

"Your Excellency, I have seen the Herr Colonel Graf von Specht. He died at ten minutes past eleven this morning."

His parade voice rang in the room; when it ceased the silence, for a space of moments, was absolute. What broke it was the voice of Von Wetten.

"Thank God!" it said, loudly and triumphantly.

The Baron swung round to him, but before he could speak Bettermann gathered up the slack of his long limbs and rose from his chair. He stood a moment, gaunt in his loose and worn clothes, impending over the seated baron.

"So that was it! Well" He paused, surveying the pair of them, the old man, the initiate and communicant of the inmost heart of the machine through which his soul had gone like grain through a mill, and the tall Prussian officer, at once the motor and millstone of that machine. And he smiled. "Well," he repeated, "there's the end of that!"

The door closed behind him; his retreating footsteps echoed in the corridor. The Baron spoke at last. He stared up at Von Wetten, his strong old face seamed with new lines.

"You thank God for that, do you?" he said.

Von Wetten returned his gaze. "Yes, Excellency," he replied.

He had screwed his monocle into his eye; it gave to his unconscious arrogance the barb of impertinence.

"You!" The Baron cried out at him. "You thank God, do you? and neither your thanks nor your God is worth the bones of a single Pomeranian grenadier! Do you know what has happened, fool?"

Captain von Wetten bent towards him, smiling slightly.

"You are speaking to Haase, of course, Excellency?"

The Baron caught himself. His face went a trifle pinker, but his mouth was hard under the clipped white moustache and the heavy brows were level.

"I will tell you what has happened," he said deliberately. "I will try to make it intelligible to you."

He held up the ivory paper-knife, its slender yellow blade strained in his two hands.

"That is Germany to-day," he said, "bending." His strong hands tightened; the paper-knife broke with a snap. "And that is Germany to-morrow broken. We have failed."

He threw the two pieces from him to the floor and stared under the pent of his brows at Von Wetten.

Their eyes engaged. But one of the pieces slid across the floor to Herr Haase's feet. Orderly and serviceable always, Herr Haase bent and picked up the broken pieces and put them back upon the table.

VIII

ALMS AND THE MAN

While she was yet dressing, she had heard the soft pad of slippers on the narrow landing outside her room and the shuffle of papers; then, heralded by a single knock, the scrape and crackle of a paper being pushed under her door. It was in this fashion that the Maison Mardel presented its weekly bills to its guests.

"Merci!" she called aloud, leaving her dressing to go and pick up the paper. A pant from without answered her and the slippers thudded away.

Standing by the door, with arms and shoulders bare, she unfolded the document, a long sheet with a printed column of items and large inky figures in francs and centimes written against them, and down in the right hand corner the dramatic climax of the total. It was the total that interested Annette Kelly.

"H'm!" It was something between a gasp and a sigh. "They 're making the most of me while I last," said Annette aloud.

Her purse was under her pillow, an old and baggy affair of shagreen, whose torn lining had to be explored with a forefinger for the coins it swallowed. She emptied it now upon the bed. The light of a Paris summer morning, golden and serene, flowed in at the window, visiting the poverty of the little room with its barren benediction and shining upon the figure of Annette as she bent above her money and counted it She was a slender girl of some three-and-twenty years, with hair and eyes of a somber brown; six weeks of searching for employment in Paris and economizing in food, of spurring herself each morning to the tone of hope and resolution, of returning each evening footsore and dispirited, had a little blanched and touched with tenseness a face in which there yet lingered some of the soft contours of childhood.

She sat down beside the money on the bed, her ankles crossed below her petticoat; her accounts were made up. After paying the bill and bestowing one franc in the unavoidable tip, there would remain to her exactly eight francs for her whole resources. It was the edge of the precipice at last. It was that precipice, overhanging depths unseen and terrible, which she was contemplating as she sat, feet swinging gently in the rhythm of meditation, her face serious and quiet. For six weeks she had seen it afar off; now it was at hand and immediate.

"Well," said Annette slowly; she had already the habit of talking aloud to herself which comes to lonely people. She paused. "It just means that today I've got to get some work. I've got to."

She rose, forcing herself to be brisk and energetic. The Journal, with its advertisements of work to be had for the asking, had come to her door with the glass of milk and the roll which formed her breakfast, and she had already made a selection of its more humble possibilities. She ran them over in her mind as she finished dressing. Two offices required typists; she would go to both. A cashier in a shop and an English governess were wanted. "Why shouldn't I be a governess?" said Annette. And finally, somebody in the Rue St. Honore required a young lady of good figure and pleasant manner for "reception." There were others, too, but it was upon these five that Annette decided to concentrate.

She put on her hat, took her money and her Journal, and turned to the door. A curious impulse checked her there and she came back to the mirror that hung above her dressing-table.

"Let's have a look at you!" said Annette to the reflection that confronted her.

She stood, examining it seriously. It was, she thought, quite presentable, a trim, quiet figure of a girl who might reasonably ask work and a wage; she could not find anything in it to account for those six weeks of refusals. She perked her chin and forced her face to look assured and spirited, watching the result in the mirror.

"Ye-es," she said at last, and nodded to the reflection. "You'll have to do; but I wish I wish you hadn't got that sort of doomed look. Good-bye, old girl!"

At the foot of the stairs, in the open door of that room which was labeled "Bureau," where a bed and a birdcage and a smell of food kept company with the roll-top desk, stood the patronne, Madame Mardel. She moved a little forth into the passage as Annette approached.

"Good morning, mademoiselle. Again a charming day!"

She was a large woman, grossly fleshy, with clothes that strained to creaking point about her body and gaped at the fastenings. Her vast face, under her irreproachably neat hair the hair of a Parisienne was swarthy and plethoric, with the jowl of a bulldog and eyes tiny and bright. Annette knew her for an artist in "extras," a vampire that had sucked her purse lean with deft overcharges, a creature without mercy or morals. But the daily irony of her greeting had the grace, the cordial inflexion, of a piece of distinguished politeness.

"Charming," agreed Annette. She produced the bill. "I may as well pay this now," she suggested.

Madame's chill and lively eyes were watching her face, estimating her solvency in the light of Madame's long experience of misfortune and despair. She shrugged a huge shoulder deprecatingly.

"There is no hurry," she said. She always said that. "Still, since mademoiselle is here."

Annette followed her into the bureau, that dimlighted sanctuary of Madame's real life. Below the half-raised blind in the window the canaries in their cage rustled and bickered; unwashed plates were crowded on the table; the big unmade bed added a flavor of its own to the atmosphere. Madame eased herself, panting, into the chair before the desk, revealing the great rounded expanse of her back with its row of straining buttons and lozenge-shaped revelations of underwear. With the businesslike deliberation of a person who transacts a serious affair with due seriousness, she spread the bill before her, smoothing it out with a practiced wipe of the hand, took her rubber stamp from the saucer in which' it lay, inked it on the pad and waited. Annette had been watching her, fascinated by that great methodical rhythm of movement, but at the pause she started, fished the required coins from the old purse, and laid them at Madame's elbow. "Merci, mademoiselle," said Madame, and then, and not till then, the stamp descended upon the paper. A flick with a scratchy pen completed the receipt, and Madame turned awkwardly in the embrace of her chair to hand it to Annette with her weekly smile. The ritual was accomplished.

"Good morning, mademoiselle. Thank you; good luck."

The mirthless smile discounted the words; the cold, avid eyes were busy and suspicious. Annette let them stare their fill while she folded the paper and tucked it into the purse; she had had six weeks of training in the art of preserving a cheerful countenance.

Then: "Good morning, madame," she smiled, with her gay little nod and reached the door in good order.

There was still Aristide, the lame man-of-all-work, who absorbed a weekly franc and never concealed his contempt of the amount. He was waiting on the steps, leaning on a broom, and turned his rat's face on her, sourly and impatiently, without a word. She paused as she came to him and dipped two fingers into the poor old purse; Aristide's pale, red-edged eyes followed them, while his thin mouth twisted into contempt.

"This is for you, Aristide," she said, and held out the coin.

He took it in his open palm and surveyed it with lifted eyebrows. "This?" he inquired.

"Yes." The insult never failed to hurt her; this morning, in particular, she would have been glad to set forth upon the day's forlorn hope without that preface of hate and cruel greed. But Aristide still stood, with the coin in his open hand, staring from it to her and she flinched from him. "Good morning," she said timidly, and slipped past.

It needed the gladness of the day, its calm and colorful warmth, to take the taste of Aristide out of her mouth and uplift her again to her mood of resolution. Her way lay downhill; the first of her advertisements gave an address at the foot of the Rue Lafayette; and soon the stimulus of the thronged streets, the mere neighborhood of folk who moved briskly and with purpose, re-strung her slackened nerves and she was again ready for the battle. And as she went her lips moved.

"Mind, now!" she was telling herself. "Today's the end the very end. You've got to get work today!"

The address in the Rue Lafayette turned out to be that of a firm of house and estate agents; it was upon the first floor and showed to the landing four ground-glass doors, of which three were lettered "Private," while the fourth displayed an invitation to enter without knocking. Upon the landing, in the presence of those inexpressive doors, behind which salaries were earned and paid and life was all that was orderly and desirable, Annette paused for a space of moments to make sure of herself.

"Now!" she said, with a deep breath, and pushed open the fourth door.

Within was an office divided by a counter, and behind the counter desks and the various apparatus of business. The desks were unoccupied; the only person present was a thin pretty girl seated before a typewriter. She looked up at Annette across the counter; her face showed patches of too bright a red on the cheekbones.

"Good morning," began Annette, with determined briskness. "I've come."

The girl smiled. "Typist?" she interrupted.

"Yes," said Annette. "The advertisement"—she stopped; the girl was still smiling, but in a manner of deprecating and infinitely gentle regret.

Annette stared at her, feeling within again that rising chill of disappointment with which she was already so familiar. "You mean" she stammered awkwardly "you mean you've got the place?"

The thin girl spread her hands apart in a little French gesture of conciliation.

"Ten minutes ago," she answered. "There is no one here yet but the manager, and I was waiting at the door when he arrived."

"Thank you," said Annette faintly. The thin girl, still regarding her with big shadowy eyes, suddenly put a hand to her bosom and coughed. The neat big office beyond the bar of the polished counter was unbearably pleasant to look at; one could have been so happily busy at one's place between those tidy desks. A sharp bell rang from an inner office; the thin girl rose. The hectic on her cheeks burned brighter.

"I must go," she said hurriedly. "He wants me. I hope you will have good luck."

The sunlight without had lost some of its quality when Annette came forth to the street again; it no longer warmed her to optimism. She stood for some moments in the doorway of the building, letting her depression and discouragement have their way with her.

"If only I might cry a bit," she reflected. "That would help a little. But I mustn't even do that!"

She had to prod herself into fresh briskness with the sense of her need, that to-day was the end. She sighed, jerked her chin up, set her small face into the shape of resolute cheerfulness and started forth again in the direction of the second vacancy for a typist.

Here, for a while, hope burned high. The office was that of a firm of thriving wine exporters and the post had not yet been filled. The partner into whose office she penetrated by virtue of her sheer determination to see someone in authority, was a stout ruddy Marseillais, speaking French in the full-throated Southern fashion; he was kindly and cheery, with broad vermilion lips a-smile through his beard.

"Yes, we want a typist," he admitted; "but I'm afraid" his amiable brown eyes scrutinized her with manifest doubt. "You have references?" he inquired.

Yes, Annette had references. She had only lost her last situation when her employer went bankrupt; the testimonial she produced spoke well of her in every sense. She gave it him to read. But what what was it in her that had inspired that look of doubt, that look she had seen so often before in the eyes of possible employers?

"Yes, it is very good." He handed the paper back to her, still surveying her and hesitating. "And you are accustomed to the machine? H'm!"

It was then that hope flared up strongly. He could not get out of it; he must employ her now. Salary? She would take what the firm offered! And still he continued to look at her with a hint of embarrassment in his regard. She felt she was trembling.

"I'm afraid" he began again, but stopped at her involuntary little gasp and shifted uneasily in his chair. He was acutely uncomfortable. An idea came to him and he brightened. "Well, you can leave your address and we will write to you. Yes, we will write to you."

And to-day was the end! Annette stared at him. "When?" she asked shortly.

The burly man reddened dully; she had seen through his pretext for getting rid of her. "Oh, in a day or two," he answered uneasily.

Annette rose. She had turned pale but she was quite calm and self-possessed.

"I I hoped to get work today," she said. "In fact, I must find it today. But will you at least tell me why you won't give me the place?"

The big man's cheery face began to frown. He was being forced to fall back on his right to employ or not to employ whom he pleased without giving reasons. Annette watched him, and before he could speak she went on again.

"I'm not complaining," she said. Her voice was even and very low. "But there's something wrong with me, isn't there? I saw how you looked at me at first. Well, it wouldn't cost you anything, and it would help me a lot, if you'd just tell me what it is that's wrong. You see, nobody will have me, and it's getting rather rather desperate. So if you'd just tell me, perhaps I could alter something, and have a chance at last."

Her serious eyes, the pallor of her face, and the level tones of her voice held him like a hand on his throat. He was a man with the cordial nature of his race, prone to an easy kindliness, who would have suffered almost any ill rather than feel himself guilty of a cruelty. But how could he speak to her of the true reason for refusing her the son in the business, the avid young debauchee whose victims were girls in the firm's employ?

"If you'd just tell me what it is, I wouldn't bother you any more, and it might make all the difference to me," Annette was saying.

She saw him redden and shift sharply in his chair; an impulse of his ardent blood was spurring him to give her the work she needed, and then so to deal with his son that he would never dare lift his eyes to her. But the instinct of caution developed in business came to damp that dangerous warmth.

"Mademoiselle!" He returned her look gravely and honestly. "Upon my word, I can see nothing whatever wrong with you nothing whatever."

"Then," began Annette, "why won't you?"

He stopped her with an upraised hand. "I am going to tell you," he said. "There is a rule in this office, and behind the rule are good and sufficient reasons, that we do not take into our employ women who are still young and pretty."

She heard him with no change of her rigid countenance. She understood, of course; she had known in her time what it was to be persecuted. She would have liked to tell him that she was well able to take care of herself, but she recalled her promise not to bother him further.

She sighed, buttoning her glove. "It's a pity," she said unhappily, "because I really am a good typist."

"I am sure of it," he agreed. "I infinitely regret, but sa y est!"

She raised her head. "Well, thank you for telling me, at any rate," she said. "Good morning, monsieur."

"Good morning, mademoiselle," he replied, and held open the door for her to pass out.

Once more the street and the sunshine and the hurry of passing strangers, each pressing by about his or her concerns. Again she stood a little while in the doorway, regarding the thronged urgency that surged in spate between the high, handsome buildings, every unit of it wearing the air of being bound towards some place where it was needed, while she alone was unwanted.

"I think," considered Annette, "that I ought to have some coffee or something, since it's the last day."

She looked down along the street; not far away the awning of a cafe showed red and white above the sidewalk, sheltering its row of little tables, and she walked slowly towards it. How often in the last six weeks, footsore and leaden-hearted, had she passed such places, feeling the invitation of their ease and refreshment in every jarred and crying nerve of her body, yet resisting it for the sake of the centimes it would cost.

She took a chair in the back row of seats, behind a small iron table, slackening her muscles and leaning back, making the mere act of sitting down yield her her money's worth. The shadow of the awning turned the day to a benign coolness; there was a sense of privilege in being thus at rest in the very street, at the elbow of its passers-by. A crop-headed German waiter brought the cafe au lait which she ordered, and set it on the table before her two metal jugs, a cup and saucer, a little glass dish of sugar, and a folded napkin. The cost was half a franc; she gave him a franc, bade him keep the change, and was rewarded with half a smile, half a bow, and a "Merci beaucoup, madame!" which in themselves were a balm to her spirit, bruised by insult and failure. The coffee was hot; its fragrance gushed up from her cup; since her last situation had failed her she was tasting for the first time food that was appetizing and dainty.

She lifted the cup. "A short life and a merry one," she murmured, toasting herself before she drank.

Six francs remained to her, and there were yet three employers to visit. The lady in need of a governess and the shop which required a cashier were at opposite ends of Paris; the establishment which desired a young lady for "reception" was between the two. Annette, surveying the field', decided to reserve the "reception" to the last. She finished her coffee, flavoring to the last drop the warm stimulation of it; then, having built up again her hopeful mood, she set out anew.

It was three hours later, towards two o'clock in the afternoon, that she came on foot, slowly, along the Rue St. Honore, seeking the establishment which had proclaimed in the Journal its desire to employ, for purposes of "reception," a young lady of good figure and pleasant manners. She had discovered, at the cost of one of her remaining francs for omnibus fares, that a 50-franc a month governess must possess certificates, that governessing is a skilled trade overcrowded by women of the most various and remarkable talents. At the shop that advertised for a cashier a floor-walker had glanced at her over his shoulder for an instant, snapped out that the place was filled, and walked away.

The name she sought appeared across the way, lettered upon a row of first-floor windows; it was a photographer's.

"Now!" said Annette. "The end this is the end!"

A thrill touched her as she went up the broad stairway of the building; the crucial thing was at hand. The morning had been bad, but at each failure there had still been a possibility ahead. Now, there was only this and nothing beyond.

A spacious landing, carpeted, and lit by the tall church-windows on the staircase, great double doors with a brass plate, and a dim indoor sense pervading all the place! Here, evidently, the sharp corners of commerce were rounded off; its acolytes must be engaging female figures with affable manners.

Annette's ringer on the bronze bell-push evoked a manservant in livery, with a waistcoat of horizontal yellow and black stripes like a wasp and a smooth, subtle, still face. He pulled open one wing of the door and stood aside to let her pass in, gazing at her with demure eyes, in whose veiled suggestion there was something satiric. Annette stepped past him at once.

"There is an advertisement in the Journal for a young lady," she said. "I have come to apply for the post."

The smooth manservant lowered his head in a nod that was just not a bow, and closed the tall door.

"Yes," he said. "If mademoiselle will give herself the trouble to be seated I will inform the master."

The post was not filled, then. Annette sat down, let the wasp-hued flunkey pass out of sight, and looked round at the room in which she found herself. It was here, evidently, that the function of "reception" was accomplished. The manservant admitted the client; one rose from one's place at the little inlaid desk in the alcove and rustled forward across the gleaming parquet, with pleased and deferential alacrity to bid Monsieur or Madame welcome, to offer a chair and the incense of one's interest and delight in service. One added oneself to the quality of the big, still apartment, with its antique furniture, its celebrities and notorieties pictured upon its walls, its great chandelier, a-shiver with glass lusters hanging overhead like an aerial iceberg. No noises entered from the street; here, the business of being photographed was magnified to a solemnity; one drugged one's victim with pomp before leading him to the camera.

"I could do it," thought Annette. "I'm sure I could do it. I could fit into all this like a like a snail into a shell. I'd want shoes that didn't slide on the parquet; and then oh, if only this comes off!"

A small noise behind her made her turn quickly. The door by which the footman had departed was concealed by a portiere of heavy velvet; a hand had moved it aside and a face was looking round the edge of it at her. As she turned, the owner of it came forward into the room, and she rose.

"Be seated, be seated!" protested the newcomer in a high emasculate voice, and she sat down again obediently upon the little spindle-legged Empire settee from which she had risen.

"And you have come in consequence of the advertisement?" said the man with a little giggle. "Yes; yes! We will see, then!"

He stood in front of her, half-way across the room, staring at her. He was a man somewhere in the later thirties, wearing the velvet jacket, the cascading necktie, the throat-revealing collar, and the overlong hair which the conventions of the theatre have established as the livery of the artist. The details of this grotesque foppery presented themselves to Annette only vaguely; it was at the man himself as he straddled in the middle of the polished floor, staring at her, that she gazed with a startled attention a face like the feeble and idiot countenance of an old sheep, with the same flattened length of nose and the same weakly demoniac touch in the curve and slack hang of the wide mouth. It was not that he was merely ugly or queer to the view; it seemed to Annette that she was suddenly in the presence of something monstrous and out of the course of Nature. His eyes, narrow and seemingly colorless, regarded her with a fatuous complacency.

She flushed and moved in her seat under his long scrutiny. The creature sighed.

"Yes," he said, always in the same high, dead voice. "You satisfy the eye, mademoiselle. For me, that is already much, since it is as an artist that I consider you first. And your age?"

She told him. He asked further questions, of her previous employment, her nationality, and so forth, putting them perfunctorily as though they were matters of no moment, and never removing his narrow eyes from her face. Then, with short sliding steps, he came across the parquet and sat down beside her on the Empire settee.

Annette backed to the end of it and sat defensively on the edge, facing the strange being. He, crossing his thin legs, leaned with an arm extended along the back of the settee and his long, large-knuckled hand hanging limp. His sheep's face lay over on his shoulder towards her; in that proximity its quality of feeble grotesqueness was enhanced. It was like sitting in talk with a sick ape.

"Curiouser and curiouser!" quoted Annette to herself. "I ought to wake up next and find he really doesn't exist."

"Mademoiselle!" The creature began to speak again. "You are the ninth who has come hither today seeking the post I have advertised. Some I rejected because they failed to conciliate my eye; I cannot, you will understand, be tormented by a presence which jars my sense."

He paused to hear her agree.

"And the others?" inquired Annette.

"A-ah!" The strange being sighed. "The others in each case, what a disappointment! Girls beautiful, of a personality subdued and harmonious, capable of taking their places in my environment without doing violence to its completeness; but lacking the plastic and responsive quality which the hand of the artist should find in his material. Resistant they were resistant, mademoiselle, every one of them."

"Silly of them," said Annette briefly. She was meeting the secret stare of his half-closed eyes quite calmly now; she was beginning to understand the furtive satire in the regard of the smooth footman who had admitted each of those eight others in turn and seen their later departure. "What was it they wouldn't do?" she inquired.

"Do!" The limp hand flapped despairingly; the thin voice ran shrill. "I required nothing of them. One enters; I view her; I seat myself at her side as I sit now with you; I seek in talk to explore her resources of sentiment, of temperament, of sympathy. Perhaps I take her hand" As though to illustrate the recital, his long hand dropped suddenly and seized hers. He ceased to talk, surveying her with a scared shrewdness.

Annette smiled, letting her hand lie where it was. She was not in the least afraid; she had forgotten for the moment the barrenness of the streets that awaited her outside, and the fact that she had come to the end of her hopes.

"And they objected to that?" she inquired sweetly.

"Ah, but you." He was making ready to hitch closer along the seat, and she was prepared for him.

"Oh, I'd let you hold them both if that were all," she replied. "But it isn't all, is it?"

She smiled again at the perplexity in his face; his hands slackened and withdrew slowly. "You haven't told me what salary you are offering," she reminded him.

"Mademoiselle you, too?"

She nodded. "I, too," she said, and rose. The man on the settee groaned and heaved his shoulders theatrically; she stood, viewing in quiet curiosity that countenance of impotent vileness. Other failures had left her with a sense of defenselessness in a world so largely populated by men who glanced up from their desks to refuse her plea for work. But now she had resources of power over fate and circumstance; the streets, the night, the river, whatever of fear and destruction the future held, could neither daunt nor compel her. She could go out to meet them, free and victorious.

"Mademoiselle!" The man on the settee bleated at her.

She shook her head at him. It was not worth while to speak. She went to the door and opened it for herself; the smooth manservant was deprived of the spectacle of her departure.

She went slowly down the wide stairs. "Nine of us," she was thinking. "Nine girls, and not one of us was what did he call it? plastic. I'm not really alone in the world, after all."

But it was very like being alone in the world to go slowly, with tired feet, along the perspectives of the streets, to turn corners aimlessly, to wander on with no destination or purpose. There was yet money in the old purse a single broad five-franc piece; it would linger out her troubles for her till to-morrow.

She would need to eat, and her room at Madame Mardel's would come to three francs; she did not mean to occupy it any longer than she could pay for it. And then the morning would find her penniless in actuality.

Her last turning brought her out to the arches of the Rue de Rivoli; across the way the trees of the Tuileries Gardens lifted their green to the afternoon sunlight. She hesitated; then crossed the wide road towards the gardens, her thoughts still hovering about the five-franc piece.

"It's a case for riotous living," she told herself, as she passed in to the smooth paths beneath the trees. "Five francs' worth of real dinner or something like that. Only I'm not feeling very riotous just now."

What she felt was that the situation had to be looked at, but that looking at it could not improve it. Things had come to an end; food to eat, a bed to sleep in, the mere bare essentials of life had ceased, and she had not an idea of what came next; how one entered upon the process of starving to death in the streets. Passers-by, strolling under the trees, glanced at her as she passed them, preoccupied and unseeing, a neat, comely little figure of a girl in her quiet clothes with her still composed face. She went slowly; there was a seat which she knew of farther on, overshadowed by a lime tree, where she meant to rest and put her thoughts in order; but already at the back of her mind there had risen, vague as night, oppressive as pain, tainting her disquiet with its presence, the hint of a consciousness that, after all, one does not starve to death pas si bete! One takes a shorter way.

A lean youth, with a black cotton cap pulled forward over one eye, who had been lurking near, saw the jerk with which she lifted her head as that black inspiration was clear to her, and the sudden coldness and courage of her face, and moved away uneasily.

"Ye-es," said Annette slowly. "Ye-es! And now Ghh!"

A bend in the path had brought her suddenly to the seat under the lime tree; she was within a couple of paces of it before she perceived that it had already its occupant the long figure of a young man who sprawled back with his face upturned to the day and slumbered with all that disordered and unbeautiful abandon which goes with daylight sleep. His head had fallen over on one shoulder; his mouth was open; his hands, grimy and large, showed half shut in his lap. There was a staring patch of black sticking plaster at the side of his chin; his clothes, that were yet decent, showed stains here and there; his face, young and slackened in sleep, was burned brick-red by exposure. The whole figure of him, surrendered to weariness in that unconscious and uncaring sprawl, seemed suddenly to answer her question this was what happened next; this was the end unless one found and took that shorter way.

"They walk till they can't walk any longer; then they sleep on benches. I could never do that!"

She stood for some seconds longer, staring at the sleeping man. Resolution, bitter as grief, mounted in her like a tide. "No, it shan't come to that with me!" she cried inwardly. "Lounging with my mouth open for anyone to stare at! No!"

She turned, head up, body erect, face set strongly, and walked away. Neither sheep-faced human grotesques in palatial offices nor all Paris and its civilization should make her other than she wished to be. She stepped out defiantly and stopped short.

The old purse was in her hand; through its flabby sides she could feel with her fingers the single five-franc piece which it yet contained. Somehow, that had to be disposed of or provided for; five francs was a serious matter to Annette. She looked round; the man in the seat was still sleeping.

Treading quietly, she went back to him, taking the coin from her purse as she went. Upon his right side his coat pocket bulged open; she could see that in it was a little wad of folded papers. "His testimonials poor fellow!" she breathed. Carefully she leaned forward and let the broad coin slip into the pocket among the papers. Then, with an end of a smile twisted into the set of her lips, she turned again and departed. Among the trees the lean youth in the black cotton cap watched her go.

A day that culminates in sleep upon a bench in a public place is commonly a day that has begun badly and maintained its character. In this case it may be said to have begun soon after nine A.M. when a young man in worn tweed clothes and carrying a handkerchief pressed to his jaw, stepped out from a taxi and into that drug-store which is nearest to the Gare de Lyon. The bald, bland chemist who presides there has a regular practice in the treatment of razor-cuts acquired through shaving in the train; he looked up serenely across his glass-topped counter.

"Good morning, monsieur," he said. "A little cut yes?"

Young Raleigh gazed at him across the handkerchief.

"No! A thundering great gash," he answered with emphasis. "I want something to patch it up with."

"Certainly certainly!" The bald apothecary had the airs of a family physician; he smiled soothingly. "We shall find something. Let me now see the cut!"

Raleigh protruded his face across the soaps and the bottles of perfume, and the apothecary rose on tiptoe to scrutinize the wound. The razor had got home on the edge of the jaw with a scraping cut that bled handsomely.

"Ah!" The bald man nodded, and sought a bottle. "A little of this" he was damping a rag of lint with the contents of the bottle "as a cleansing agent first. If monsieur will bend down a little so."

Daintily, with precision and delicacy, he proceeded to apply the cleansing agent to the cut; at the first dab the patient leapt back with an exclamation.

"Confound you!" he cried. "This stuff burns like fire."

"It will pass in a moment," soothed the chemist. "And now, a little patch, and all will be well."

His idea of a suitable dressing was two inches of stiff and shiny black plaster that gripped at the skin like a barnacle and looked like a tragedy. Raleigh surveyed the effect of it in a show-case mirror gloomily.

"I wonder you didn't put it in a sling while you were about it," he remarked ungratefully. "People'll think I've been trying to cut my throat."

"Monsieur should grow a beard," counseled the chemist as he handed him his change.

Raleigh grunted, disdaining, retort, and passed forth to his waiting cab. The day had commenced inauspiciously. The night before, smoking his final cigarette in his upper berth in the wagon-lit, he had tempted Providence by laying out for himself a programme and a time schedule; and it looked as if Providence had been unable to resist the temptation. The business of the firm in which he was junior partner had taken him to Zurich; he had given himself a week's holiday in the mountains, and was now on his way back to London. The train was due to land him in Paris at half-past eight in the morning, and his plans were clear. First, a taxi to the Cafe de la Paix and breakfast there under the awning while the day ripened towards the hours of business; then a small cigar and a stroll along the liveliness of the boulevard to the offices of the foundry company, where a heart-to-heart talk with the manager would clear up several little matters which were giving trouble. Afterwards, a taxi across the river and a call upon the machine-tool people, get their report upon the new gear-steels and return to the Gare du Nord in time to catch the two o'clock train for Calais.

He had settled the order of it to his satisfaction before he pulled the shade over the lamp and turned over to sleep; and then, next morning, he had gashed himself while shaving, and the train was forty minutes late.

"These clothes" there was a narrow slip of mirror between the front windows of the taxi which reflected him, a section at a time "these clothes 'ud pass," he considered gloomily, considering their worn and unbusinesslike quality. "But with this" his fingers explored his chin "folks'll think we only do business between sprees."

The manager of the foundry company was a French engineer who had been trained in Pittsburg, a Frenchman of the new style, whose silky sweetness of manner was the mask of a steely tenacity of purpose. He had a little devilish black moustache, waxed at the points, like an earl of melodrama, and with it a narrow cheerless smile that jeered into futility Raleigh's effort to handle the subject on a basis of easy good fellowship. The heart-to-heart talk degenerated into a keen business controversy, involving the consultation of letter-files; it took more time than Raleigh had to spare; and in the end nothing was settled.

"You catch the airly train to London?" inquired the manager amiably, when Raleigh was leaving.

"Yes," replied Raleigh warmly. "I'm going to get out of this while I've got my fare left."

"Bon voyage," said the Frenchman smilingly. "You will present my compliments to your father?"

"Not me," retorted Raleigh. "I'm not going to let him know I saw you."

The machine-tool people, to whom his next visit was due, were established south of the river, a long drive from the boulevards. They were glad to receive him; there was a difficulty with some of the new steels, and they took him into the shops that he might see and appreciate the matter for himself. In the end it was necessary for Raleigh to reset the big turret lathe and demonstrate the manner of working, standing to the machine in his ancient tweed clothes nobody offered him overalls while the swift belting slatted at his elbow and fragments of shaved steel and a fine spray of oil welcomed him back to his trade. The good odor of metal, the engine-room smell, filled his nostrils; he was doing the thing which he could do best; it was not till it was finished that he looked at his watch and realized that the last item of his time-table had gone the way of the first, and he had missed the two o'clock train.

He paid off his return cab in the Place de la Concorde and stood doubtfully on the curb, watching it skate away with the traffic. His baggage had gone on by the two o'clock train; he was committed now to an afternoon in those ancient clothes with the oily stigma of the workshop upon them. His hands, too, were black from his work; he had slept badly in the train and done without a bath. In the soft sunlight that rained upon those brilliant streets he felt foul and unsightly.

He yawned, between a certain afternoon drowsiness and a languid depression.

"I'll wander up to the Meurice an' get a wash, anyhow," he decided, and turned to stroll through the Tuileries Gardens towards the hotel. He went slowly; it was pleasant among the trees, and when a seat in the shadows offered itself he sank down into it.

"I'll sleep all right in the train to-night," he thought, shoving back his cap.

There were children playing somewhere out of sight; their voices came to him in an agreeable tinkle. He crossed one leg over the other and settled himself more comfortably; he had plenty of time to spare now. His eyes closed restfully.

The touch that roused him was a very gentle one, scarcely more than a ghost of a sensation, the mere brush of a dexterous hand that slid as quietly as a shadow along the edge of his jacket pocket and groped into it with long clever fingers, while its owner, sitting beside him on the bench, gazed meditatively before him with an air of complete detachment from that skilled felonious hand. Raleigh, waking without moving, was able for a couple of seconds to survey his neighbor, a slim white-faced youth with a black cotton cap slouched forward over one eye. Then, swiftly, he caught the exploring hand by the wrist and sat up.

"Your mistake," he said crisply. "There's nothing but old letters in that pocket."

The youth at the first alarm tried to wrench loose, writhing in startled effort like a pronged snake, with all his smooth, vicious face clenched in violent fear. Raleigh gave a twisting jerk to the skinny wrist and the struggle was over; the lad uttered a yelp and collapsed back on the seat.

"Be good," warned Raleigh in easy French; "be good, or I'll beat you, d'you hear?"

The youth sniffed, staring at him with eyes in which a mere foolish fear was giving place to cunning. He was a creature flimsy as paper, a mere lithe skinful of bones, in whom the wit of the thief supplied the place of strength. He was making now his hasty estimate of the man he had to deal with.

"Well," demanded Raleigh, "what have you got to say for yourself?"

"Monsieur!" the youth struck into an injured whine. "I meant no harm, but I was desperate; I have not eaten today" his eyes noted the amused contempt on Raleigh's face, and he poised an instant like a man taking aim "and when I saw the lady slip the money into monsieur's pocket while he slept, and reflected that he would never even know that he had lost it."

"Eh?" Raleigh sat up. The thief suppressed a smile. "What lady, espece de fourneau? What are you talking about?"

"It's not a minute ago," replied the youth, discarding the whine. "See, she is perhaps not out of sight yet, if monsieur will look along the path. No, there she goes that one!"

His hand was free now; he was using it to point with; but he made no attempt to escape.

"She approached monsieur while he slept, walking cautiously, and slipped the money it was a five-franc piece, I think into his pocket. Yes, monsieur, that was the pocket."

He smiled patronizingly as Raleigh plunged a hand into the pocket in question, fumbled among the papers there, and drew out the coin and stared at it. He had the situation in hand now; he could get rid of this strong young man as soon as he pleased.

"She is going out of the gate now, monsieur," he said.

Raleigh turned. At the farther end of the path the woman who had been pointed out to him was close to the exit; in a few seconds more she would be gone. He could see of her nothing save her back that and a certain quality of carriage, a gait measured and deliberate.

He threw a word to the thief, who stood by with his hands in his pockets and an air of relishing the situation. "All right; you can go," he said, and started upon the chase of the secret bestower of alms.

"And me?" the outraged thief cried after him in tones of bitterness. "And me? I get nothing, then?"

The serge-clad back was disappearing through the gates into the welter of sunlight without; Raleigh gathered up his feet and sprinted along the tree shaded path. He was going to understand this business. He picked up the view of the serge-clad back again, walking towards the bridge, hastened after it and slowed down to its own pace when he was still some ten yards behind.

"Why, it's a girl!"

Somehow, he had counted upon finding an elderly woman, some charitable eccentric who acquired merit by secret gifts. He saw, instead, a slim girl, neatly and quietly clad, whose profile, as she glanced across the parapet of the bridge, showed pearl-pale in the shadow of her hat, with a simple and almost childlike prettiness of feature. There was something else, too, a quality of the whole which Raleigh, who did not deal in fine shades, had no words to describe to himself. But he saw it, nevertheless a gravity, a character of sad and tragic composure, that look of defeat which is prouder than any victory; it waked his imagination.

"Something wrong!" he said to himself vaguely, and continued to follow.

At the southern end of the bridge she turned her back to the sun and went east along the quay where the second-hand booksellers lounged beside their wares. She neither hurried nor slackened that deliberate pace of hers; Raleigh, keeping well behind, his wits at work acutely, wondered what it reminded him of, that slow trudge over the pavements. It was when the booksellers were left behind that an incident enlightened him.

She stopped for a minute and leaned upon the parapet; he crossed the road to be out of sight in case she should look back. She had been carrying in her hand a purse, and now he saw her open it and apparently search its interior, but idly and without interest as though she knew already what to expect of it. Then she closed it and tossed it over the parapet into the river.

"Ah!" Sudden comprehension rushed upon him; he knew now what that slow, aimless gait suggested to him. He recalled evenings in London, when he walked or drove through the lit streets and saw, here and there, the figures of those homeless ones who walked walked always, straying forward in a footsore progress till the night should be ripe for them to sit down in some corner. And then, that shadow in her face, that mouth, tight-held but still drooping; her way of looking at the river! His hand, in his pocket, closed over the five-franc piece which she had dropped there; he started across the road to accost her forthwith, but at that moment she moved on again, and once more he fell into step behind her.

There is a point, near the Ile de la Cite, where the Seine projects an elbow; the quay goes round in a curve under high houses; a tree or two overhangs the water, and there is a momentary space of quiet, almost a privacy at the skirts of bristling Paris. Here, commonly, men of leisure sit through the warm hours, torpidly fishing the smooth green depth of water below; but now there was none. The girl followed the elbow round and stopped at the angle of it. She leaned her arms on the coping and gazed down at the quiet still water below.

She was looking at it with such a preoccupation that Raleigh was able to come close to her before he spoke. He, too, put an arm on the parapet at her side.

"Looks peaceful, doesn't it?" he said quietly.

The girl's head rose with a jerk, and she stared at him, startled. The words had been deftly chosen to match her own thoughts; and for the while she failed to recognize in this tall young man the sprawling figure of the slumberer in the Tuileries Gardens.

"I, I who are you?" she stammered. "What do you want?"

He was able to see now that her pale composure was maintained only by an effort, that the strain of it was making her tremble. He answered in tones of careful conventionality.

"I'm afraid I startled you," he said. "I'm sorry. I shouldn't have ventured to speak to you at all if you hadn't—" He paused. "You don't happen to remember me at all?" he asked.

"No," said Annette. "If I hadn't, what?"

He slipped a hand into his pocket and drew forth the five-franc piece. The broad palm it lay on was still grimy from the workshop.

"I happened to fall asleep in the Tuileries this afternoon," he said. "Idiotic thing to do, but—."

"Oh!" The color leapt to her face. "Was that you?"

Raleigh nodded. "You had hardly moved away when a man who had been watching you tried to pick my pocket and woke me in doing so. He told me what he'd seen and pointed you out."

Annette gazed at him in tired perplexity. When he was on his feet, the condition of his clothes and hands and the absurd black patch on his chin were noticeable only as incongruities; there was nothing now to suggest the pauper or the outcast in this big youth with the pleasant voice and the strongly tanned face.

"I, I made a mistake," she said. "I saw you sleeping on the bench and I thought a little help, coming from nowhere like that you'd be so surprised and glad when you found it." She sighed. "However, I was wrong. I'm sorry."

"I'm not!" Raleigh put the money back in his pocket swiftly. "I think it was a wonderful idea of yours; it's the most splendid thing that ever happened to me. There was I, grumbling and making mistakes all day, playing the fool and pitying myself, and all the time you were moving somewhere within a mile or two, out of sight, but watching and saying: 'Yes, you're no good to anybody; but if the worst comes to the worst you shan't starve. I'll save you from that!' I'll never part with that money."

Annette shook her head; weariness inhabited her like a dull pain. "I didn't say that" she answered; "you weren't starving, and you don't understand. It doesn't matter, anyhow."

"Please," said Raleigh. He saw that she wanted to get rid of him, and he had no intention of letting her do so. "It matters to me, at any rate. But there is one thing I didn't understand."

She did not answer, gazing over her clasped hands at the water, across whose level the spires and chimneys of the city bristled like the skyline of a forest.

"It was while I was following you here, wondering whether I might speak to you," he continued. "I was watching you as you went, and it seemed to me that you were well, unhappy; in trouble or something. And then, back there on the quay, I saw you open your purse and throw it into the river."

He paused. "There was a hole in it," said Annette shortly, without turning her head.

"But" he spoke very quietly "you are in trouble? Yes, I know I'm intruding upon you" she had moved her shoulders impatiently "but haven't you given me just the shadow of a right? Your gift it might have saved my life if I'd been what you thought; I might have fetched up in the Morgue before morning. Men do, you know, every day women, too!" Her fingers upon the parapet loosened and clasped again at that. "You can't tie me hand and foot with such an obligation as that and leave me plante la."

"Oh!" Annette sighed. "It's nothing at all," she said. "But, as you want so much to know I'm a typist; I'm out of work; I've been looking for it all day, and I'm disappointed and very tired."

"And that's really all?" demanded Raleigh.

"All!" She turned to look at him at last, meeting his steady and penetrating eyes quietly. She had an impulse to tell him what was comprehended in that "all"; to speak deliberately plain words that should crumple him into an understanding of her tragedy. But even while she hesitated there came to her a sense that he knew more than he told; that the grey eyes in the red-brown face had read more of her than she was willing to show. She subsided.

"Yes, that's all," she said.

He nodded, a quick and business-like little jerk of the head. "I see. I've been worrying you, I'm afraid; but I'm glad I made you tell, because I can put that all right for you at once, as it happens."

The girl, leaning on the wall, drew in a harsh breath and turned to him. Young Raleigh, who had written a monograph on engineering stresses, had still much to learn about the stresses that contort and warp the souls of men and women. He learned some of it then, when he saw the girl's face deaden to a blanker white and the flame of a hungry hope leap into her eyes. He looked away quickly.

"You mean you can?"

He hushed her with his brisk and matter-of-fact little nod.

"I mean I can find you a situation in a business office as a typist," he said explicitly. "Wasn't that what you wanted?"

"Yes, yes." She was trembling; he put one large, grimy hand upon her sleeve to steady her. "Oh, please, where is the office? I'll go there at once, before."

"Hush!" he said. "It's all right. We'll get a taxi and I'll take you there. It's the Machine-Tool and Gear-Cutting Company; I don't know what they pay, but—."

"Anything," moaned Annette. "I'll take anything."

"Well, it's more than that," he smiled. "A typist with Raleigh and Son at her back isn't to be had every day of the week."

A taxicab drifted out of a turning on to the quay a hundred yards away; Raleigh waved a long arm and it came towards them.

"And after we've fixed this little matter," suggested Raleigh, "don't you think we might go somewhere and feed? I can get a sketchy kind of wash at the office while you're talking to the manager; and I'm beginning to notice that I didn't have my lunch to-day."

"I didn't either," said Annette, as the taxi slid to a standstill beside them. "But, oh! you don't know you don't know all you're doing for me. I'll never be able to thank you properly."

Raleigh opened the door of the cab for her. "You can try," he said. "I'm in Paris for three days every fortnight."

The taxicabs of Paris include in their number the best and the worst in the world. This was one of the latter; a moving musical-box of grinding and creaking noises. But Annette sank back upon its worn and knobly cushions luxuriously, gazing across the sun-gilt river to the white, window-dotted cliffs of Paris with the green of trees foaming about their base.

"Oh, don't you love Paris?" she cried softly.

"I do," agreed Raleigh, warmly, watching the soft glow that had come to her face. "I can't keep away from it."

IX

THE DARKENED PATH

The captain reached a hand forth and touched the mate's arm.

"Sit down, James," he said quietly.

The mate made a curious quick grimace and sat forthwith. "Shove off," ordered the captain.

Johnny Cos, the yellow, woolly-haired boatman, plying his oars, sat perforce in face of his passengers and close to them. He would have preferred it otherwise; there had been something in the mate's face which daunted him. He glanced at it again furtively as he pulled away from the square-sterned American schooner which had ridden over the bar in the twilight of dawn and anchored, spectral and strange, in Beira Harbor. The mate's face was strong and sunburnt, the face of a man of lively passions and crude emotions; but as he sat gazing forth at the little hectic town across the smooth harbor, it had a cast of profound and desperate unhappiness. Johnny Cos had not words to tell himself what he saw; he only knew, with awe and a certain amount of fear, that he moved in the presence of something tragic.

"James," began the captain again.

The mate withdrew his miserable eyes from the scene. "What?"

"There ain't any reason why" began the captain, and paused and Hooked doubtfully upon the faithful Johnny Cos. "D'you speak English?"

"Yes, sar," replied Johnny, ingratiatingly. "You want good 'otel, Cap'n? Good, cheap 'otel? I geeve you da card; 'Otel Lisbon, sar. All cap'n go there."

"No," said the captain shortly. "We can talk better when we get ashore, James," he added to the mate.

"Ver' good 'otel, Cap'n; ver' cheap" coaxed Johnny Cos. "You want fruit, Cap'n: mango, banan', coconut, orange, grenadeel, yes? I geeve you da card, Cap'n ver' cheap!"

"That'll do," said the captain. "I don't want anything. Get a move on this boat o' yours, will you?"

Johnny Cos sighed and resigned himself to row in silence, only murmuring at intervals: "'Otel Lisbon; good, ver' good, an' cheap!" When that murmur, taking courage to grow audible, drew the mate's eye upon him, he stopped short in the middle of it and murmured no more.

"You c'n wait to take me aboard again," said the captain, when the wharf was reached; and the two men went slowly together into the town, along the streets of ankle-deep sand, towards the office of the consul.

It was an hour later that the loafers on the veranda of the Savoy Hotel observed their slow approach. They had done whatever business they had with the consul. They were deep in talk; the captain's grizzled head was bent toward his shorter companion, and something of the mate's trouble reflected itself in his hard, strongly-graven face. In the merciless deluge of sunlight, and upon the openness of the street, they made a singular grouping; they seemed to be, by virtue of some matter that engrossed and governed them, aloof and remote, a target set up by Destiny.

By the steps of the hotel the captain paused, wiping the shining sweat from his face. The eavesdroppers in the long chairs cocked their ears.

"James," they heard him say; "it's bad, it's just as bad as it can be. But it ain't no reason to go short of a drink with a saloon close handy."

He motioned with his head towards the shade of the long veranda, with the bar opening from it and its bottles in view. The mate, frowning heavily, nodded, and the pair of them entered and passed between the wicker chairs with the manner of being unconscious of their occupants.

From within the bar their voices droned indistinctly forth to the listeners.

"Leavin' you here," they heard the captain say; "James, I'm sorry right through; but you said yourself."

"Sure;" the mate's voice answered hoarsely. "Here or Hell or anywhere, what's the difference to me now?"

After that they moved to the window, and what they said further was indistinguishable. The loafers on the veranda exchanged puzzled looks; they lacked a key to the talk they had heard. When at last the two seamen departed they summoned forth the barman for further information. But that white-jacketed diplomat, who looked on from the sober side of the bar at so much that was salient to the life of Beira was not able to help them.

"I couldn't make out what was troublin' them," he said, playing with the diamond ring on his middle finger. "They was talking round and round it, but they never named it right out. But it seems the younger one has been paid off. He looks bad, he does."

"Well," said a man of experience from his chair; "he'll be drunk tonight, and then we'll hear."

"H'm!" The barman paused on his way back to his post. "When I see that feller drunk, I'm goin' to climb a tree. I got no use for trouble."

But the mate's conduct continued to be as unusual as his words overheard on the hotel veranda. He did not accompany the captain back to the ship, and in the afternoon he was seen sitting on the parapet of the sea-wall, his face propped in his hands, staring out across the shining water of the harbor. The vehement sun beat down upon his blue-coated back and the hard felt hat that covered his head; he should have been in an agony of discomfort and no little danger, clad as he was; but he sat without moving, facing the water and the craft that lay at their anchors upon it. It was Father Bates, the tall Scottish priest, who saw him and crossed the road to him.

"My friend," the priest accosted him, with a light tap on the shoulder. "You'll die the sooner if you take your hat off. But you'll die anyhow if you go on sitting here."

At his touch the mate looked round sharply. The tall white-clad Father, under his green-lined sun umbrella, rested a steady look on his face.

"You're in trouble, I'm afraid," said the priest. "Is there anything a man can do for you?"

"No!" The word came hoarsely but curt from the mate's throat. "Leave me alone!"

The tall priest nodded. "Nothing a man can do, eh?" he said. "Well, then you know who can help you, don't you?"

The miserable rebellious eyes of the young man hardened.

"Leave me alone," he growled. "Say, you're a kind of a missionary, ain't you? Well, I don't want none of your blasted cant, see?"

The Father smiled. "I know how you feel. My name is Father Bates, and anyone will show you where I live. Bates don't forget! And I really wouldn't sit much longer in that sun, if I were you."

A sound like a snarl was his answer as he passed on. Looking back before he turned the corner, he saw that the mate had returned to his old posture, brooding in his strange and secret sorrow over the irresponsive sea.

He was still there at sunset when the schooner went out, holding himself apart from the little group of Beira people who halted to watch her departure. Upon her poop a couple of figures were plain to sight, and one of these waved a hand towards the shore as though to bid farewell to the man they left behind. The mate, however, made no response. He watched unmoving while she approached the heads and glided from view, her slender topmasts lingering in sight over the dull green of the mangroves, with the sunset flush lighting them delicately. Then she was gone, like a silent visitor who withdraws a presence that has scarcely been felt.

The mate crossed the road and addressed the man who stood nearest.

"Where's the deepo?" he demanded, abruptly. "The railway station."

The other gave directions which the mate heard, frowning. Then, without thanking his guide, he turned to walk heavily through the foot-clogging sand in the direction indicated.

It was a hundred and fifty miles up the line that he next emerged to notice, at Mendigos, that outpost set in the edge of the jungle, where the weary telegraphists sweat through the sunny monotony of the days and are shaken at night by the bitter agues that infest the land.

The mate dropped from the train here, still clad as at Beira in thick, stifling sea-cloth and his hard hat, though his collar was now but a limp frill. He came lurching, on uncertain feet, into the establishment of Hop Sing, the only seller of strong drink at Mendigos. The few languid, half-clad men who lounged within looked up at him in astonishment. He pointed shakily towards a bottle on the primitive bar. "Gimme some of that," he croaked, from a parched throat.

The smiling Chinaman, silk-clad and supple, poured a drink for him, watched him consume it, and forthwith poured another. With the replenished tumbler in his hand, the mate returned his look.

"What you starin' at, you Chow?" he demanded.

The subtle-eyed Chinaman ceased neither to smile nor to stare.

"My t'ink you velly sick man. Two shillin' to pay, please."

"Sick!" repeated the mate. "Sick! You you know, do ye?"

The idle men who lounged behind were spectators to the drama, absorbed but uncomprehending. They saw the fierce, absurdly-clad sailor, swaying on his feet with the effects of long-endured heat and thirst, confronting the suave composure of the Chinaman as though the charge of being unwell were outrageous and shameful.

"Say," he demanded hoarsely, "it, it don't show on me."

The Chinaman made soothing gestures. "My see," he answered. "But dem feller belong here, him not see nothing. All-a-light foh him. Two shillin' to pay, please."

The mate dragged a coin from his pocket and dropped it on the bar. He turned at last to the others, as though he now first noticed them.

"What's back of here?" he asked abruptly, motioning as he spoke to the still palms which poised over the galvanized iron roofs.

"How d'you mean?" A tall, willowy man in pajamas answered him surprisedly. "There's nothing beyond here. It's just wild country."

"No white men?" asked the mate.

"Lord, no!" said the other. "White men die out there. It's just trees and niggers and wild beasts and fevers." He looked at the mate with a touch of amusement breaking through his curiosity. "You weren't thinking of goin' there in that kit were you?"

The mate finished his drink and set his glass down.

"I am goin' there," he answered.

"But look here!" The telegraphists broke into a clamor. "You've been too long in the sun; that's what's the matter with you. You can't go up there, man; you'd be dead before morning."

The tall man, to whom the mate had spoken first, had a shrewd word to add. "If it's any little thing like murder, dontcher know, why the border's just a few hours up the line."

"Murder!" exclaimed the mate, and uttered a bark of laughter.

They were possibly a little afraid of him. He had the physique of a fighter and the presence of a man accustomed to exercise a crude authority. Their protests and warnings died down; and, after all, a man's life and death are very much his own concern in those regions.

"D'you think he's mad?" one of them was whispering when the mate turned to Hop Sing again.

"Set up the drinks for them," he commanded. "I'll not wait meself, but here's the money."

"You not dlink?" asked the Chinaman, as the mate laid the coins on the counter.

"No," was the reply. "No need to spoil another glass."

He gave a half nod to the other men, but no word, pulled his hard hat forward on his brow, and walked out to the aching sunlight, and towards a path that led between two iron huts to the fringe of the riotous bush. The telegraphists crowded to look after him, but he did not turn his head. He paused beneath the great palms, where the ground was clear; then the thigh-deep grass, which is the lip of the bush, was about him, grey, dry as straw, rustling as he thrust through it with the noise of paper being crumpled in the hands. A green parrot, balancing clown-like on a twig, screamed raucously; he glanced up at its dazzle of feathers. Then the wall of the bush itself yielded to his thrusting, let him through, and closed behind his blue-clad back. Africa had received him to her silence and her mystery.

"Well, I'm blowed!" The tall telegraphist stared at the place where he had vanished. "I say, you chaps, we ought to go after him."

No one moved. "I shouldn't care to come to my hands with him," said another. "Did you did you see his face?"

They had all seen it; the speaker was voicing the common feeling.

"It's like drinkin' at a wake," observed the tall man, his glass in his hand. "Well, here's to his memory!"

"His memory," they chorused, and drank.

But the end of the tale came later. It was told in the veranda of Father Bates's house at Beira, by Dan Terry, as he lay on his cot and drank in the air from the sea in life-restoring draughts. He had been up in the region of lost and nameless rivers for three years of fever and ague and toil, and now he was back, a made man ready to be done with Africa, with square gin bottles full of coarse gold to sell to the bank, and a curious story to tell of a thing he had seen in the back country.

It was evening when he told it, propped up on his pillows, with the blankets drawn up under his chin, and his lean, leathery face, a little softened by his fever, fronting the long, benevolent visage of Father Bates. The Father had a deckchair, and sprawled in it at length, listening over his deep Boer pipe. A faint, bitter ghost of an odor tainted the still air from the mangroves beyond the town, and there was heard, like an undertone in the talk, the distant slumberous murmur of the tide on the beach.

"But how did you first get to hear of him?" the Father was asking, carrying on the talk.

"Oh, that was queer!" said Dan. "You see, I was making a cut clean across country to that river of mine, and, as far as I could tell, I was in a stretch of land where there hasn't been one other white man in twenty years. Bad traveling it was swamp, cane, and swamp again for days; the mud stinking all day, the mist poisoning you all night, the cane cutting and scratching and slashing you. It was as bad as anything I've seen yet. And it was while we were splashing and struggling through this that I saw, lying at the foot of an aloe of all created things an old hat. I thought for a moment that the sun had got to my brain. An old, hard, black bowler hat it was, caved in a bit, and soaked, and all that, but a hat all the same. I couldn't have been more surprised if it had been an iceberg. You see, except my own hat, I hadn't seen a hat for over two years."

Father Bates nodded and stoked the big bowl of his pipe with a practiced thumb.

"It might ha' meant anything," Dan went on; "a chap making for my river, for instance. So the next Kaffir village I came to I went into the matter. I sat down in the doorway of the biggest hut and had the population up before me to answer questions."

"They were willing?" asked the Father.

"I had a gun across my knees," explained Dan; "but they were willing enough without that. And a queer yarn they had to tell, too; I couldn't quite make it out at first. It began with an account of a village hit by smallpox close by. Their way of dealing with smallpox is simple: they quarantine the infected village by posting armed men round it until all the villagers are starved to death or killed by the smallpox. Then they burn the village. It costs nothing, and it keeps the disease under. This village, it seems, was particularly easy to deal with, since it stood three hundred yards from the nearest water, and the water was placed out of bounds.

"It must have been about the third day after the quarantine was declared that the, the incident occurred. A man and a girl, carrying empty waterpots, had come out of the village towards the stream. The armed outposts, with their big stabbing assegais ready in their hands, ordered them back, but the poor creatures were crazed with thirst and desperate. They were pleading and crying and still creeping forward, the man first, the girl a few steps behind, mad for just water. What happened first was in the regular order of things in those parts. The fellows on guard simply waited, and when the man was up to them one stepped forward and drove the thirty-inch blade of a stabbing assegai clean through him. Then they stood ready to do the same to the girl as soon as she arrived.

"She had tumbled to her knees at the sight of the killing, and was still crying and begging piteously for water. They said she held out her arms to them, and bowed her head between. After a while, when they did not answer, she got to her feet and stood looking at the dead body stretched in the sun, the long blades of the spears, and the shining of the water beyond. It was as though she was making up her mind about them, for at last she picked up her waterpot and came forward towards her sure and swift death. The assegai-men were so intent on her that none of them seem to have heard a man who came out of the bush close behind them. One of them, as I was told, had actually flung back his arm for the thrust and the girl, she hadn't even flinched! The thing was within an inch of being done; the stabbing assegai goes like lightning, you know; she must have been tasting the very bitterness of death. The man from the bush was not a second too soon. The first they knew of him was a roar, and he had the shaft of the assegai in his hand and had plucked it from its owner.

"He must have moved like a young earthquake, and bellowed like a full-grown thunderstorm. All my informants laid stress on his voice; he exploded in their midst with an uproar that overthrew their senses, and whacked right and left with fist and foot and assegai. He was a white man; it took them some seconds to see that through the dirt on him; he was clad in rags of cloth, and his head was bare, and he raged like a sackful of tiger-cats. He really must have been something extraordinary in the way of a fighter, for he scattered a clear dozen of them, and sent them flying for their lives. One man said that when he was safe he looked back. The white man, with the assegai on his shoulder, was stumping ahead into the infected village, and the girl she was lying down at the edge of the water drinking avidly. She hadn't even looked up at the fight."

Father Bates nodded. "Poor creatures," he said. "Yes?"

"Well, the cordon being broken, those of the villagers who weren't too far gone to walk on their feet promptly scattered, naturally, and no one tried to stop them. When at last the people from the neighboring kraals plucked up courage to go and look at the place, they found there only the bodies of the dead. The white man had gone, too. They never saw him again, but from time to time there came rumors from the north and east tales of a wanderer who injected himself suddenly into men's affairs, withdrew again and went away, and they remembered the white man who roared. He was already passing into a myth.

"I couldn't make head nor tail of the thing; but one point was clear. Since this white man had neither Kaffirs nor gear he couldn't hurt my river, and that was what chiefly mattered to me just then. I might have forgotten him altogether, but that I came on his tracks again, and then, to finish with, I saw the man himself."

"Eh?" Father Bates looked up.

"I'm telling you the whole thing, Padre. You keep quiet and you'll hear."

The sad evening light was falling, and the faint breeze from the sea had a touch of chill in it.

"Keep your blankets up, Dan," said the Father.

"You bet," replied Dan. "Well, about this fellow I'm telling you of! He must have been getting a reputation for uncanniness from every village he touched at. By the time I came up with the scene of his next really notable doings he was umtagati in full form supernatural, you know, a thing to be dreaded and conciliated. And I don't wonder, really. Here was a man without weapons, bareheaded in the sun, speaking no word of any native language, alone and nearly naked, plunging ahead through that wild unknown country and no harm coming to him. You can't play tricks of that sort with Africa; the old girl holds too many trumps; but this chap was doing it. It was against Nature.

"He'd made his way up to a place where I always expect trouble. There is, or rather, there was then a brute of a chief there, a fellow named N'Komo, who paid tribute to M'Kombi, and was sort of protected and supported by him. He was always slopping over his borders with a handful of fighting men and burning and slaughtering and raping among the peaceful kraals. A devil he was, a real black devil for cruelty and lust. He had just started on a campaign when this lonely white man arrived in the neighborhood, passing through a bit of district with N'Komo's mark on it in the form of burned huts and bodies of people. A man N'Komo had killed was a sight to make Beelzebub sick. Torture, you know; mutilation beastliness! The white man must have seen a good many such bodies.

"N'Komo and his swashbucklers had slept the night in a captured kraal, and were still there in the morning when the white man arrived. I know exactly the kind of scene it was. The carcasses of the cattle slaughtered for meat would be lying all over the place between the round huts, and bodies of men and women and children with them. The place would be swarming with the tall, black spearmen, each with a skin over his shoulder and about his loins; there would be a fearful jabber, a clatter of voices and laughter and probably screams, horrible screams, from some poor nigger whose death they'd be dragging out, hour after hour, for their fun. Near the main gate N'Komo was holding an indaba with his chief bucks. I've seen him many times a great coal-black brute, six feet four in height, with the flat, foolish, good-natured-looking face that fooled people into thinking him a decent sort. I wish I'd shot him the first time I saw him.

"Well, the indaba, the council, you know was in full swing when up comes this white man, running as if for his life, and wailing, wailing! The Kaffir who told me had seen it from where he was lying, tied hand and foot, waiting his turn for the firebrands and the knives. He said: 'He wailed like one who mourns for the dead!' There was a burnt kraal not a mile away, so one can guess what he had been seeing and was wailing about. 'His face,' the nigger told me, 'was like the face of one who has lived through the torment of N'Komo and is thirsty for death; a face to hide one's eyes before. And it was white and shining like ivory!' He came thus, pelting blindly at a run, into the midst of N'Komo's war indaba.

"He picked out N'Komo as the chief man there in a moment; that was easy enough, and he broke into a torrent of words, gesticulating and pointing back in the direction from which he had come. Telling him of what he had seen, of course poor beggar! Can't you imagine him, with those tall surprised black soldiers all round him and the great dangerous bulk of negro king before him, trying to make them understand, trembling with horror and fury, raging in homely useless English against the everyday iniquity of Africa? Can't you imagine it, Padre?"

"Ssh! You'll get a temperature," warned Father Bates. "Yes; I can imagine it. It makes me humble."

"You see, I know what had maddened him. The first work of N'Komo's I ever saw was a young mother and a baby dead and and finished with, and it nearly sent me off my head. If I'd been half the man this poor beggar was I'd have had N'Komo's skin salted and sun-dried before I slept. He he didn't wait to mourn about things; he went straight ahead to find the man who had done them and deal with him.

"Probably they took him for a lunatic; at any rate, they soon began to laugh at him, shaking and talking in their midst. He was a new thing to have sport with, and N'Komo presently leaned forward, grinning, touched him on the arm, and pointed. The white man's eyes followed the black finger to where a poor devil lay on the ground, impaled by a stake through his stomach. It was N'Komo's way of telling him what to expect, and he understood. He stopped talking.

"The nigger who saw it all and told me about it said that when he had looked round on all the horrors he turned again towards N'Komo, and at the sight of his eyes N'Komo ceased to grin. His big brute face went all to bits, as a Kaffir's does when he is frightened. But the white man made a little backward jerk with his hand that's what it seemed like to the nigger who told me and suddenly, from nowhere in particular, a big pistol materialized in his grip. He must have been pretty clever at the draw. His hand came up, there was a smart little crack, a spit of smoke, and N'Komo, the great war chief, was rolling on the ground, making horrible noises like like bad plumbing, with half his throat shot away, and the man who had done it was backing towards the main gate with the big revolver swinging to right and left across the group of warriors.

"And he got away, too. That, really, is the most wonderful part of the whole thing. I expect that as soon as N'Komo was settled, the usual row and the usual murders began by various would-be successors. By night they had all started north again, on a hot-foot race to occupy and hold the head kraal, and the country was clear of them, and the white man's credit as a magic worker stood higher than ever. He could have had anything he liked in any of the kraals for the asking; he could have been law-giver, king, and god. But he was off in the bush again, alone and restless and mysterious, with his ivory-white face and his eyes full of pain and anger."

"Aye," said Father Bates. "Pain and anger that's what it was! And at last you saw him yourself, didn't you?"

"Yes," said Dan. "I saw him. I was at my river then, combing the gold out of it, when a Kaffir trekking down told me of him. He was at a kraal fifty miles away two days' journey, lying, up with a hurt foot. The gold was coming out of that river by the bottleful; it wasn't a thing to take one's eyes off for a moment; but a white man, the white man who had killed N'Komo well, I couldn't keep away. I spun a yarn to my men about lion spoor that I wanted to follow, and off I went by myself and did that fifty miles of bush and six-foot grass and rocks in thirty hours, which was pretty good, considerin'. It was afternoon when I came through a patch of palms and saw the kraal lying just beyond.

"I hadn't much of an idea what kind of man I expected to see. I rather fancy I expected to be disappointed to find him nothing out of the way after all, and to learn that nine-tenths of the yarns about him were just nigger lies. I was thinking all that as I stopped in the palms' shade to mop the sweat out of my hat, and then I saw him!

"He was passing between me and the huts, a strange lame figure, leaning on a stick, with a few rags of clothing bound about him. His head, with its matted thick hair, was bare to the thresh of the sun; he was thick-set, shortish, slow-moving, a sorrowful and laborious figure. I saw the shine of his bare skin, and even the droop and sorrow of his heavy face. I stood and watched him for perhaps a minute in the shadow under those great masts of palms; I saw him as clearly as I see you; and suddenly a light came to me and I knew I understood it all. His loneliness, his pain and anger, his wanderings in that savage wilderness, the wild misery of his eyes and the ivory-white of his stricken face I understood completely. He had run away from the sight of men of his own color he would have no use for me. So then and there I turned and went back through the palms and started on the trek for my own camp. It was all I could do for him."

"But," said Father Bates, "you've not said what it was that you saw."

"Padre," said Dan; "that poor, poor fellow, who loomed to the Kaffirs like a great and merciful god, he was a leper as white as snow!"

"Holy saints defend us!" The Father made a startled motion of crossing himself, staring at Dan's lean, somber face in a blankness of consternation. "So that's what it was, then! A leper!"

"That's what it was," said Dan. "I've seen it before in the East."

"He said," continued the Father "he said he had no use for my blasted cant. And he hadn't, he hadn't! He knew more than I."

X

MISS PILGRIM'S PROGRESS

The double windows of the big office overlooked the quays of Nikolaieff and the desk was beside them; so that the vice-consul had only to turn his head to see from his chair the wide river and its traffic, with the great grain-steamers, like foster-children thronging at the breast of Russia, waiting their turn for the elevators, and the gantries of the shipyards standing like an iron filigree against the pallor of the sky. The room was a large one, low-ceilinged, and lighted only upon the side of the street; so that a visitor, entering from the staircase, looked as from the bottom of a well of shadow across the tables where the month-old American newspapers were set forth to the silhouette of the vice-consul at his roll-top desk against his background of white daylight.

Mr. Tim Waters, American citizen in difficulties, leaned upon the top of the desk and pored absorbedly across the head of his country's representative at the scene beyond the window. A tow-boat with a flotilla of lighters was at work in midstream; there was a flash of white foam at her forefoot, and her red-and-black funnel trailed a level scarf of smoke across the distance. It was a sketch done vigorously in strong color, and he broke off the halting narrative of his troubles to watch if with profound unconscious interest.

Selby, the vice-consul, shifted impatiently in his chair. He was a small, dyspeptic, short-sighted man, and he was endeavoring under difficulties to give the impression that he had no time to spare.

"Well," he snapped; "go on. You were walking peaceably along the street, you said. What comes next?"

Tim Waters turned mild eyes upon him, withdrawing them from the tow-boat with patient reluctance.

"There was one o' them dvorniks" (doorkeepers), he resumed in a voice of silky softness. "He was settin' outside his gate on one o' them stools they have. And he was talkin' to one o' them istvostchiks." (cabmen).

His thin, sun-browned face, furrowed with whimsical lines, with its faint-blue eyes that wandered from his hearer to the allurement of the window and back again, overhung the desk as he spoke, drawling in those curiously soft tones of his an unconvincing narrative of sore provocation and the subsequent fight. He was a man in the later twenties, lean and slack-limbed; the workman's blouse of coarse linen, belted about him, and the long Russian boots which he wore, gave him, by contrast with the humor and sophistication of his face and the controlled ease of his attitude as he lounged, something of the effect of a man in fancy dress. Actually he belonged to the class familiar to missionaries and consuls of world-tramps, those songless troubadours for whom no continent is large enough and no ocean too wide. With his slightly parted lips of wonder and interest, a pair of useful fists and a passport granted by the American Minister in Spain, he had worked his way up the Mediterranean to the Levant, drifted thence by way of the Black Sea to Nikolaieff, and remained there ever since. Riveter in the shipyards, winch driver on the wharves, odd-man generally along the waterside, he and his troubles had come to Selby's notice before.

The vice-consul sniffed and stared unsympathetically as the recital wandered unhurried to its end. For him, the picaroon who leaned upon his desk was scarcely more than a tramp; Selby had respectability for a religion; and his beaky, irritable face, behind the glasses that straddled across his nose, answered Tim Waters's mild conciliatory gaze with stiff hostility. The dvornik and the istvostchik, it seemed, had laughed loudly and significantly as Waters went by, and he had turned to inquire into the joke.

"Because, y'see, Mr. Selby, them Russians just don't laugh in a general way, except they're wantin' to start something. An' I heard 'em say 'Amerikanetz' just as plain as I can see you settin' there. So, a' course, I knowed it was me they was pickin' on." The fight had followed; Tim Waters, while he told of it, raised the hand in which he held his cap and looked thoughtfully at a row of swollen and abraded knuckles; and lastly, the police had intervened.

"It was that big sergeant with the medals," said the victim. "Come at me with his sword, he did. Seems like it ain't safe to be an American citizen in this town, Mr. Selby."

"Does it?" Selby sat back sharply in his chair, his ragged moustache bristling, his glasses malevolently askew on his nose. "You're a mighty fine example of an American citizen, aren't you? Say, Waters, you don't think you can put that over again, do you?"

"Eh?" Tim Waters opened his pale blue eyes in the mildest surprise. "Why, Mr. Selby?" he began, fumbling in his pocket. The vice-consul interrupted him with a snarl.

"Now you don't want to pull that everlasting passport of yours on me again," he cried. "Every crook and hobo that's chased off a steamer into this town has got papers as good as yours, red seal an' all. You seem to think that bein' an American citizen's a kind of license to play hell and then come here to be squared. Well, I'm going to prove to you that it's not."

Waters was watching him as he spoke with something of that still interest which he had given to the scene beyond the window. Now he smiled faintly.

"But say, Mr. Selby," he protested gently. "It it ain't the sergeant I'm worried about. I'll get him all right. But there's what they call a protocol fer breakin' up that istvostchik, an' you bein' our consul here."

Selby rose, jerking his chair back on its castors. "Cut that out," he shrilled. "Your consul, eh? Your kind hasn't got any consul, not if you had forty passports see? You get out o' this office right now; and if they hand you six months with that protocol."

He was a ridiculous little man when he was angry; the shape of him as he stood, pointing peremptorily across the room to the door, rose grotesque and pitiable against the window. The wanderer, still leaning on the desk, looked over at him with lips parted as though he found a profit of interest even in his anger.

"And you can tell your friends, if you got any," fulminated the vice-consul, "that this place isn't."

He broke off short in mid-word; the rigid and imperative arm with which he still pointed to the door lost its stiffening; he made a snatch at his sliding glasses, saved them, and stood scaring. Waters turned his head to look likewise.

"This is the American Consulate?" inquired a voice from the doorway.

For the moment neither answered, and the newcomer came down between the tables towards the light of the window.

Of the two men, it was assuredly Waters, who had followed the lust of the eye across the continents, who was best able to flavor and relish that entry and approach. For him, stilly intent and watchful, it was as though a voice, the voice which had spoken from the shadowy doorway, had incarnated itself and become visible, putting on a form to match its own quality, at once definite and delicate. The newcomer moved down the room with a subdued rustling of skirts, resolving at last into a neat and appealing feminine presence that smiled confidently and yet conciliatorily and offered a hand towards Selby.

"It is the American Consulate, isn't it?" she asked again.

Selby, ruffled like an agitated hen, woke to spasmodic movement, and took the hand.

"Why, yes," he answered, pushing towards her the chair he had not offered to Waters and erupting forthwith into uneasy volubility. "This is it. Sit down, madam; sit right down and tell me what I can do for you."

The girl, still smiling, took the seat he gave her; across the desk-top, Waters, unmoving, his battered hand grasping his peaked Russian cap, gazed upon her absorbedly.

"Just got in, have you?" inquired Selby fussily.

"Yes," she answered. "I got in this morning by the boat from Odessa. You see, I've come up from Bucharest, and as I don't know very much about Russia, I thought."

Selby, seated again in his chair of office, his fingers judicially joined, nodded approvingly. "You just naturally came along to your consul," he finished for her. "Quite right, Miss, er."

"Pilgrim," supplied the girl.

"Miss Pilgrim?" he hesitated. She nodded. "Well, Miss Pilgrim, if there's any information I can give you, or assistance, or, or advice, I'll be very happy to do what I can. You're, er, traveling alone?"

"Yes," she replied, with her little confirming nod.

He had forgotten for the while the mere existence of Waters, brooding wordlessly over them, and Waters after his manner, had forgotten everything in the world. The girl between them, sitting unconscious and tranquil under their converging gaze, had snared their faculties. She was perhaps twenty-four, and both Selby and Waters, when afterwards they used to speak of her, always insisted on this, not pretty. She was fair in a commonplace way, middle-sized and inconspicuous, the fashion of young woman who goes to compose the background of life. She raised to the light of the window a face of creamy pallor, with large serious grey eyes, and lips of a gentle and serene composure; but it was not these that redeemed her from being merely negligible and made her the focus of the two men's eyes. It was rather a quality implicit in the whole of her as she sat, feminine and fragile by contrast with even the meager masculinity of Selby, with a suggestion about her, an emanation, of steadfastness and courage as piteous and endearing as the bravery of a lost child. In Selby, staled and callous long since to all those infirmities of the wits or the purse which are carried to a consul as to a physician, there awoke at sight of her all that was genial and protective in his sore and shriveled soul; in Waters, who shall say what visions and interpretations?

She looked from one to the other of them with her trustful eyes. On Waters they seemed to dwell for a moment as though in question.

"Yes," she repeated; "I came alone; there wasn't anybody to come with me." Her voice, mild and pleasant, corresponded to the rest of her. "I've been working down in Rumania for nearly a year, in the Balkan Bank, and before that I was in Constantinople. But I've always wanted to see Russia; I'd heard and read so much about it; so" with a little explanatory shrug of her shoulders "I came."

Waters's still eyes widened momentarily; he, at any rate, understood. He knew, contentedly and well, that need to see, the unease of the spirit that moves one on, that makes of the road a home and of every destination a bivouac. His chin settled upon his crossed arms as he continued to take stock of this compatriot of the highways.

"Oh!" Selby was enlightened and a little disconcerted. This was not turning out as he had expected. He had diagnosed a tourist, and now discovered that he had been entertaining a job-seeker unawares. But the girl's charm and appeal held good; she was looking at him trustfully and expectantly, and he surrendered. He set his glasses straight with a fumbling hand and resumed his countenance of friendly and helpful interest.

"Then, you propose to, er, seek employment here in Nikolaieff," he inquired.

"Yes," she answered serenely. "Typist and stenographer, or secretary or translator in French and German and Rumanian" she was numbering off the occupations on her fingers as she listed them "or even governess, if there isn't anything else. But it seems to me, with the English steamers coming here all the time and the shipbuilding works, there ought to be some office I could get into."

Selby pursed his lips doubtfully.

"You don't know of anything?", she asked. "That's what I came in to see you about if you happened to know of anything? Because our consuls hear of pretty nearly everything that's going on, don't they?"

It wasn't flattery; her good faith was manifest in her face and voice; and Selby suppled under it like a stroked cat.

"I wouldn't say that, Miss Pilgrim," he demurred coyly. He paused. Her mention of shipping offices disturbed him. He had much business with shipping offices; and he was picturing to himself, involuntarily and with distaste, that gentle courage bruising itself upon the rough husks of managers and their like, peddling itself from one noisy Russian office to another, wearing thin its panoply of innocence upon evil speech and vile intention. There were the dregs of manhood in him, for all his narrowness and feebleness, and the prospect offended him like an indecency.

"No, there's only one job I know of in Nikolaieff that you could take," he said abruptly. "And that's right here in this office."

He had said it upon a rare impulse of generosity; all men are subject to such impulses; and he halted upon the word for his reward. She rendered it handsomely.

"Oh!" she cried, her grey eyes shining and all her pale and gentle face alive with sudden enthusiasm. "Here in the Consulate?" She spoke the word as a devotee might speak of a temple. "That, oh, that's glorious!"

It was utterly satisfactory; Selby swelled and bridled.

"Er, secretary and stenographer," he said largely. "I had a young man here a while since, but I let him go. He couldn't seem to be respectful. And, er, as to terms, Miss Pilgrim."

"Yes?" murmured Miss Pilgrim, as respectfully as he could wish.

But the vice-consul did not continue. In his moment of splendor, it may be that he became aware that only a part of his audience was applauding, and his eyes had fallen on Waters. Till that moment he had actually forgotten him; he seized now on an occasion to be still more impressive.

"Hey, you Waters!" he cried commandingly. "What you waitin' there for? Didn't you hear me tell you to clear out of this? Go on, now; an' don't let me see you in this office again!"

She failed to come up to his expectations this time; she looked puzzled and distressed and seemed to shrink. Waters, removing his eyes from her face, stood deliberately upright. His vagueness and dreaminess gathered themselves into gravity. His lips moved as though on the brink of an answer, but he said nothing.

"Go on!" yapped Selby again.

"I'm goin'," replied Waters, turning from him.

He sent the girl a look that was a claim upon her. "Pleased to meet ye," he said clearly. "Me name's Waters; I'm an American too."

Selby bounced in his chair behind him, squeaking and spluttering; the girl, surprised and uncertain, stammered something. But her face, for all her embarrassment, acknowledged his claim. He took his reply from it, nodded slowly in satisfied comprehension and walked past her towards the door. His worn blouse glimmered white in the shadows of the entry; and he was gone.

Behind him, the office was suddenly uncomfortable and cheerless. Selby was no longer sure of himself and the figure he had cut; the girl looked at him with eyes in which he read a doubt.

"You don't want to take any notice of that fellow," he blustered. "He'd no right to speak to you. He's just a tough in trouble with the police and wanting me to fix it for him. He won't come here again in a hurry."

"But" she hesitated. "Isn't he an American?" she ventured.

"Huh!" snorted Selby. "Americans like him are three for a nickel round here."

"Oh!" she murmured, and sat looking at him while he plunged into the question of "terms." His glasses wobbled on his nose; his hands moved jerkily as he talked, fidgeting with loose papers on his desk; but his weak eyes did not return her gaze.

Nikolaieff, which yet has a quality of its own, has this in common with other abiding places of men that life there shapes itself as a posture or a progress in the measure that one gives to it or receives from it. Tim Waters, who fed upon life like a leech, returned to it after a six weeks' enforced absence (the protocol had valued a damaged istvostchik at that price) with a show of pallor under the bronze on his skin and a Rip van Winkle feeling of having slumbered through far-reaching changes. During his absence the lingering southern autumn had sloped towards winter; the trees along the sad boulevard were already leafless; the river had changed from luminous blue to the blank hue of steel. The men in the streets went fortified with sheepskins or furs; Waters, still in his linen blouse, with hands sunk deep in his pockets and shoulders hunched against the acid of the air, passed among them as conspicuous as a naked man, marking as he moved the stares he drew across high, raised collars.

He was making his way across the city to his old haunts by the waterside; he crossed the Gogol Street through its brisk, disorderly traffic of trams and droschkies and gained the farther sidewalk hard by where a rank of little cabs stood along the gutter. A large sedate officer, moving like a traction-engine, jostled him back into the gutter; he swore silently, and heard a shout go up behind him, a blatant roar of jeers and laughter. Startled, he turned; the istvostchiks, the padded, long-skirted drivers of the little waiting cabs, were gathered together in the roadway; their bearded and brutal faces, discolored with the cold, were agape and hideous with their laughter; and in the forefront of them, pointing with a great hand gloved to the likeness of a paw, stood and roared hoarsely the particular istvostchik on whose account he had suffered the protocol and the prison. The discord of their mirth rilled the street; the big men, padded out under their clothes to a grotesque obesity, their long coats hanging to their heels giving them the aspect of figures out of a Noah's Ark, drew all eyes. The beginnings of a crowd gathered to watch and listen.

"The Amerikanetz," the foremost istvostchik was roaring. "Look at him! Look at his clothes! Just out of prison Look at him!"

Everybody looked; the word "Amerikanetz" fled from lip to lip like a witticism. Waters, stunned by the suddenness of it all, daunted and overwhelmed, turned to move away, to get out of sound and hearing. Forthwith a fresh howl went up. He caught at his self-possession and turned back.

The moment had epic possibilities; the istvostchiks were not fewer than eight in number and the crowd was with them. Waters's face was dark and calm and his movements had the deliberate quiet of purpose. Another instant and Nikolaieff would have been gladdened and scandalized by something much more spectacular than a pogrom. The leading istvostchik, still pointing and bellowing, was inviting disaster; when from behind him, ploughing through the onlookers', came the overdue policeman, traffic baton in hand.

"Circulate, circulate!" he cried to the loiterers, waving at them with his stick. "It is not permitted to congregate. Circulate, gentlemen!"

He advanced into the clear space of roadway behind the rearmost cab, between Waters and his tormentors. His darting official eye fell on the former, standing in his conspicuous blouse, his thin face tense and dire.

"And this?" he demanded. "What is this?"

A chorus of explanations from the istvostchiks answered him. "Amerikanetz," they told him, "just out of prison!" They thronged round him, bubbling over with the story, while he stood, trim and armed, his hard, neat face arrogant under the sideways-tilted peak of his cap, hearing them augustly. Then he smiled.

"Tak!" he said briefly. "So!" He turned on Waters, coming round on him with a movement like a slow swoop. Never was anything so galling as the air he had of contemptuous and amused comprehension.

"You march!" he ordered. "Get off this street!" He pointed with his white-painted baton to the nearest turning. "Don't say anything, now," he warned. "March!"

Waters hesitated. The istvostchiks, still hopeful of sport, pressed nearer. To disobey and resist meant being cut down and stamped to death under their heavy boots. Across the policeman's pointing arm, Waters saw the face of his enemy, expectant, avid, bestial with hideous and cruel mirth. He regarded it for a moment thoughtfully. Then, with a shrug, he turned and moved in the direction he had been ordered to go.

Again, behind him, there was that jeering outcry, as the policeman, smiling indulgently and watching his departure, seemed to preside over the chorus.

He came at length, going slowly, to the water side. It was dark by then; the sheds of the wharves shut out the river and made a barrier against the sweep of the wind. From over their roofs came the glare of the high arc-lamps at the wharf-edge and the masts and the rigging of ships lifted into view. The stridency of day was over in the shabby street; its high houses, standing like cliffs, showed tier upon tier of windows, dimly lighted or dark, while from under the feet of the buildings, from cellar-saloons to traktirs below the street-level, there spouted up the ruddiness of lamplight and the jangle of voices. There was a smell in the sharp air of ships and streets blended, the aromatic freshness of tar, the sourness of crowds and uncleanliness.

Waters, halting upon the cobbles, sniffed with recognition and unstiffened his mind as he gazed along the dreary street. He was here, on his own ground; somewhere in the recesses of those gaunt houses he would sleep that night, and next day he would wedge himself back into his place in that uneasy waterside community and all would be as before. He shivered under the lee of the sheds as he stood, looking, scarcely thinking, merely realizing the scene in its evening disguise.

Down the street towards him, walking with strong and measured steps that resounded upon the cobbles, vague under the shadow of the sheds, came a man. Waters glanced casually in his direction as he came near, aware of him merely as in shape that inhabited the darkness, a dim thing that fitted in with the hour and the furtive street. Then the man was close to him and visible.

"By gosh!" exclaimed Waters aloud.

It was, of all possible people, "the sergeant with the medals." He stared at him helplessly.

"Nu!" cried the sergeant heartily. He possessed all that patronizing geniality which policemen can show to evil-doers, as to colleagues in another department of the same industry. "You are back again yes? And how did you find it up there?"

Waters swallowed and hesitated. The sergeant was a vast man, blond as a straw and bearded like an Assyrian bull, the right shape of man to wear official buttons. His short sword hung snugly along his leg in its black, brass-tipped scabbard; his medals, for war-service in the army, for exemplary conduct, for being alive and in the police at the time of the Tsar's coronation and so forth, made a bright bar on the swell of his chest. A worthy and responsible figure; yet the sum of him was to Waters an offence and a challenge.

He found his tongue. "About the same as you left it, I guess," he answered unpleasantly.

The big man laughed, standing largely a-straddle with the thumbs of his gloved hands hooked into his sword-belt. He was rosy as a pippin and cheery as a host.

"It has done you good," he declared. "For one thing, I can see that you speak Russian better now oh, much better! It is a fine school. By and by, we will send you up for six months, and after that nobody will know you for an Amerikanetz. Ah, you will thank me some day!"

Waters heard him stonily and nodded with meaning.

"You bet I will," he replied. "And when I'm through with you, you'll know just how grateful I am." The need for words with a taste to them mastered him. He broke into his own tongue. "You'll get yours, you big slob!"

"Eh?" The sergeant cocked an ear alertly, "Beek slab? What is that in Russian?"

"It's your middle name," retorted Waters cryptically and made to move on.

"Do svidania!" called the sergeant mockingly, raising his voice to a shout. "Till we meet again! Because I shall be watching you, Votters; I shall be."

"Here!" Waters wheeled on him, hands withdrawn from his pockets and cleared for action.

"You start bellerin' at me in the street that way an' I'll just about."

There was no cohort of hostile istvostchiks here, and anger ached in him like a cancer. He stepped up to the sergeant with a couple of long, cat-footed strides and the out-thrust jaw of war. But the sergeant, instead of bristling and giving battle, held up one large, leather-clad hand with the motion of hushing him.

"St!" he clicked warningly. "Not now! Be orderly, Votters. See your lady-consul!"

"What?" Waters halted, taken by surprise, and turned his head. The sergeant, rigid and formal upon the instant, was saluting. Upon the high sidewalk, a dozen paces away, a girl was passing; she acknowledged the sergeant's salute with a small bow. Her eyes seemed to fall on Waters and she stopped.

"Why, it's" she began, and hesitated as though at a loss for his name. She stood, inspecting the grouping of the pair in the road, the massive sergeant and his slighter, more vivid companion. "Is there is there anything the matter?"

Waters turned his back upon the sergeant and moved slowly towards her, peering at her where she waited in the growing darkness.

"Not with me," he answered.

"Oh!" It was, of course, Miss Pilgrim, the girl whom he had watched across the top of the vice consul's desk. She stood above him now at the edge of the high sidewalk, whence the deep cobbled revetment of the gutter sloped like a fortification. Gazing at her with all his eyes, he identified again, like dear and long-remembered landmarks, the poise of her head, the fragile slope of her shoulders, the softly lustrous pallor of her face. Even her attitude, perched over him there and leaning a little towards him, was a thing individual and characteristic.

"I wondered," she said. "I thought, perhaps."

"We are just talking" Waters reassured her. "Him and me's old friends."

He endeavored to be convincing; but it happened that she had seen as she approached the motion with which he had turned on the sergeant a moment before, and she still waited.

"Perhaps," she suggested then in her pleasant voice, "if you could spare the time, you'd walk along a little way with me?"

He smiled. It was protection she was offering him, the shield of her company, dropping it from above like a gentle gift, like a flower let fall from a balcony. She saw the white gleam of his smile in his shadowed face and made a small, quick movement as though she shrank. Waters made haste to accept.

"With you, Miss Pilgrim? Why, sure I will," he replied warmly, and strode across the gutter to her side.

To the sergeant, watching dumbly this pairing and departure, he said nothing; he did not even turn to enjoy his face.

It was strange to pass along that familiar street with her, to glance down at her and see her forward bent face in profile against the dark doorways leading to interiors whose secrets he knew. The drinking dens were noisy at their feet; the tall houses were dark and sinister above them. He heard her breath as she walked at his elbow in the vicious chill of the evening and out upon the water, visible between the sheds as a low green and a high white light sliding, slowly across the night, an outgoing steamer wailed like a hoarse banshee. Once upon a time he had seen the Black Hundred come roaring and staggering along that street under the eyes of the ships, and had backed into one of the doorways past which they now walked to fight for his life. The memory of it came curiously to him now, as the girl at his side led him on, hurrying to bring him to safety.

They turned a corner ere she spoke to him again, and advanced along a street which showed a vista of receding darkness, beaded by the dull house-lamps set over the courtyard gates. Not till then did she slacken the hurry of her gait. She lifted her face towards him.

"But there was something, wasn't there?" she asked. "Between you and that policeman, I mean. You weren't really just chatting?"

Waters shrugged the policeman into the void.

"It's nothin' that you'd need to worry about, Miss Pilgrim," he answered. "He don't amount to anything."

She was still looking at him. She had on a big muffling coat and her face lifted out of the high collar of it.

"But" she paused. "I was watching, you for a minute; I saw you go back to talk to him," she said. "That's why I stopped. You see, that day in the office, I was ever so sorry."

"Oh, that!" Waters was vaguely embarrassed; he was not used to sympathy so openly expressed. "You mean Selby an' all that? That didn't hurt me."

But she would not be denied. "It hurt me," she answered. "To see you go out like that, so quietly, after asking for help and nobody to say a word for you! I've been hoping ever since that I'd see you so that I'd be able to tell you. Of course," she added, in the tone of one who makes reasonable allowances, "of course, Mr. Selby's in a difficult position; he has to consider the authorities. Naturally, being our consul, he'd like to do his best for all Americans; but he has to be careful. You can understand that, can't you?"

"Why, sure!" agreed Waters warmly. "It's mighty good of you to feel like that about me, Miss Pilgrim; and I ain't blamin' Selby any. He was born like that, I guess sort o' poor white trash and his folks didn't find it out in time to smother him. But I wish I was consul here for a time and he'd come to me to have me fix somethin' for him. I'd cert'nly like to have him know how it feels."

"Ah, but I know," she said earnestly. "I can guess like having no home or friends or even a country of your own to belong to. Like finding out suddenly that Uncle Sam wasn't your uncle after all! Tell me, was it what they did to you, I mean was it very bad?"

He smiled a little wryly, looking down into her serious face.

"Well, it wasn't very good," he answered. "It wasn't meant to be. It ain't often these people get a white man to practice on, an' they sure made the most o' the chance. But it didn't kill me; and, anyway, there ain't any reason why it should trouble you, Miss Pilgrim."

He had a feeling that he preferred her to be immune from the knowledge and understanding of such things, to be and remain a mere eyeful of delicate and stimulating feminine effect. But upon his words she half halted, turning to him; she drew a hand from her muff and her fingers touched his sleeve.

"No reason?" she repeated. "Ah, but there is! There is a reason. I haven't got any official position or anything to lose at all. I don't have to consider anybody. So next time if there is a next time I want you to come straight away to me."

He stared at her, not understanding her sudden excitement. "To you, Miss Pilgrim? You mean come round to Selby's again?"

"No, no!" She shook her head impatiently. "You know it's no use to go there. But I live close by here; I'm taking you there now; and I want you to come to me. Then I'll see the Chief of Police for you; I know him quite well."

"So do I," said Waters. "He's a crook. But say, Miss Pilgrim, I don't just see."

She interrupted him. "I'll explain what I mean and then you'll see that it's all right. But now I want you to come home and have a glass of tea and see where I live. It's Number Thirteen only two houses more. You will come, won't you?"

"I'll be glad to," answered he.

The house to which she brought him had a cavernous courtyard arch like a tunnel, outside whose gates the swaddled dvornik huddled upon the sheltered side of the arch. Of all his body, only his eyes moved as they approached, pivoting under his great hood to scan them and follow them through the gate. Within, the small court was a pit of gloom roofed by the windy sky; a glass-paneled door let them in to a winding stone stair with an iron handrail that was greasy to the touch. It was upon the second floor that Miss Pilgrim halted and put a key into a door.

There was a hall within, a narrow passage cumbered with big furniture, wardrobes and the like, which had obviously overflowed from the rooms. At the far end of it, a door was ajar, letting out a slit of bright light and a smell of cabbage. Miss Pilgrim opened a nearer door, reached for the switch and turned to summon Waters where he waited in the entry, browsing with those eager eyes of his upon this new pasture.

"Here's where you'll come when you want me," she said.

He entered the room, walked as far as the middle of it and looked about him. To his sensitive apprehension, whetted to fineness in the years of his wandering and gazing, it was as though a chill and dead air filled the place, a suggestion as of funerals. Opposite the door, two tall windows, like sepulchral portals, framed oblongs of the outer darkness; and the white-tiled stove in the corner was like a mausoleum. The cheap parquet of the floor had a clammy gleam; a tiny icon, roosting high in a corner, showed a tawdry shine of gilding; the whole room, square and lofty, with its sparse furniture grouped stiffly about its emptiness, was gaunt and forbidding. Of a personality that should be at home within it and leave the impress of its life upon the place, there was not a sign; it was the corpse of a room. Waters turned from his scrutiny of it towards Miss Pilgrim, standing yet by the door and clear to see at last in the light. She smiled at him with her pale, quiet face, and he marked how, when she ceased to smile, her mouth drooped and her face returned to shadow. "That's Selby," he told himself hotly. "Selby done that to her!"

There was another door in the corner, near the white stove. It stood a few inches open, revealing nothing. But as he glanced towards it, it seemed to him that he detected in the lifeless air a nuance of fragrance, something elusive as a shade that emanated from the farther room, and had in its very slightness and delicacy a suggestion of femininity. He knew that it must be her bedroom that lay beyond the door, and he found himself wondering what that was like.

Presently he was seated by the little sham mahogany table, upon which the big brass samovar steamed and whispered, listening to her and watching her. She gave him his glass of the pale-yellow Russian tea that neither cheers nor inebriates, but merely distends and irrigates, and sat over against him, sipping at her glass and returning his gaze with her steady eyes.

"I've only had this room a little time," she remarked. "I've had just a bedroom before. But I had to have somewhere for people to come the people who can't go to Mr. Selby, I mean. You know what they call me at the Police Bureau? Mr. Selby's the vice-consul and I'm the vice-vice. So this," her gaze traveled round the barren room with gentle complacency "this is my Vice-vice Consulate."

"Oh!" Waters looked up at her over the rim of his glass with a changed interest. "The vice-vice? That's a pretty good name. Then you've been doin' this for fellers already?"

He marked a faintness of pink that dawned for a moment in her face at the question. She smiled involuntarily and a little ruefully.

"Well," she hesitated; "I've tried, but I'm afraid I haven't actually done anything for anybody. I haven't had a real chance yet. But, anyhow, there's this room all ready and there's me; and any American who can't go to Mr. Selby for help can come here."

He nodded.

"It was really from you I got the idea," she went on; "when you went out of the Consulate like that and there was nowhere you could go. And later on, there was a sailor from one of the ships, and afterwards a man who said he was a Mormon missionary; and Mr. Selby wouldn't couldn't see his way to do anything for them. The sailor was brought in by two policemen, though he was only a boy! He couldn't speak a word of Russian, of course, and it made me so sorry to think of him all alone with those people, having things done to him and not understanding anything. So, after hours, I went round to see the Chief of Police."

Waters moved a little on his chair. Her face had a mild glow of enthusiasm which touched it with sober beauty. He shook his head.

"He's no good," he said. "You hadn't oughter gone to him by yourself."

"But," Miss Pilgrim protested, "lots of people have said that, and it's all wrong. It was he that nicknamed me the 'vice-vice,' and now all the police in the streets salute me when they see me. Even that first time, before I knew him or anything, he was just as nice as he could be. He was in his office, writing at a table under a lamp, and he just looked up at me, hard and well, taking stock of me, you know, while I told him who I was and what I'd come for. And then he gave me a chair and sat and listened to everything I'd got to say, leaning on his elbow and watching me close. I suppose a Chief of Police gets used to watching people like that."

"I, I wouldn't wonder," answered Waters vaguely. He was seeing, in a swift vision, that interview, with the black-browed man in uniform under the lamp, listening and staring.

"I told him how I felt about it," Miss Pilgrim continued, "and how, since there wasn't anybody else to speak for the boy, I'd come along to see if I could do anything. And when I'd finished he let me go on till I hadn't another word to say that I could think of! he just bowed and said he'd have been delighted to oblige me, but the sailor's captain had been in and paid his fine and taken him away three hours before. Then he sent for glasses of tea and we sat and had a talk, and I got him to say I could always come again when I wanted to. But, you see, if it hadn't been for the captain."

"Sure," agreed Waters. "They'd have turned the kid loose for you. And the Mormon? Seems to me I seen that Mormon, unless there's a couple of them strayin' around. How did you fix it for him?"

Again, at the query, that ghost of pink showed on her cheeks.

"Oh, he—he wasn't very nice," she answered. "He was a big stout man, with a curly black beard like fur growing close to his face all round and shiny round knobs of cheek bulging out of it. I never did get to hear just what the trouble was with him, because when he was telling Mr. Selby, he looked round at me first and then bent over the desk and whispered. Whatever it was, it made Mr. Selby very angry; he simply bounced out of his chair and shouted the man right out of the room. And the man, I couldn't help being sorry for him, just went walking backwards, fending Mr. Selby off with his hands, with his mouth open and his eyes staring, looking as helpless and aghast as could be. And when he got to the door, he burst out crying like a little child."

Waters smacked his knee. "That's him," he cried. "That's the feller! He was up the river same time as me, an' gettin' plenty to cry for, too. But what in what made you try to do anything for one o' them?"

"He said he was an American citizen," answered Miss Pilgrim; "and Mr. Selby wouldn't help him; so he was qualified. What made it difficult in his case was that somehow I never found out what he'd done; and the Chief of Police was queer about him too. I remember once that he told me that if he were to let the man go, he'd be afraid to sleep at nights, for fear he'd hear children's voices weeping in the dark. I couldn't get anything else out of him. And the next time I went, they'd found out that the Mormon wasn't an American at all; he'd just been in the States for a couple of years and then come back to Russia. So there wasn't any more I could do."

Waters put his empty glass upon the square iron tray by the samovar. He reached under his chair for his cap.

"That's so," he agreed. "You couldn't do nothin' for that feller. Maybe you'll land with the next one."

He smiled at her across the little table. He understood now why the gaunt room reflected nothing of her. It was a city of refuge she had built and the refugees had failed to come; it was a makeshift temple of her patriotism and her pity. He caught her small answering smile, noting with what a docility of response her lips shaped themselves to it. No doubt she had smiled just as obediently at the "Mormon."

"It's a great idea, too," he went on. "Maybe Selby's all right as far as he goes, but he certainly don't go very far. This here" he gathered the room into his gesture "starts off where he stops. It's great!"

It was good to see her brighten under the brief praise.

"Then you see now what I meant when I told you to come here to me?" she asked. "Because I'll do everything I can, and the Chief of Police will always listen to me. And you will come, won't you, if you should happen ever to need help or or anything?"

"Why, you bet I will," he promised heartily. "I reckon I got a right to. You're my vice-vice and we don't want to waste a room like this."

Watching her while he spoke, he had to hold down a smile which threatened to show. She needed somebody in trouble and she was relying on him.

She left open the door for him while he went down the winding staircase, that he might have light to see his way. When he was at the bottom, he looked up, to see her head across the handrail, silhouetted above him and still oddly recognizable and suggestive of her. Her voice came down to him, echoing in the well of the stairway.

"Good night," it said. "You won't, you won't forget?"

He was smiling as he went forth through the long hollow of the arch to the dim street; the huddled dvornik with his swiveling eyes saw him, his face lifted to the light of the numbered house-lamp, still with the shape of a smile inhabiting his lips. The night wind, bitter from the water, met him as he went, driving through the meagerness of his clothes, and still he smiled, cherished his mood like a treasure. And below his mirth, cordial as a testimony of friendship, there endured the memory of the barren and lifeless room, waiting for its fulfillment.

In the lodging which he discovered for himself, he lay that night upon his crackling mattress, hands under his head, smoking a final cigarette and staring up at the map of stains upon the ceiling. It had been a day tapestried with sensations; there was much for the thoughtful mind of a connoisseur of life to dwell upon; but, as he lay, in that hour of his leisure, the memory that persisted in him was of the inner door in the dull room where he had drunk tea and talked with the girl, and all the suggestion and enticement of it. He wished that for a moment he could have looked beyond it and viewed just once the delicate and fragrant privacy which it screened. The outer room had a purpose as plain as a kitchen; the girl in it had shown him of herself only that purpose; the rest of her was shut from him.

He pitched the end of his cigarette from him, turning his head to watch it roll to safety in the middle of the bare floor.

"I'll go after a job in the morning," he said half aloud to the emptiness of the mean chamber, and turned to sleep upon the resolution.

It was nearing noon of the next day when, following the trail of that redeeming job, he went towards the Mathieson yards. While he was yet afar off he could see between the roofs the cathedral-like scaffolding clustering around the shape of a ship in the building; the rapid-fire of the hammers and riveting guns at work upon her, plates was loud above the noises of the street. But he went slowly; he had already been some hours upon his quest, and there was a touch of worry and uncertainty in his face. It seemed that the world he had known so well had changed its heart. The gatekeeper at the wharves where he formerly had driven a winch had refused to admit him, and at the Russian foundry he had been curtly ordered away. Policemen had hailed him familiarly and publicly, and twice passing istvostchiks had swerved their little clattering vehicles to the curb to jeer down into his face as they rumbled by. The smudged impress of a rubber-stamp upon his passport and three lines of sprawling Russian handwriting recording his conviction and punishment had marked him with the local equivalent of the brand of Cain; henceforward he was set apart from other men. He pondered it as he went in an indignant bewilderment; it was strange that others should find him so different when he knew himself to be the same as ever.

The Scottish foreman-shipwright in the yard office looked up from his standing-desk, lifting, to the light of the open door a red monkey-face comically fringed with coppery whiskers, and stared at him ferociously with little stone-blue eyes. He listened in fierce stillness while Waters put forward his request to be taken on.

"It's you, is it?" he said then. "I know ye. When did they let ye out?"

"Yesterday," answered Waters wearily. "Say, boss, it was only for beatin' up an istvostchik, and I got to have a job."

The fiery monkey-face, pursed in sourest disapproval, did not relax a line. "Yesterday an' now ye come here! Well, we're no' wantin' hands just now, d'ye see? An' if we was, we'd no' want you. So now ye know!"

The angry mask of a face continued to lower at him unwaveringly; it was almost bitter and righteous enough to be funny. Waters surveyed it for a space of moments with a faint interest in its mere grotesqueness; it did not change nor shift under his scrutiny, but continued to glare inhumanly like a baleful lamp. He humped a thin shoulder in resignation and turned away. When he was halfway to the gate, he heard behind him the foreman ordering the gatekeeper not to admit him in future.

Passing again along the cobbled street, he halted suddenly and gazed about him like a man seeking. Everything was as it had been before, from the folk moving in it to the pale sky over it. The little shops, showing idealized pictures of their wares on painted boards beside their doors for the benefit of a public that could not read; the cluster of small gold domes on a church at the corner; the great bearded laboring men in their filthy sheepskins; the Jews, sleek and furtive; the cabman who doffed his hat and crossed himself as he drove by a shrine there was not a house nor a man that he could not identify and classify. He had come back to them from the pain and labor of his imprisonment confident of what he should find; and it was as if a home had become hostile and unwelcoming.

"Guess I'll have to be movin' outta this town," he told himself. "Seems as if I'd stopped here long enough!"

He had time to confirm this judgment in the days that followed. The approach of winter was bringing its inevitable slackness to all work carried on in the open air, and the big works could afford to be scrupulous about the characters of the men they engaged; and the little tradesmen feared the ban of the police. His slender store of money came to an end, and but for occasional jobs of wood-splitting as the supplies of winter fuel came in, it would have been difficult merely to live. As it was, he dragged his belt tighter about the waist of the old linen blouse and showed to the daylight a face whose whimsicality and vagueness were darkened with a touch of the saturnine. He showed it likewise to Miss Pilgrim when one day she passed him at the noon hour, hurrying past the corner on which he stood, wrapped to the eyes in her greatcoat.

She recognized him suddenly and stopped.

"Good morning," she said. "It's, it's a cold day, isn't it?"

Waters had his back to the wall for shelter, and though he stood thus out of the wind, the air drenched him with its chill like water. He smiled slowly with stiff lips at the brisk outdoor pink in her cheeks.

"This ain't cold," he answered. "You won't call this cold when you've been through a winter here."

"No," she agreed. "I suppose I won't." She shifted diffidently, looking at him with her frank eyes. "Are you getting along all right," she asked.

He smiled again; in her meaning there was only one kind of "all right" and "all wrong." "Why, yes," he replied. "I'm all right, Miss Pilgrim; an' if I wasn't, I'd know where to come."

She nodded eagerly. "Yes; I don't want you to forget. I I'll always be glad to do everything I can."

"Sure; I know that," he replied. "An' you? You makin' out all right too, Miss Pilgrim? That Vice-vice-Consulate o' yours keepin' you pretty busy?"

The brisk pink flooded across her face in a quick flush, and her mouth drooped. But her eyes, as always, were steady against his.

"There hasn't been anybody yet," she answered, with a look that deprecated his smile.

He hastened to be sympathetic. "Too bad!" he said. "With a room like that all ready an' waitin' too. But maybe it's only that things is kind o' slack just now; somebody'll be cuttin' loose pretty soon and you'll get your turn all right."

She made to move on, but paused again to answer.

"The room will always be there if you if anybody wants it," she said. "Even if nobody ever comes, it shall always be ready, at least. That's all I can do."

She bade him farewell, with the little nod she had, and passed on, muffling her chin down into her great cloth collar. Waters looked after her with a frown of consideration. He was forgetting for the moment that he was cold, that he had fed inadequately upon gruel of barley, that he was all but penniless in an expensive and hostile world. There was astir in his being, as he watched the slight overcoated figure of the girl, that same protective instinct which had galvanized even Selby into generosity; it never fails to make one feel man enough to cope with any array of ills. There crossed and tangled in his mind a moving web of schemes for aiding and consoling her.

Each of them had for a character vagueness of method and utter completeness of result, but none amounted to a programme. Waters, for all his brisk record, was not a man of action; he was rather a mechanism jolted abruptly into action by the impulses of a detached and ardent mind. It was chance, the ironic chance whose marionettes are men and women, and not any design of his, which turned his feet that evening towards the room that was always to be waiting and ready.

He was returning towards his lodging after an afternoon of looking for work, tired, wearing a humor in tune with the early dark and the empty monotony of the streets by which he went. The few folk who were abroad in them went by like shy ghosts; the high fronts of the houses were like barricades between him and all the comfort and security in the world. There was mud in the roads and his boots were no longer weather-proof. Life tasted stale and sour.

An empty droschky, going the same way as himself, came bumping along the gutter behind him, the driver singing hoarse and broken snatches of song. He moved from the edge of the pavement to be clear of mud-splashes as it passed him, and heard, without further concern, the vehicle draw up level with him and the whistle and slap of the whip as the istvostchik light-heartedly tortured his feeble horse.

"Her eyes are cornflowers," proclaimed the istvostchik melodiously; "her lips are-" He was abreast of Waters as he broke off. Five feet of uneven and slimy sidewalk separated them. Waters looked up; a house-lamp was above, dull and steady as a foggy star; and it showed him, upon the box of the droschky, his enemy, the mainspring of all his troubles. He halted short.

The istvostchik had recognized him likewise. He was something short of drunk, but his liquor was lively in him, and he wrenched his poor specter of a horse to a standstill. Upon his seat, padded hugely in his gown, he had a sort of throned look, a travesty of majesty; his whip was held like a scepter.

They stared at one another for a space of three or four breaths. Waters was frankly aghast; this, upon the top of his other troubles, was overwhelming. The istvostchik ruptured the moment with a brassy yell.

"Wow!" he howled. "My Amerikanetz, the Foreigner, the jail-bird! Look at him, brothers!" He waved his whip as though the darkness were thronged with auditors. "Look at the jail-bird!"

From the gate below the dull lamp a dvornik poked his head forth. Waters had a sense that every door and window in the street was similarly fertile in heads.

"Stop that!" he called to the istvostchik. "That's enough, now."

The man upon the little cab rolled on his seat in a strident ecstasy of eloquence, brandishing arm and whip abroad above the back of the drooping horse.

"He tried to fight me, and first I beat him terribly oh, terribly! and then I made a protocol and sent him to prison. See him?" he bellowed. "See the jail-bird? See the dog?"

Waters swore helplessly. A month before, upon a quarter of such provocation, he would have flashed into fight; but cold, hunger and friendlessness had damped the tinder in him. He made to go on and get away from it all; he started quickly.

"Come back, jail-bird!" howled the istvostchik.

"I haven't done with you, my golubchik, my little prison-rat. Come back here to me when I bid you. What, you won't? Get on, you!"

The last was to the horse, accompanied by a rending slash with the whip. The wretched animal jerked forward, and Waters backed to the wall as his enemy clattered down upon him again.

"That'll do you," he warned as the cabman dragged his horse to a standstill once more. "I'm not lookin' for trouble. You be on your way!"

The immense ragged-edged voice of the istvostchik descended upon him, drowning his protest.

"He runs away from me, this Amerikanetz! He runs away, because when I find him I beat him I beat him whenever I find him. See now, brothers, I am beating him!"

And out of the tangle of his gesticulations, the whip-lash swooped across the sidewalk and cut Waters heavily across the neck.

In the mere surprise of it and the instance of the pain, Waters made a noise like a yelp, a little spurt of involuntary sound. And then the tinder lighted.

"Beating him!" intoned the istvostchik, mighty in his moment. "Beat."

It was the last coherent syllable which he uttered in the affair. With a rush Waters cleared the sidewalk and was upon him, had him by the pulp of clothes which enveloped him and tore him across the wheel to the ground. They went down together across the curb, legs in the gutter among the wheels, a convulsive bundle of battle that tore apart and whirled together again as the American, with all the long-compressed springs of his being suddenly released and vibrant, poured his resentment and soul-soreness into his fists and found balm for them in the mere spite of hitting somebody.

It was a short fight. The istvostchik, even under his padding, was a biggish man and vicious with liquor; he grappled at his antagonist earnestly enough, to drag him down and bite and worry and kick in the manner of his kind. But the breast of the worn linen blouse ripped in his clutch and a pair of man-stopping punches on the mouth and the eye drove him backwards towards the wall. It was then he began to squeal.

There were spectators by now, dvorniks who came running and passers-by upon the other side who appeared from nowhere as though suddenly materialized. There was a sparse circle of them about the fight when it ceased, with the istvostchik down and flattened in the angle of the wall and the pavement, making small timid noises like a complaining kitten. Waters, with the mist of battle clearing, from his eyes, saw them all about him, dark, well-wrapped figures, watching him silently or whispering together. He sensed their profound disapproval of him and his proceedings.

"That'll keep you quiet for a while," he spoke down to the wreck of the istvostchik.

Only moans answered him; he grunted and turned to go. From the nearest group of spectators a single figure detached itself and moved towards him, blocking his path. It revealed itself at close quarters as a stout, middle-aged man, prosperously fur-coated, with a spike of dark beard the inevitable public-spirited citizen of the provinces.

"You must explain this disturbance," he said to Waters importantly. "You must wait here and explain yes, and show your papers. You cannot walk away like this!"

His companions pressed nearer interestedly. Waters could not know the figure he cut, with his torn blouse which even in the gloom showed stains of the mud and blood of the combat.

"Get out of my way!" was all his answer.

"Your papers," persisted the stout man. "I," he puffed his chest, "I am in the Administration; I require to see your papers. Produce them!"

The pale oblong of his fat face wagged at Waters peremptorily; he quite obviously felt himself a spokesman for order and decency and the divinely ordained institution of "papers."

"I said get out o' my way," said Waters clearly. He put the flat of his hand against the stout man's fur-coated chest, shoved, and sent him staggering back on his heels among his supporters. Without looking towards him again, he passed through them and continued his way. He heard the chorus of their indignation break out behind him.

It followed him, a cackle of outraged respectability, with here and there an epithet distinguishable like a plum in a pudding. "Ruffian," they called him, "assassin," "robber," and so forth, the innocuous amateur abuse of men who have learned their bad language from their newspapers. It was not till he had gone a hundred yards, and the noise of their lamentation had a little died down, that there emerged out of the blur of it a voice that was quite clear.

"Hi, you there!" It rang with the note of practiced authority. "Halt, d'you hear? Halt!"

The tones were enough, without the fashion of the words, to tell him that a policeman had arrived on the scene. He looked back and saw that the group of citizens was flowing along the sidewalk towards him, a black moving blot. He could not distinguish the policeman, but he knew that the others must be escorting him, coming with him to see the finish.

There was a corner some thirty or forty yards farther on. Waters jammed his cap tighter on his head, picked up his heels and sprinted for it.

"Halt, there!" shouted the policeman. "Halt-I'll shoot!"

Waters was at the corner when the shot sounded, detonating, like a cannon in the channel of the street. Where the bullet went he did not guess; he was round the corner, running in the middle of the street for the next turning, with eyes alert for any entrance in which he might find a refuge. But the firing had had its intended effect of bringing every dvornik to his gate, and there was nothing for it but to run on. He heard the chase round the corner behind him and the policeman's 'repeated shout; the skin of his back crawled in momentary expectation of another shot that might not go wild; and then, with the next corner yet twenty yards away, came the idea.

The mere felicity of it tickled him like a jest in the midst of all his stress; he spent hoarded breath in a gasp of laughter.

Around the corner that lay just ahead of him, for which he was racing, was the street in which Miss Pilgrim lived, with her outer room that was always ready and waiting. Without design or purpose he had run towards it; an inscrutable fate, whimsical as his own humor, had herded him thither. Well, he would go there! The matter was slight, after all; she would explain the whole matter to her Chief of Police, how the istvostchik had been the assailant and so forth; he would be released, and her self-appointed function of "vice-vice" would shine forth justified and vindicated. It all fell out as dexterously as a conjuring trick.

"Halt!" yelled the policeman. "I know you, halt!"

But he did not shoot again; those southern policemen lack the fiber that will loose bullet after bullet along a dark street; and Waters had yet a good lead as he rounded the next corner and came into cover. The house he sought was near by; as he cleared the angle, he dropped into a swift walk that the new row of dvorniks might not mark him at once for a fugitive, and strode along sharply under the wall where it was darkest. He passed Number Seventeen without a sign from its dvornik, and in the gate of Number Fifteen two dvorniks were gossiping and did not turn their heads as he passed. The arch of Number Thirteen, the house he sought, was close at hand when the pursuit came stamping round the corner behind him; he heard their cries as he slipped in through the half-open gate of the arch. The chance that had brought him hither was true to him yet, for there was no dvornik on watch; the man had chosen that moment of all others to step over to gossip with his neighbor of Number Fifteen.

He paused in the blackness of the courtyard to listen whether the pursuit would pass by, and heard it arrive outside the gate, jangling with voices. It had gathered up the dvornik on its way. Waters, with a hand upon the door that opened to the staircase, heard the brisk voice of the policeman questioning him in curt spurts of speech, and the dvornik's answers. "Of course, he might have gone in. There is an Amerikanka here, from the Consulate, and he might have gone to her." Then the policeman, cutting the knot: "We'll soon see about that!" He waited no longer, but entered and darted up the stair; he must at all costs not be caught before he got to Miss Pilgrim.

It was the thought of her and the expectation of her welcome to the barren room that made him smile as he climbed. Muddy, penniless and hunted, he knew himself for one that brought gifts; he was going to make her rich with the sense of power and benevolence. He was half-way up the second flight, at the head of which she lived, when he heard the policeman and his following of citizens enter below him and the stamp of their firm ascending feet on the lower steps. He took the remaining stairs three at a time. Upon the landing, the door of the flat stood ajar.

Gently, with precautions not to be heard below, he pushed it open, uncovering the remembered view of the furniture-cluttered passage, with the doors of rooms opening from it and the kitchen door at the end. The kitchen door was closed now; there was no sound anywhere within the place. Nearest to him, on the left of the passage, the door of the room in which he had drunk tea was open and dark.

He tapped nervously with his nails upon the door, hearing from below the approaching footsteps of the hunters.

"Miss Pilgrim," he called in a loud whisper along the passage. "Miss Pilgrim!"

The bell-push was a button somewhere in the woodwork and he could not find it. He tapped and whispered again. The others were at the foot of the second flight now; in a couple of seconds the turn of the staircase would let them see him, and he would be captured and dragged away from her very threshold. He had a last agony of hesitation, an impulse swiftly tasted and rejected, to try a rush down the stairs and a fight to get through and away; and then he stepped into the flat and eased the door to behind him. Its patent lock latched itself with a small click unheard by the party whose feet clattered on the stone steps.

There was a clock somewhere in the dwelling that ticked pompously and monotonously, and no other sound. Standing inside the door, in that hush of the house, he was oppressed by a sense of shameful trespass; he glanced with trepidation towards the kitchen, dreading to see someone come forth and shriek at the sight of him. Supposing Miss Pilgrim were out! Then from the landing came a smart insistent knock upon the door, and within the flat a bell woke and shrilled vociferously. He turned; the room that was always to be ready was at his side, and he fled on tiptoe into its darkness.

He got himself clear of the door, moving with extended hands across its creaking parquet till he touched the cold smoothness of the tiled stove, and freezing to immobility as he heard the kitchen door open. Quick footsteps advanced along the passage; to him, checking, his breath in the dark, listening with every nerve taut, it was as though he saw her, the serene poise of her body as she walked, the pathetic confidence of her high-held head, so distinctive and personal was even the noise of her tread on the boards. Presently, when she had sent the policeman away, he would see her and make her the gift of his request and watch her face as she received it from him.

The latch clicked back under her hand, and she was standing in the entry, confronting the policeman and his backing of citizens.

"Yes?" he heard her say, with a note of surprise at the sight of them. "Yes? What is it?"

The policeman's voice, with the official rasp in it, answered, spitting facts as brief as curses. "Man evading arrest aggravated assault believed to be a certain American apparently escaped this direction." It was like a telegram talking. Then, from his escort, a corroborating gabble.

He could imagine her look of rather puzzled eagerness. "An American?" she exclaimed. Then, as she realized it and its possibilities possibly also the fact that already when an American was sought for it was to her door that they came "oh!"

"Require you to produce him," injected the policeman, "if here! He is here yes?"

"No," she answered; "nobody has come here yet."

There seemed to be a check at that; the effect of her, standing in the doorway, made insistence difficult. The loud clock ticked on, and, at the background of the whole affair, the citizens on the landing maintained a subdued and unremarked murmur among themselves.

"He came this way," observed the policeman tenaciously. "He was seen to pass the next house." And a voice chimed in, melancholy, plaintive, evidently the voice of the dvornik who had been discovered absent from his post: "Yes, I saw him."

"Well," Miss Pilgrim seemed a little at a loss. "He's not here." She paused. "I have two rooms here," she added; "this" she must be pointing to the dark open door beside her "and my bedroom. You can look in this room, if that is what you want."

Waters heard the answering yap of the policeman and the shuffle of feet. He turned in panic; there was no time to reason with events. A step, and his groping hands were against that inner door, which yielded to their touch. Even in the chaos of his wits, he was aware of that subtle odor he had perceived before, that elusive fragrance which seemed a very emanation of chaste girlhood and virgin delicacy. He was inside, leaving the door an inch ajar, as the switch clicked in the outer room and a narrow jet of light stabbed through the opening.

"You see, there is nobody," Miss Pilgrim was saying.

The citizens, faithful to the trial, had crowded in. The policeman grunted doubtfully.

Waters, easing his breath noiselessly, let his eyes wander. The streak of light lay across the floor and up over the counterpane of a narrow wooden bed, then climbed the wall across the face of a picture to the ceiling. Beyond its illumination, there were dim shapes of a dressing-table and a wash-hand-stand, and there were dresses hanging on the wall beside him behind a sheet draped from a shelf. A window, high and double-paned, gave on the courtyard. Through it he could see the lights shining in curtained windows opposite.

"That?" It was Miss Pilgrim answering some question. "That is my bedroom. No; you must not go in there!"

There was a hush and a citizen said "Ah!" loudly and knowingly. Waters, listening intently, frowned.

"I must look," said the policeman curtly.

"But" her voice came from near the door, as though she were standing before it, barring the way to them, "you certainly shall not look. It is my bedroom, and even if your man had come here" she broke off abruptly. "You see he is not here," she added.

"I must look," repeated the policeman in exactly the same tone as before. "It is necessary."

"No," she said. "You must take my word. If you do not, I shall complain tomorrow morning to the consul and to the Chief of Police and you shall be punished."

"H'm!" The policeman was in doubt; she had spoken with a plain effect of meaning what she said, and a policeman's head upon a charger is a small sacrifice for a courteous Chief to offer to a lady friend. He tried to be reasonable with her.

"It was because he was seen to come this way," he argued. "He passed the next house and the dvornik this man here! saw him. He had committed an assault, an aggravated assault, on an istvostchik and evaded arrest. And he came this way."

"He is not here, though," replied Miss Pilgrim steadily. "Nobody at all has been here this evening. I give you my word."

The Russian phrase she used was "chestnoe slovo," "upon my honorable word." Waters caught his breath and listened anxiously.

"I give you my honorable word that he is not here," she affirmed deliberately.

"Now what do you know about that?" exclaimed Waters helplessly.

From the rear of the room somebody piped up acutely: "Then why may the policeman not look, since nobody is there?" Murmurs of agreement supported the questioner.

Miss Pilgrim did not answer. It was to Waters as though she and the policeman stood, estimating each other, measuring strength and capacity. The policeman grunted.

"Well," he said, "since you say, upon your honorable word but I must report the matter, you understand." He paused and there followed the rustle of paper as he produced and opened his notebook.

"Your names?" he demanded.

"Certainly," agreed Miss Pilgrim, in a voice of extreme formality. But she moved to the bedroom door and drew it conclusively shut before she replied.

Waters drew deep breaths and shifted his weight from one foot to the other. From the farther room he could hear now no more than confused and inarticulate murmurings; but he was not curious about the rest. He knew just what was going on the fatuous interrogatory as to name, surname, age, birthplace, nationality, father, mother, trade, married or single, civil status, and all the rest of the rigmarole involved in every contact with the Russian police. He had seen it many times and endured it himself often enough. Just now he had another matter to think of.

"Honorable word!" he repeated. "It's a wonder she couldn't find something different to say. Now I got to fool her. I got to, I."

The window showed him the pit of the courtyard; its frame was not yet caulked with cotton-wool and sealed with brown paper for the winter. He got it open and leaned out, feeling to either side for a spout, a pipe, anything that would give him handhold to climb down by. There was nothing of the kind; but directly below him he could make out the mass of the great square stack of furnace-wood built against the wall. From the sill to the top of the stack was a drop of full twenty feet.

He measured it with his eyes as best he could in the darkness. It was a chance, a not impossible one, but ugly enough. At any rate, it was the only one, if he were to get out and leave that "honorable word" untarnished. It never occurred to him that she might take it less seriously than he.

Waters, who dreamed, who stood by and gazed when life became turbulent and vivid, did not hesitate now. There was time for nothing but action, if he was to substitute a worthy sacrifice for his spoiled gift.

Seated upon the sill, he managed to draw the inner window shut and to latch it through the ventilating pane; the outer one he had to leave swinging and trust that she might find or not demand an explanation for it. This done, he was left, with his back to the house, seated upon the sill, a ledge perhaps a foot wide, with his legs swinging above the twenty-foot drop. In order to make it with a chance for safety, he had so to change his posture that he could hang by his hands from the sill, thus reducing the sheer fall by some six feet.

The dull windows of the courtyard watched him like stagnant eyes as, leaning aside, he labored to turn and lower himself. His experience at sea and upon the gantries in the yards should have helped him; but the past days, with their chill and insufficient food, had done their work on nerve and muscle, and he was still straining to turn and get his weight on to his hands when he slipped.

In the outer room, the catechism was running, or crawling, its ritual course.

"Father's nationality?" the policeman was inquiring, with his notebook upheld to the light and! a stub of flat pencil poised for the answer. A noise from the courtyard reached him. "What's that?" he inquired.

"Sounds like wood slipping off the stack," volunteered a citizen, and the dvornik, whose business it had been to pile it, and who had trouble enough on his hands already, sighed and drooped.

"American, of course," replied Miss Pilgrim patiently.

Below in the courtyard, Waters sat up and raised a hand to where something wet and warm was running down his cheek from under his hair, and found that it hurt his wrist when he did so. He rose stiffly, cursing to himself at the pain it caused him. Above him, the windows of the room that was always to be ready and waiting were broad and bright and heads were visible against them. He felt himself carefully and discovered that he could walk.

"Huh! Me for the roads goin' south outta this," he soliloquized, as he hobbled towards the gate; "an' startin' right now!"

He paused at the entry to the arch and looked back at the windows again.

"Honorable word!" he repeated bitterly, nursing his injured wrist. "Wouldn't that jar you?"

He moved out through the gale slowly and painfully.

XI

THE CONNOISSEUR

The office of the machine-tool agency, where Mr. Baruch sat bowed and intent over his desk, was still as a chapel upon that afternoon of early autumn; the pale South Russian sun, shining full upon its windows, did no more than touch with color the sober shadows of the place. From the single room of the American Vice-Consulate, across the narrow staircase-landing without, there came to Mr. Baruch the hum of indistinguishable voices that touched his consciousness without troubling it. Then, suddenly, with a swell-organ effect, as though a door had been flung open between him and the speakers, he heard a single voice that babbled and faltered in noisy shrill anger.

"Out o' this! Out o' this!" It was the unmistakable voice of Selby, the vice-consul, whose routine day was incomplete without a quarrel. "Call yourself an American you? Coming in here."

The voice ceased abruptly. Mr. Baruch, at his desk, moved slightly like one who disposes of a trivial interruption, and bent again to the matter before him. Between his large, white hands, each decorated with a single ring, he held a small oblong box, the size of a cigar-case, of that blue lacquer of which Russian craftsmen once alone possessed the secret. Battered now by base uses, tarnished and abraded here and there, it preserved yet, for such eyes as those of Mr. Baruch, clues to its ancient delicacy of surface and the glory of its sky-rivaling blue. He had found it an hour before upon a tobacconist's counter, containing matches, and had bought it for a few kopeks; and now, alone in his office, amid his catalogues of lathes and punches, he was poring over it, reading it as another man might read poetry, inhaling from it all that the artist, its maker, had breathed into it.

There was a telephone at work in the Vice-Consulate now a voice speaking in staccato bursts, pausing between each for the answer. Mr. Baruch sighed gently, lifting the box for the light to slide upon its surface. He was a large man, nearing his fiftieth year, and a quiet self-security a quality of being at home in the world was the chief of his effects. Upon the wide spaces of his face, the little and neat features were grouped concisely, a nose boldly curved but small and well modeled, a mouth at once sensuous and fastidious, and eyes steadfast and benign. A dozen races between the Caspian and the Vistula had fused to produce this machine-tool agent, and over the union of them there was spread, like a preservative varnish, the smoothness of an imperturbable placidity.

Footsteps crossed the landing, and there was a loud knock on his door. Before Mr. Baruch, deliberate always, could reply, it was pushed open and

Selby, the vice-consul, his hair awry, his glasses askew on the high, thin bridge of his nose, and with all his general air of a maddened bird, stood upon the threshold.

"Ah, Selby, it is you, my friend!" remarked Mr. Baruch pleasantly. "And you wish to see me yes?"

Selby advanced into the room, saving his eyeglasses by a sudden clutch.

"Say, Baruch," he shrilled, "here's the devil of a thing! This place gets worse every day. Feller comes into my office, kind of a peddler, selling rugs and carpets and shows a sort of passport; Armenian, I guess, or a Persian, or something; and when I tell him to clear out, if he doesn't go and throw a kind of a fit right on my floor!"

"Ah!" said Mr. Baruch sympathetically. "A fit yes? You have telephoned for the gorodski pomosh the town ambulance?"

"Yes," said Selby; "at least, I had Miss Pilgrim do that, my clerk, you know."

"Yes," said Mr. Baruch; "I know Miss Pilgrim. Well, I will come and see your peddler man." He rose. "But first see what I have been buying for myself, Selby." He held out the little battered box upon his large, firm palm. "You like it? I gave forty kopeks for it to a man who would have taken twenty. It is nice yes?"

Selby gazed vaguely. "Very nice," he said perfunctorily. "I used to buy 'em, too, when I came here first."

Mr. Baruch smiled that quiet, friendly smile of his, and put the box carefully into a drawer of his desk.

The American Vice-Consulate at Nikolaief was housed in a single great room lighted by a large window at one end overlooking the port and the wharves, so that, entering from the gloom of the little landing, one looked along the length of it as towards the mouth of a cave. Desks, tables, a copying-press and a typewriter were all its gear; it was a place as avidly specialized for its purpose as an iron foundry, but now, for the moment, it was redeemed from its everyday barrenness by the two figures upon the floor near the entrance.

The peddler lay at full length, a bundle of strange travel-wrecked clothes, suggesting a lay figure in his limp inertness and the loose sprawl of his limbs. Beside him on the boards, trim in white blouse and tweed skirt, kneeled the vice-consul's clerk, Miss Pilgrim. She had one arm under the man's head, and with the other was drawing towards her his fallen bundle of rugs to serve as a pillow. As she bent, her gentle face, luminously fair, was over the swart, clenched countenance of the unconscious man, whose stagnant eyes seemed set on her in an unwinking stare.

Mr. Baruch bent to help her place the bundle in position. She lifted her face to him in recognition. Selby, fretting to and fro, snorted.

"Blamed if I'd have touched him," he said. "Most likely he never saw soap in his life. A hobo that's what he is just a hobo."

Miss Pilgrim gave a little deprecating smile and stood up. She was a slight girl, serious and gentle, and half her waking life was spent in counteracting the effects of Selby 's indigestion and ill-temper. Mr. Baruch was still stooping to the bundle of rugs.

"Oh, that'll be all right, Mr. Baruch," she assured him. "He's quite comfortable now."

Mr. Baruch, still stooping, looked up at her.

"I am seeing the kind of rugs he has," he answered. "I am interested in rugs. You do not know rugs no?"

"No," replied Miss Pilgrim.

"Ah! This, now, is out of Persia, I think," said Mr. Baruch, edging one loose from the disordered bundle. "Think!" he said. "This poor fellow, lying here he is Armenian. How many years has he walked, carrying his carpets and rugs, all the way down into Persia, selling and changing his goods in bazaars and caravanserais, and then back over the Caucasus and through the middle of the Don Cossacks all across the Black Lands carrying the rugs till he comes to throw his fit on Mr. Selby's floor! It is a strange way to live, Miss Pilgrim, yes?"

"Ye-es," breathed Miss Pilgrim. "Ye-es."

He smiled at her. He had a corner of the rug unfolded now and draped over his bent knee. His hand stroked it delicately; the blank light from the window let its coloring show in its just values. Mr. Baruch, with the dregs of his smile yet curving his lips, scanned it without too much appearance of interest. He was known for a "collector," a man who gathered things that others disregarded, and both Miss Pilgrim and Selby watched him with the respect of the laity for the initiate. But they could not discern or share the mounting ecstasy of the connoisseur, of the spirit which is to the artist what the wife is to the husband, as he realized the truth and power of the coloring, its stained-glass glow, the justice and strength of the patterning and the authentic silk-and-steel of the texture.

"Is it any good?" asked Selby suddenly. "I've heard of 'em being worth a lot sometimes thousands of dollars!"

"Sometimes," agreed Mr. Baruch. "Those you can see in museums. This one, now I would offer him twenty rubles for it, and I would give perhaps thirty if he bargained too hard. That is because I have a place for it in my house."

"And he'd probably make a hundred per cent, on it at that," said Selby. "These fellows."

The loud feet of the ambulance men on the stairs interrupted him. Mr. Baruch, dragging the partly unfolded rugs with him, moved away as the white clad doctor and his retinue of stretcher-bearers came in at the door, with exactly the manner of the mere spectator who makes room for people more directly concerned. He saw the doctor kneel beside the prostrate man and Miss Pilgrim hand him one of the office tea-glasses; then, while all crowded round to watch the process of luring back the strayed soul of the peddler, he had leisure to assure himself again of the quality of his find. The tea-glass clinked against clenched teeth. "A spoon, somebody!" snapped the doctor. The cramped throat gurgled painfully; but Mr. Baruch, slave to the delight of the eye, was unheeding. A joy akin to love, pervading and rejoicing his every faculty, had possession of him. The carpet was all he had deemed it and more, the perfect expression in its medium of a fine and pure will to beauty.

The peddler on the floor behind him groaned painfully and tatters of speech formed on his lips.

"That's better," said the doctor encouragingly.

Mr. Baruch dropped the rug and moved quietly towards the group.

The man was conscious again; a stretcher-bearer, kneeling behind him, was holding him in a half sitting posture, and Mr. Baruch watched with interest how the tide of returning intelligence mounted in the thin mask of his face. He was an Armenian by every evidence, an effect of weather-beaten pallor appearing through dense masses of coal-black beard and hair one of those timid and servile off-scourings of civilization whose wandering lives are daily epics of horrid peril and adventure. His pale eyes roved here and there as he lay against the stretcher-bearer's knee.

"Well," said the doctor, rising and dusting his hands one against the other, "we won't need the stretcher. Two of you take him under his arms and help him up."

The burly Russian ambulance men hoisted him easily enough and stood supporting him while he hung between them weakly. Still his eyes wandered, seeking dumbly in the big room. The doctor turned to speak to the vice-consul, and Miss Pilgrim moved forward to the sick man.

"Yes?" she questioned, in her uncertain Russian. "Yes? What is it?"

He made feeble sounds, but Mr. Baruch heard no shaped word. Miss Pilgrim, however, seemed to understand.

"Oh, your rugs!" she answered. "They're all here, quite safe." She pointed to the bundle, lying where it had been thrust aside. "Quite safe, you see."

Mr. Baruch said no word. The silken carpet that he had removed was out of sight upon the farther side of the big central table of the office. The peddler groaned again and murmured; Miss Pilgrim bent forward to give ear. Mr. Baruch, quietly and deliberately as always, moved to join the conference of the doctor and Selby. He was making a third to their conversation when Miss Pilgrim turned.

"One more?" she was saying. "Is there one more? Mr. Baruch, did you— Oh, there it is!"

She moved across to fetch it. The peddler's eyes followed her slavishly. Mr. Baruch smiled.

"Yes?" he said. "Oh, that carpet! He wants to sell it yes?"

"He isn't fit to do any bargaining yet," replied Miss Pilgrim, and Mr. Baruch nodded agreeably.

The doctor and Selby finished their talk, and the former came back into the group.

"Well, take him down to the ambulance," he bade the men.

They moved to obey, but the sick man, mouthing strange sounds, seemed to try to hang back, making gestures with his head towards the disregarded bundle that was the whole of his earthly wealth.

"What's the matter with him?" cried the doctor impatiently. "Those rugs? Oh, we can't take a hotbed of microbes like that to the hospital! Move him along there!"

"And I'm not going to have 'em here," barked Selby. The peddler, limp between the big stretcher bearers, moaned and seemed to shiver in a vain effort to free himself.

"Wait, please!" Miss Pilgrim came forward. She had been folding the silken rug of Mr. Baruch's choice, and was now carrying it before her. It was as though she wore an apron of dawn gold and sunset red.

The pitiful man rolled meek imploring eyes upon her. She cast down the rug she carried upon the others in their bundle and stood over them.

"I'll take care of them," she said. "They will be safe with me. Do you understand? Me!" She touched herself upon her white-clad bosom with one hand, pointing with the other to the rugs.

The man gazed at her mournfully, resignedly. Martyrdom was the daily bread of his race; oppression had been his apprenticeship to life. It was in the order of things as he knew it that those who had power over him should plunder him; but, facing the earnest girl, with her frank and kindly eyes, some glimmer of hope lighted in his abjectness. He sighed and let his head fall forward in a feeble motion of acquiescence, and the big men who held him took him out and down the stairs to the waiting ambulance.

"Well!" said Selby, as the door closed behind the doctor. "Who wouldn't sell a farm and be a consul. We'd ought to have the place disinfected. What do you reckon to do with that junk, Miss Pilgrim?"

Miss Pilgrim was readjusting the thong that had bound the rugs together.

"Oh, I'll take them home in a droschky, Mr. Selby," she said. "I've got a cupboard in my rooms where they can stay till the poor man gets out of hospital."

"All right," snarled Selby. "It's your troubles." He turned away, but stopped upon a sudden thought. "What about letting Baruch take that rug now?" he asked. "He's offered a price and he can pay it to you."

"Certainly," agreed Mr. Baruch. "I can pay the cash to Miss Pilgrim and she can pay it to the poor man. He will perhaps be glad to have some cash at once when he comes out."

Miss Pilgrim, kneeling beside the pack of rugs, looked doubtfully from one to the other. Mr. Baruch returned her gaze benignly. Selby, as always, had the affronted air of one who is prepared to be refused the most just and moderate demand.

"Why," she began hesitatingly, "I suppose-" Then Selby had to strike in.

"Aren't worrying because you said you'd look after the stuff yourself, are you?" he jeered.

Mr. Baruch's expression did not alter by so much as a twitch; there was no outward index of his impulse to smite the blundering man across the mouth.

The hesitancy upon Miss Pilgrim's face dissolved in an instant and she positively brightened.

"Of course," she said happily. "What can I have been thinking of? When the poor man comes out Mr. Baruch can make his own bargain with him; but till then I promised!"

Selby, with slipping glasses awry on his' nose, gaped at her.

"Promised!" he repeated. "That that hobo."

Mr. Baruch intervened.

"But, Selby, my friend, Miss Pilgrim is quite right. She promised; and it is only two or three days to wait, and also it is not the only rug in the world. Though," he added generously, "it is a nice rug yes?"

Miss Pilgrim smiled at him gratefully; Selby shrugged, and just caught his glasses as the shrug shook them loose.

"Fix it to suit yourselves," he snarled, and moved away toward his untidy desk by the window.

The pale autumn sun had dissolved in watery splendors as Mr. Baruch, with the wide astrakhan collar of his overcoat turned up about his ears, walked easily homeward in the brisk evening chill. There were lights along the wharves, and the broad waters of the port, along which his road lay, were freckled with the spark-like lanterns on the ships, each with its little shimmer of radiance reflected from the stream. Commonly, as he strolled, he saw it all with gladness; the world and the fullness thereof were ministers of his pleasure; but upon this night he saw it absently, with eyes that dwelt beyond it all. Outwardly, he was the usual Mr. Baruch; his slightly sluggish benevolence of demeanor was unchanged as he returned the salute of a policeman upon a corner, but inwardly he was like a man uplifted by good news. The sense of pure beauty, buried in his being, stirred like a rebellious slave. Those arabesques, that coloring, that texture thrilled him like a gospel.

It was in the same mood of abstraction that he let himself into his flat in the great German-built apartment-house that overlooked the "boulevard" and the thronged river. He laid aside his overcoat in the little hall, conventional with its waxed wood and its mirror, clicked an electric-light switch and passed through a portiere into the salon, which was the chief room of his abode. A large room, oblong and high-ceilinged, designed by a man with palace architecture that obsession of the Russian architect on the brain. He advanced to it, still with that vagueness of sense, and stopped, looking round him.

It was part of the effect which Mr. Baruch made upon those who came into contact with him that few suspected him of a home, a domesticity of his own; he was so complete, so compactly self-contained, without appanages of that kind. Here, however, was the frame of his real existence, which contained it as a frame contains a picture and threw it into relief. The great room, under the strong lights, showed the conventional desert of polished parquet floor, with sparse furniture grouped about it. There was an ivory-inlaid stand with a Benares brass tray; a Circassian bridal linen-chest stood against a wall; the tiles of the stove in the corner illustrated the life and martyrdom of Saint Tikhon. Upon another wall was a trophy of old Cossack swords. Before the linen-chest there stood a trunk of the kind that every Russian housemaid takes with her to her employment a thing of bent birchwood, fantastically painted in strong reds and blues. One buys such things for the price of a cocktail.

Mr. Baruch stood, looking round him at the room. Everything in it was of his choosing, the trophy of some moment or some hour of delight. He had selected his own background.

"Ah Samuel!"

He turned, deliberate always. Between the portieres that screened the opposite doorway there stood the supreme "find" of his collection. Somewhere or other, between the processes of becoming an emperor in the machine-tool trade of southern Russia and an American citizen, Mr. Baruch so complete in himself, so perfect an entity had added to himself a wife. The taste that manifested itself alike on battered blue lacquer and worn prayer-rugs from Persia had not failed him then; he had found a thing perfect of its kind. From the uneasy Caucasus, where the harem-furnishers of Circassia jostle the woman-merchants of Georgia, he had brought back a prize. The woman who stood in the doorway, one strong bare arm uplifted to hold back the stamped leather curtain, was large a great white creature like a moving statue, with a still, blank face framed in banks of shining jet hair. The strong, lights of the chamber shone on her; she stood, still as an image, with large, incurious eyes, looking at him. All the Orient was immanent in her; she had the quiet, the resignation, the un-hope of the odalisque.

"Samuel," she said again.

"Ah, Adina!" And then, in the Circassian idiom, "Grace go before you!"

Her white arm sank and the curtains swelled together behind her. Mr. Baruch took the chief of his treasures into his arms and kissed her.

The room in which presently they dined was tiny, like a cabinet particulier; they sat at food like lovers, with shutters closed upon the windows to defend their privacy. Mr. Baruch ate largely, and his great wife watched him across the table with still satisfaction. The linen of the table had been woven by the nuns of the Lavra at Kiev; the soup-bowls were from Cracow; there was nothing in the place that had not its quality and distinction. And Mr. Baruch fitted it as a snail fits its shell. It was his shell, for, like a snail, he had exuded it from his being and it was part of him.

"I saw a carpet to-day," he said abruptly. There was Black Sea salmon on his plate, and he spoke above a laden fork.

"Yes?" The big, quiet woman did not so much inquire as invite him to continue. Mr. Baruch ate some salmon. "A carpet yes," he said presently. "Real like Diamonds, like you, Adina, I no mistake."

At the compliment, she lowered her head and raised it again in a motion like a very slow nod. Mr. Baruch finished his salmon without further words.

"And?" Upon her unfinished question he looked up.

"Yes," he said; "surely! In a few days I shall bring it home."

Her large eyes, the docile eyes of the slave-wife, acclaimed him. For her there were no doubts, no judgments; the husband was the master, the god of the house. Mr. Baruch continued his meal to its end.

"And now," he said presently, when he had finished, "you will go to bed."

She stood up forthwith, revealing again her majestic stature and pose. Mr. Baruch sat at his end of the table with his tiny cup of coffee and his thimble-like glass before him. He lifted his eyes and gazed at her appreciatively, and, for a moment, there lighted in his face a reflection of what Selby and Miss Pilgrim might have seen in it, had they known how to look, when first he realized the silken glories of the carpet. The woman, returning his gaze, maintained her pale, submissive calm.

"Blessings upon you!" he said, dismissing her.

She lowered her splendid head in instant obedience.

"Blessings," she replied, "and again blessings! Have sweet sleep, lord and husband!"

He sat above his coffee and his liqueur and watched her superb body pass forth from the little room. She did not turn to look back; they are not trained to coquetry, those chattel-women of the Caucasus. Mr. Baruch smiled while he let the sweetish and violently strong liqueur roll over his tongue and the assertively fragrant coffee possess his senses. His wife was a "find," a thing perfect of its sort, that satisfied his exigent taste; and now again he was to thrill with the joy of acquisition. There were rugs in the room where he sat one draped over a settee, another hanging upon the wall opposite him, one underfoot each fine and singular in its manner He passed an eye over them and then ceased to sec them. His benevolent face, with all its suggestive reserve and its quiet shrewdness, fell vague with reverie. It was in absence of mind rather than in presence of appetite that he helped himself for the fourth time to the high-explosive liqueur from the old Vilna decanter; and there flashed into sight before him, the clearer for the spur with which the potent drink rowelled his consciousness, the vision of the silk carpet, its glow, as though fire were mixed with the dyes of it, the faultless Tightness and art of its pattern, the soul-ensnaring perfection of the whole.

It was some hours later that he looked into his wife's room on his way to his own. She was asleep, her quiet head cushioned upon the waves of her hair. Mr. Baruch, half-burned cigar between his teeth, stood and gazed at her. Her face, wiped clean of its powder, was white as paper, with that deathlike whiteness which counts as beauty in Circassia; only the shadows of her eyelids and the broad red of her lips stained her pallor. Across her breast the red and blue hem of the quilt lay like a scarf.

Mr. Baruch looked at the arrangement critically. He was a connoisseur in perfection, and something was lacking. It eluded him for a moment or two and then, suddenly, like an inspiration, he perceived it. The rug the thing delicate as silk, with its sheen, its flush of hues, with the white slumbering face above it! The picture, the perfect thing he saw it!

The woman in the bed stirred and murmured.

"Blessings upon you," said Mr. Baruch, and smiled as he turned away.

"Bl-essings," she murmured sleepily, without opening her eyes, and sighed and lay still once more.

The heart of man is a battle-ground where might is always right and victory is always to the strongest of the warring passions. And even a saint's passion to holiness is hardly stronger, more selfless, more disregardful of conditions and obstacles than the passion of the lover of the beautiful, the connoisseur, toward acquisition. In the days that followed, Mr. Baruch, walking his quiet ways about the city, working in the stillness of his office, acquired the sense that the carpet, by the mere force of his desire, was somehow due to him a thing only momentarily out of his hands, like one's brief loan to a friend. Presently it would come his way and be his; and it belongs to his sense of security in his right that not once, not even when he remembered it most avidly, did he think of the expedient of buying it from the sick peddler by paying him the value of it.

Another man would probably have gone forthwith to Selby, told him the secret, and enlisted his aid; but Mr. Baruch did not work like that. He allowed chance a week in which to show its reasonableness; and not till then, nothing having happened, did he furnish himself, one afternoon, with an excuse, in the form of a disputed customs charge, and cross the narrow landing to the American Vice-Consulate.

Selby was there alone at his disorderly desk by the window, fussing feebly among the chaos of his tumbled papers, and making a noise of desperation with his lips like a singing kettle.

"Ah, Selby, my friend!" Mr. Baruch went smilingly forward. "You work always too much. And now come I with a little other thing for you. It is too bad yes?"

"Hallo, Baruch!" returned Selby. "You're right about the working. Here I keep a girl to keep my papers in some kind of a sort of order and I been hunting and digging for an hour to find one of 'em. It gets me what she thinks I pay her for! Hoboes an' that kind o' trash, that's her style."

Mr. Baruch had still his agreeable, mild smile, which was as much a part of his daily wear as his trousers. He could not have steered the talk to better purpose.

"Hoboes?" he said vaguely. "Trash?"

Selby exploded in weak, sputtering fury, and, as always, his glasses canted on the high, thin bridge of his nose and waggled in time to each jerk of words.

"It's that hobo, you saw him, Baruch, that pranced in here and threw a fit and a lot of old carpets all over my floor. Armenian or some such thing! Well, they took him to the hospital and this afternoon he hadn't got more sense than to send a message over here."

Mr. Baruch nodded.

"Ah, to Miss Pilgrim, yes? because of her very kind treatment."

Selby caught his glasses as they fell.

"Huh!" he sneered malevolently. "You'd have to be a hobo before you'd get kindness from her. Hard-luck stories is the only kind she believes. 'I'll have to go, Mr. Selby,' she says. And she goes—and here's me hunting and pawing around—"

"Yes," agreed Mr. Baruch; "it is inconvenient. So I will come back tomorrow with my matter, when you shall have more time. Then the poor man, he is worse or better?"

"You don't suppose I been inquiring after him, do you?" squealed Selby.

"No," replied Mr. Baruch equably, "I do not suppose that, Selby, my friend."

The street in which Miss Pilgrim had her rooms was one of the long gullies of high-fronted architecture running at right angles to the river, and thither portly, handsomely overcoated, with the deliberateness of a balanced and ordered mind in every tread of his measured gait went Mr. Baruch. He had no plan; his resource and personality would not fail him in an emergency, and it was time he brought them to bear. One thing he was sure of he would take the carpet home that night.

At the head of two flights of iron-railed stone stairs, he reached the door of the flat which he sought. Two or three attempts upon the bell-push brought no response, and he could hear no sound of life through the door. He waited composedly. It did not enter his head that all the occupants might be out; and he was right, for presently, after he had thumped on the door with his gloved fist, there was a slip-slap of feet within and a sloven of a woman opened to him.

Mr. Baruch gave her his smile.

"The American lady is in? I wish to speak to her." The woman stood aside hastily to let him enter. "Say Gaspodin Baruch is here," he directed blandly.

It was a narrow corridor, flanked with doors, in which he stood. The woman knocked at the nearest of these, opened it, and spoke his name. Immediately from within he heard the glad, gentle voice of the consul's clerk.

"Surely!" it answered the servant in Russian; then called in English, "Come in, Mr. Baruch, please!"

He removed his hat and entered. An unshaded electric-light bulb filled the room with crude light, stripping its poverty and tawdriness naked to the eye its bamboo furniture, its imitation parquet, and the cheap distemper of its walls. But of these Mr. Baruch was only faintly aware, for in the middle of the floor, with brown paper and string beside her, Miss Pilgrim knelt amid a kaleidoscope of tumbled rugs, and in her hand, half folded already, was the rug.

She was smiling up at him with her mild, serene face, while under her thin, pale hands lay the treasure.

"Now this is nice of you, Mr. Baruch," she was saying. "I suppose Mr. Selby told you I'd had to go out."

Mr. Baruch nodded. He had let his eyes rest on the rug for a space of seconds, and then averted them.

"Yes," he said. "He said it was some message about the poor man who was ill, and I think he was angry."

"Angry?" Miss Pilgrim's smile faded. "I'm, I'm sorry for that."

"So," continued Mr. Baruch, "as I have to go by this way, I think I will call to see if I can help. It was some paper Mr. Selby cannot find, I think."

"Some paper?" Miss Pilgrim pondered. "You don't know which it was?"

Mr. Baruch shook his head regretfully. Between them the rug lay and glowed up at him.

"You see," continued Miss Pilgrim, "it's this way, Mr. Baruch. That poor man in the hospital doesn't seem to be getting any better yet, and he's evidently fretting about his rugs. They're probably all he's got in the world. So this afternoon they telephoned up from the hospital to say he wanted me to send down one in particular, the thinnest one of them all. That's this one!"

She showed it to him, her fingers feeling its edge. There was wonder in his mind that the mere contact of it did not tell her of its worth.

"I'm afraid it's the one you wanted to buy," she said. "The one you said was worth thirty rubles. Well, of course, it's his, and since he wanted it I had to get it for him. I couldn't do anything else, could I, Mr. Baruch?"

Mr. Baruch agreed.

"It is very kind treatment," he approved. "So now you pack it in a parcel and take it to the hospital before you go back to find Mr. Selby's paper yes? Mr. Selby will be glad."

A pucker of worry appeared between the girl's frank brows and she fell swiftly to folding and packing the rug.

"If if only he hasn't left the office before I got there!" she doubted.

Mr. Baruch picked up the string and prepared to assist with the packing.

"Perhaps he will not be gone," he said consolingly. "He was so angry I think the paper would be important, and he would stay to find it yes?" Miss Pilgrim did not seem cheered by this supposition. "Well," said Mr. Baruch then, "if it should be a help to you and the poor man, I can take this parcel for you and leave it in the gate of the hospital when I go past this evening."

He had a momentary tremor as he made the proposal, but it was not doubt that it would be accepted or fear lest his purpose should show through it. He felt neither of these; it was the thrill of victory that he had to keep out of his tone and his smile.

For it was victory. Miss Pilgrim beamed at him thankfully.

"Oh, Mr. Baruch, you are kind!" she cried. "I didn't like to ask you, but you must be a thought reader. If you'd just hand it in for Doctor Semianoff, he'll know all about it, and I can get back to Mr. Selby at once. And thank you ever so much, Mr. Baruch!"

"But," protested Mr. Baruch, "it is a little thing—it is nothing. And it is much pleasure to me to do this for you and the poor man. Tonight he will have it, and tomorrow perhaps he will be better."

They went down the stairs together and bade each other a friendly good night in the gateway.

"And I'm ever so much obliged to you, Mr. Baruch," said Miss Pilgrim again, her pale face shining in the dusk.

Mr. Baruch put a fatherly hand on her sleeve.

"Hush! You must not say it," he said. "It is I that am happy."

Half an hour later, he found what he sought in a large furniture store on the Pushkinskaia, an imitation Persian rug, manufactured at Frankfurt, and priced seventeen rubles. With a little bargaining the salesman was no match for Mr. Baruch, at that he got it for fifteen and a half. He himself directed the packing of it, to see that no store-label was included in the parcel; and a quarter of an hour later he delivered it by cab to the dvornik at the hospital gate for Doctor Semianoff. Then he drove homeward; he could not spare the time to walk while the bundle he held in his arms was yet unopened nor its treasure housed in his home.

His stratagem was perfect. Even if the Armenian were to make an outcry, who would lend him an ear?

It would appear it could easily be made to appear that he was endeavoring to extort money from Miss Pilgrim upon a flimsy pretext that a worthless rug had been substituted for a valuable one, and the police would know how to deal with him. Mr. Baruch put the matter behind him contentedly.

The majestic woman in his home watched him impassively as he unpacked his parcel and spread the rug loosely across a couple of chairs in the salon. In actual words he said only: "This is the carpet, Adina, for your bed. Look at it well!" She looked obediently, glancing from it to his face, her own still with its unchanging calm, and wondered dully in her sex-specialized brain at the light of rapture in his countenance. He pored upon it, devouring its rareness of beauty, the sum and the detail of its perfection, with a joy as pure, an appreciation as generous, as if he had not stolen it from under the hands of a sick pauper and a Good Samaritan.

That night he stood at the door of his wife's room. "Blessings upon you!" he said, and smiled at her in acknowledgment of the blessings she returned. A brass-and-glass lantern contained the electric light in the chamber; it shone softly on all the apparatus of toilet and slumber, and upon the picture that was Mr. Baruch's chief work of art the marble-white face thrown into high relief by the unbound black hair and the colors, like a tangle of softened and subdued rainbows, that flowed from her bosom to the foot of the bed. He crossed the floor and bent and kissed her where she lay.

"Wonderful!" he said to her. "You are a question, an eternal question. And here" his hand moved on the surface of the rug like a caress "is the answer to you. Two perfect things two perfect things!"

"Blessings!" she murmured.

"I have them," he said; "two of them," and he laughed and left her.

He did not see Miss Pilgrim the following day or the next; that was easy for him to contrive, for much of his business was done outside his office. It was not that he had any fear of meeting her; but it was more agreeable to his feelings not to be reminded of her part in the acquisition of the carpet. Upon the third day, he was late in arriving, for his wife had complained at breakfast of headache and sickness, and he had stayed to comfort her and see her back to bed for a twenty-four hours' holiday from life. On his way he had stopped at a florist's to send her back some flowers.'

He was barely seated at his desk when there was a knock upon his door and Miss Pilgrim entered.

He smiled his usual pleasant welcome at her.

"Ah, Miss Pilgrim, good morning, I am glad to see you. You will sit down yes?"

He was rising to give her a chair he was not in the least afraid of her when something about her arrested him, a trouble, a note of sorrow.

"Mr. Baruch" she began.

He knew the value of the deft interruption that breaks the thread of thought.

"There is something not right?" he suggested. "I hope not." With a manner of sudden concern, he added: "The poor man, he is worse no?"

Miss Pilgrim showed him a stricken face and eyes brimming with tears.

"He's, he's dead!" she quavered.

"See, now!" said Mr. Baruch, shocked. "What a sad thing and after all your kind treatment! I am sorry, Miss Pilgrim; but it is to remember that the poor man has come here through much hardship yes? And at the least, you have given him back his rug to comfort him."

"But" Miss Pilgrim stayed his drift of easy, grave speech with a sort of cry "that's the cause of all the trouble and danger and you only did it to help me. You must come with me to the town clinic at once. Mr. Selby's gone already. There'll be no danger if you come at once."

"Danger?" repeated Mr. Baruch. "I have not understood." But though in all truth he did not understand, a foreboding of knowledge was chill upon him. He cleared his throat. "What did he die of?"

Miss Pilgrim's tears had overflowed. She had a difficulty in speaking. But her stammered words came as clearly to his ears as though they were being shouted.

"Smallpox!"

He sat down heavily in the chair whence he had risen to receive her, and Miss Pilgrim through her tears saw him shrivel in a gust of utter terror. All his mask of complacency, of kindly power, of reticence of spirit fell from him; he gulped, and his mouth sagged slack. She moved a pace nearer to him.

"But it'll be all right, Mr. Baruch, if you'll just come to the clinic at once and be vaccinated. It's only because we touched him and the rugs. There isn't any need to be so frightened."

She could not divine the vision that stood before his strained eyes the white face of a woman, weary with her ailment, and the beautiful thing that blanketed her, beautiful and venomous like a snake. His senses swam. But from his shaking lips two words formed themselves:

"My wife!"

"Oh, come along, Mr. Baruch!" cried Miss Pilgrim. "Your wife hasn't touched the rugs. She'll be perfectly all right!"

He gave her a look that began abjectly but strengthened as it continued to something like a strange sneer. For he was a connoisseur; he knew. And he was certain that Fate would never leave a drama unfinished like that.

XII

THE DAY OF OMENS

The velvet-footed, rat-faced valet moved noiselessly in the bedroom, placing matters in order for his master's toilet. He had drawn the curtains to admit the day and closed the window to bar out its morning freshness, and it was while he was clearing the pockets of the dress clothes that he became aware that from the alcove at his back, in which the bed stood, eyes were watching him. Without hurry, he deposited a little pile of coins on the edge of the dressing-table and laid the trousers aside; then, with his long thief's hands hanging open in obvious innocence, he turned and saw that his master had waked in his usual uncanny fashion, returning from slumber to full consciousness with no interval of drowsiness and half-wakefulness. It was as if he would take the fortunes of the day by surprise. His wonderful white hair, which made him noticeable without ever making him venerable, was tumbled on his head; he looked from his pillow with the immobility and inexpressiveness of a wax figure.

To his valet's murmured "good morning," he frowned slightly, as if in some preoccupation of his thoughts.

"What sort of day is it?" he asked, without replying to the greeting.

"It is fine, M'sieur le Prince," answered the valet; "a beautiful day."

"H'm!" The Prince de Monpavon lifted himself on one silk-sleeved elbow to see for himself. The window was on the west side of the building, so that from the bed one looked as through a tunnel of shadow to a sunlight that hung aloof and distant. He surveyed it for a space of minutes with a face of discontent, then fell back on his pillows.

"Thought it was raining," he remarked. "Something feels wrong about it. What time is it?"

"It is twenty minutes past eleven, M'sieur le Prince," replied the servant. "I will fetch M'sieur le Prince's letters. And M. Dupontel has telephoned."

"Eh?" The Prince's hard eyes came round to him swiftly, but not soon enough to see that movement of his right hand that gave him the appearance of deftly pocketing some small object concealed in the palm of it. "What does he say?"

"He will be here at noon, and hopes that M'sieur le Prince will go to take lunch with him."

The Prince nodded slowly, and the valet, treading always as if noise were a sacrilege, passed out of the room to fetch the letters. The Prince lifted his head to pack the pillow under it more conveniently, and waited in an appearance of deep thought. Under the bedclothes the contour of his body showed long, and slender, and his face, upturned to the canopy of the bed, was one upon which the years of his age had found slight foothold. It had the smooth pallor of a man whose chief activities are indoors: it was wary, nervous, and faintly sinister, with strong, dark eyebrows standing in picturesque contrast to the white hair. The figure he was accustomed to present was that of a man established in life as in a stronghold.

He was neither youthful nor elderly, but mature. Without fortune or rich connections, he had contrived during nearly thirty years to live as a man of wealth; he had seen the game ecarte go out and bridge come in; and had so devised the effect he made that he was still more eminent as a personality than as a gambler. Though he played in many places, he was careful not to win too much in any of them, and rather than press for a debt he would forgive it.

The rat-faced valet reappeared, carrying a salver on which were some half dozen envelopes. The Prince took them, and proceeded to examine them before opening them, while the valet, still with his uncanny noiselessness, continued his interrupted preparations. Two of the letters the Prince tossed to the floor forthwith; he knew them for trifling bills. Of the others, there was one with the name of a Paris hotel printed on the flap which appeared to interest him. He had that common weakness for guessing at a letter before opening it which princes share with scullions; and in the case of this one there was something vaguely familiar in the handwriting to which he could not put a name. He stared at it thoughtfully, and felt again a momentary stirring within him of that ill ease with which he had waked from sleep, which had made him doubt that the day was bright. Like all gamblers, he found significance in things themselves insignificant. Impatiently he abandoned his speculations and tore the envelope open; then turned upon his elbow to look at the signature.

"Parbleu!" he exclaimed.

The valet turned at the sound, but his master had forgotten his existence. The man, his hands still busy inserting studs in a shirt, watched with sidelong glances how the Prince had thrown off his languor and leaned above his letter, startled and absorbed.

"MY DEAR MONPAVON [read the Prince]: For the first time since our parting, nearly a generation ago, I am once more in Paris, of which the very speech has become strange in my mouth. I return as a citizen of the United States, a foreigner; you will perhaps recognize me with difficulty; and I would hardly give you that trouble were it not for the engagement which is outstanding between us an engagement which you will not fail to recall. It was concluded upon that evening on which we saw each other last, when, having lost to you all that remained to me to lose, you offered me my revenge whenever I should choose to come for it. Well, I have come for it. I will call upon you as soon as possible. I hope such visits are still as welcome to you as once they were."

And at the tail of the letter there sprawled the signature, bold and black: "JULES CARIGNY."

"Tiens!" exclaimed the Prince.

The valet moved. "M'sieur le Prince spoke?" he queried.

"No!" said the Prince impatiently. He glanced up from his letter at the man's sly, secret face. "But by the way have you ever heard of a Monsieur Carigny?"

It was with something like the empty shell of a smile that the man answered. "Everybody who knows M'sieur le Prince has heard of him," he said suavely.

"H'm!" the Prince grunted doubtfully, but he knew it was true. Everybody had heard of Carigny and the revenge that was due to him; impossible to refuse it to him now.

There are incidents in every man's life concerning which one can never be sure that they are closed; in such a life as that of the Prince de Monpavon there are many. The affair of Carigny, nearly thirty years before, was one of them. While he stared again at the letter, there rose before the Prince's eyes a vision of the evening upon which they had parted in a great; over-ornate room with card-tables in it, and a hanging chandelier of glass lusters that shivered and made a tinkling bell-music whenever the door opened. It had been a short game. It was a season of high stakes, and Carigny, as a loser, had doubled and doubled till the last quick hand that finished him. He was a slim youth, with a face smooth and pale. He sat back in his chair, with his head hanging, staring with a look of stupefaction at the cards that spelled his ruin, his finish, and his exile. About him, some of the onlookers began to talk loudly to cover his confusion, and their voices seemed to restore him. He blinked and closed his mouth, and sat up. "Well," he said, then, "there's an end of that!"

The Prince had answered with some conventional remark, the insincere regrets of a winner for the loser's ill fortune, and had added something about giving Carigny his revenge.

The other smiled a little and shook his head. "You are very good," he had answered; "but at present that is impossible. Some day, perhaps."

He paused. He had risen from his chair, and, though the evening was yet young, he had the look of a man wearied utterly. All the room was watching him; it was known that he had lost all.

"Whenever you like," the Prince had replied.

Carigny nodded slowly. "It may be a long time," he said. "I can see that it may be years. But, since you are so good, some day we will play once more. It is agreed?"

"Certainly; it is agreed," said the Prince.

Carigny smiled once more. He had a queer, ironic little smile that seemed to mock its own mirth. Then, nodding a good night here and there, he had gone toward the door, tall and a little drooping, between the men who stood aside to give him passage, strangely significant and notable at that final moment. At the door he had turned and looked toward the Prince.

"Au revoir!" he had said.

And the Prince, concerned not to fail in his attitude, not to make the wrong impression upon those who watched, had matched his tone carefully to Carigny's as he replied: "Au revoir!"

The thing had touched men's imaginations. The drama of that promised return, years ahead, had made a story; it had threatened the Prince with notoriety. He had had to live dexterously to escape it to play little and with restraint for many months afterward. It had had to be suffered to exhaust itself, to die lingeringly. It had lain in its grave for nearly thirty years; and now, like a hand reaching out from a tomb, came this letter. The incident was not closed.

"No wonder," said the Prince to himself, as he knotted his necktie before the mirror "no wonder the day felt wrong! There is bad luck in the very air. I must be very careful today."

M. Dupontel, waiting for him in the salon, saw him enter between the folding doors with a face upon which his distaste of the day had cast a shadow. Dupontel was no more than twenty-five, and the Prince was one of his admirations and his most expensive hobby. He rose from his seat, smiling, surveying, the other's effect of immaculate clothing, fine bearing, and striking looks, and marking the set of his countenance.

"You look very correct today," he remarked pleasantly.

The Prince nodded without humor. "It is one of my days for being correct," he answered. "I feel it in the air it is a day to be on my guard. I have these sensations sometimes not often, mercifully! and I have learned to pay attention to them."

Dupontel smiled again. "To me it seems a cheerful day," he said. "And you begin it well, at any rate."

"How, then?" The Prince, coaxing on his grey gloves, turned narrowed eyes upon him. "In what way do I begin it well?"

Dupontel produced a pocket-book from the breast of his coat. "I have to settle with you over last evening," he said. "Two thousand, wasn't it? I call that beginning any day well."

He dropped the notes upon the little table where the Prince's hat and cane lay.

The Prince picked up the notes.

"Thanks!" he said. He looked at the young man almost with curiosity. "Sure it's convenient?"

For answer, Dupontel showed him his pocketbook, with still half a dozen thousand-franc notes in it.

"I see," said the Prince.

He still hesitated for a moment or two, as if touched by some compunction, before he put the notes into his pocket. It had occurred to him vaguely that he might propitiate his fortune by sacrificing this money make himself, as it were, by a timely generosity, the creditor of good luck. But it was not the kind of thing he was used to do.

"Eh bien!" he said, and put the notes out of sight.

"And now," said Dupontel, "let us eat."

"Yes," said the Prince slowly. "That is the next thing, I suppose. And presently I will tell you a reason why this is a day to be careful of."

In the elevator that bore them toward the street, he began of a sudden to search his pockets. Dupontel, watching, him in surprise, saw a real worry replace the customary lofty impassivity of his face.

"You have lost something?" he asked.

"Yes," answered the Prince shortly. "Take us up again at once," he ordered the attendant.

"I will not keep you a moment," he said to Dupontel, when the elevator had reached his own floor again, and he entered his apartment quickly.

He found his valet still in the bedroom, putting it deftly in order, always with that secret and furtive quality of look and movement. The Prince, tall, notably splendid in person, halted in the doorway; the man, mean, little, shaped by servile and menial uses, stopped in the middle of the room and returned his gaze warily. There was an instant of silence.

"I had a coin," began the Prince. "A gold coin, not a French one! I had it in my pocket last night. Where is it?"

Never was anything so shallow as the other's pretence of distressed ignorance. It was as if he scarcely troubled to dissemble his amusement and malice.

"But I have not seen it, M'sieur le Prince," he said. "If M'sieur le Prince wishes, I will search. Doubtless."

"I am in a hurry," interrupted the Prince. "It is a Mexican coin worth ten francs only." He held out a coin. "Here is a ten-franc piece. Be quick."

They were equals for the moment; the relationship was plain to both of them. With no failing of his countenance, the valet drew the missing, piece from his pocket.

"Mexican?" he said. "I thought it was Spanish."

The coins changed hands. Neither of them failed in his attitude; they were well matched.

The Prince rejoined Dupontel with his Mexican gold piece still in his hand.

"It was this I had left behind," he said, showing the thin-worn gold disc. "It is well, a talisman of mine, a sort of mascot. I was nearly going without it. Rather than do that I would stay at home."

Dupontel laughed. "You are superstitious, then?" he said lightly. "It is not much to look at, your talisman."

The Prince shook his head; it seemed impossible to make him smile that morning.

"That is true," he agreed, "but a man must put faith in something. When you have heard what I have to tell you, you will understand that."

The streets, those lively streets of Paris that mask the keenness of their commerce with so festive a face, were sunlit as they passed on their way, and along the boulevards the trees were gracious with young green. They went at the even and leisurely pace which is natural in that city of many halting-places two men worth turning to look at, so perfectly did each, in his particular way, typify his world. Both were tall, easy-moving, sure and restrained in every gesture. Dupontel at twenty-five, for all the boyishness that sometimes showed in him, had already his finished personal effect; and the Prince, white-haired, dark-browed, with a certain austerity of expression, was as complete a thing as a work of art.

"Then what is it, exactly, that you fear from this Carigny?" asked Dupontel, when the Prince had told him of the letter. "I have heard the story, of course; but I never heard he was dangerous."

"It is not he that is dangerous," said the Prince.

"What, then?"

The Prince shook his head doubtfully. Such men as he seldom have a confidant, but he was used to speak to Dupontel with more freedom than to any other.

"Things are dangerous," he answered. "There is bad luck about; I tell you, I feel it. And now, this business of Carigny cropping up, rising like a ghost of the past to demand a reckoning!" He shuddered; it was like the shudder of a man who feels a sudden chill. "A reckoning!" he repeated. "At this rate, one is never quit of anything."

They were nearing the restaurant at which they were to lunch. Dupontel touched his companion lightly on the arm.

"You are depressed," he said. "You must gather your forces, Monpavon. You mustn't let Carigny find you in a state like this; it would make things easy for him."

The Prince made a weary little gesture of assent. "I shall be ready for him," he said. "If only-"

"If only what?"

They were at the door of the restaurant. A page like a scarlet doll held open the door for them; a Swiss, ornately uniformed, stood frozen at the salute. The Prince's somber eyes passed unseeing over these articles of human furniture.

"If only I don't get a sign," he said; "like going out without my Mexican coin, you know that would be a sign. If only I can avoid that and a couple of other things I'll be ready enough for Monsieur Carigny when he comes."

"Tiens!" said Dupontel. "You and your signs, c'est epatant!"

He was amused, and even a little contemptuous. He had not yet been long enough at play to reach that stage when the gambler is the servant of small private fetishes when an incident at the beginning of the day can fill him with fears or hopes, and all life has a meaning which expresses itself in the run of the cards.

They took their places at the table reserved for them. Waiters stood aloof, effacing themselves, prepared to pounce upon their smallest need and annihilate it. Dupontel breathed a number as he sat down, and the rotund and reverend wine-waiter, wearing a chain of office, tried to express in his face respectful esteem for a man who could give such an order.

"You need a stimulant, an encouragement," said Dupontel, leaning across to the Prince. "Therefore I have ordered for us."

He had his hands joined under his chin and his elbows on the table. The Prince, with something like a crisp oath, snatched at the salt-cellar which his movement would have overset, and saved it saved it with grains of salt sliding on the very rim, but none fallen to the table. He made sure of this fact anxiously.

"That was a near thing," he said, looking up at Dupontel. There was actually color in his face.

"Another fraction of a second and" His gesture completed the sentence.

"My dear fellow!" remonstrated Dupontel.

"That was the second," said the Prince. "First I nearly left my coin at home that was my servant's doing. Then the salt is all but spilled my friend does that. If I had a wife, I should expect to owe the third danger to her. Who will bring it to me, I wonder?"

"You are extraordinary, with your signs and dangers," said Dupontel. "I never heard you speak like this before. And, in any case, you have averted two perils."

"I have averted two," agreed the Prince. "You are right; that in itself is almost a sign. It it gives me hope for the third the blind man."

"Eh? The blind man? What blind man?"

The Prince took a spoonful of soup.

"Sometimes I forget how young you are," he said. "A blind man, of course, is nothing to you. You give him an alms, touching his hand when you put the money into it, and go on to the club to play bridge. But if I, by any chance of the street, were to touch a blind man, I should go home and go to bed. I have my share of prudence me! and that is a risk I do not take. No!"

He interrupted himself to drink from his glass, while Dupontel sat back and prepared, with a gesture of utter impatience, to be contemptuous and argumentative.

"Carigny," said the Prince, setting his glass down, "Carigny, in the old days, believed that too. But he was not prudent. That night we played, that last night of which he writes in his letter, there was a blind man who begged of him. And when he would have dropped a franc in his hand, the creature groped suddenly for the coin. We were walking to the club together, and I saw it, standing aside meanwhile. It was an old debris of a man, who begged in a voice that whispered and croaked, and his hand was shriveled and purple, and it wavered and trembled as he held it out. Because he was blind, with eyelids swollen and discolored, Carigny said, as he drew the money from his pocket: 'Here is a franc, my friend!' Then the old creature groped, as I have said, with a jerk of his inhuman claw, and grabbed the money from Carigny before he could let it fall, and I saw their hands touch. Carigny would not have played that night but that we had appointed to play."

"You could have let him off till next day," said Dupontel.

The Prince shook his head. "In those times," he said, "it was not the custom to break one's engagements neither to break them nor to allow them to be broken."

"I should like to see this Carigny of yours," said Dupontel thoughtfully. "When do you expect him to call on you?"

"His letter says 'as soon as possible,'" answered the Prince. "That constitutes in itself an engagement which Carigny will not fail to keep. He will come this afternoon."

Their meal achieved itself perfectly, like a ritual There arrived the time when the Prince set down his tiny coffee-cup and leaned back detachedly, while the waiter with the bill went through his celebrated impersonation of a man receiving a favor. Together they passed out between the great glass doors to the street.

"You will walk?" inquired Dupontel.

"As usual," said the Prince. It was his custom to pass the time between lunch and the hour when he was likely to find a game of bridge in strolling; it served for exercise.

"But," suggested the young man, "you might meet a blind man! Wouldn't it be better to go straight to the club?"

"And meet one on the way there?" The Prince shook his head. "No, my friend. That is a chance one must take. One can, however, keep one's eyes open."

In the Place de la Concorde they actually did meet a blind man a lean, bowed man feeling his way along the curb with a stick deftly enough, so that, as he was on the wrong side of the sidewalk, it would have been easy enough to brush against him in passing. It was the Prince who first perceived him approaching. He touched Dupontel and pointed.

"Parbleu!" exclaimed Dupontel. He looked strangely at the blind bearer of fate and then at his companion. The Prince was smiling now, but not in mirth.

"Let us make room for him," he said; and they stepped into the roadway to let him pass.

What was strange was that when he came abreast of them he paused, with his face nosing and peering in his blindness, and felt before him with an extended hand, as if he had expected to find something in his way. The hand and the skinny wrist, protruding from the frayed sleeve and searching the empty air, affected Dupontel unpleasantly; they touched the fund of credulity in him which is at the root of all men who believe in nothing. He watched the blind man like an actor in a scene till he moved on again, with his stick tracing the edge of the curb and his strained face unresponsive to the sunlight.

"What was he doing?" he asked, then.

The Prince's wry smile showed again. "Doing?" he repeated, "why, he was feeling for me."

Dupontel shrugged, but not in disapproval this time. His imagination was burdened with a new sense of his companion's life, complex with difficulties, haunted by portents like specters of good and evil fortune.

"But, at all events, he did not touch you!" he said at last.

"No!" The Prince swung his cane, drawing up his tall, trim figure, and stepping out briskly. "No, he did not touch me. They dog me, these, these tokens of the devil; but I am not caught. It is I that save myself. After all, mon cher, it seems possible that this may be Carigny's bad day not mine!"

Dupontel had not meant to accompany the Prince to his club that day; his purpose had been to leave him at the door and go elsewhere. But it was possible that his meeting with Carigny might be something which it would be well to have seen; and, besides, his affairs were gaining a strange hue; glamour was in them. He felt a little thrill when the massive club porter, approaching them in the hall, spoke Carigny's name.

"Monsieur Carigny telephoned," said the porter. "He particularly desired that Monsieur le Prince should be told, as soon as he arrived, that Monsieur Carigny would call at half-past four."

The Prince nodded. "I shall be upstairs, in the card-room," he answered, and passed on.

In the card-room were several men of the Prince's who had known Carigny in his Paris days, while there was scarcely a man present who had not heard some version of the Carigny story. To certain of them the Prince spoke of the visit he was expecting. He had decided that, since the meeting was not by any means to be avoided or hidden, it would best serve him to announce it to take his part in the drama and squeeze it of what credit he could. It spread through the room and through the club like a scandal. There was a throng in the room, expectant, hungry for the possibility of a scene. In the recess of a tall window, the Prince, superb in his self-possession, a figure in a world of players that was past, with his pale, severe face impassive under his white hair, made the crowd of them seem vulgar and raucous by contrast with him. Dupontel, watching him, had a moment of consternation; the Prince seemed a thing too supremely complete, too perfect as a product of his world, to risk upon the turn of the cards.

A club servant entered, bearing a card on a salver, and the talk stilled as he presented it to the Prince. He, in converse with a veteran who had known Carigny, took the card and held it in his fingers without looking at it while he finished what he was saying. All eyes were on him; it was a neat piece of social bravado. He glanced at the card at last.

"Announce Monsieur Carigny," he said to the servant, and went on talking. Dupontel felt like cheering him. The talk resumed, in a changed key.

The door opened, and the servant was once more visible, standing back against it, not without a sense of his importance as, say, a scene-shifter in the play. His voice, rolling the r, was a flat bellow of ceremony.

"Monsieur Car-rigny," he announced, "and Monsieur Georges Car-rigny!"

Every one turned. Through the door which the servant held open there advanced two men. The first was bearded, a large man, definitely elderly, who walked with a curious deliberation of tread and looked neither to the right nor to the left. The younger, following at his elbow, was possibly Dupontel's age. In him, not the clothes alone, but the face, keen lipped, quiet-eyed, not quite concealing its reserves of vitality under its composure, proclaimed the American.

The men in the room, moving aside, made an avenue from the door to the window in which, the Prince stood. The Prince came along it to greet his guest. As they halted, face to face, Dupontel saw that the young stranger touched the elder on the arm.

The Prince seemed to have doubts. He remembered Carigny as a slim youth; the stranger was burly, with a bush of beard and a red face.

"It is Carigny?" inquired the Prince, hesitating.

The stranger smiled. "Yes," he answered. "Monpavon, is it not?"

Even his French had changed, become the French of a foreigner.

"You have been a long time coming for your revenge," said the Prince. "But you are welcome always, Carigny."

He held out his hand, and again the young man touched the elder. As if he hesitated to join hands with the Prince, Carigny gave his hand, slowly, awkwardly; but his grip, when he had done it, was firm. They stood, clasping hands, under the inquisitive eyes of the others.

"Since we are to play," said Carigny, "you must allow me to present you to my son. He does not play; I have discouraged him. But he will read my cards for me. You do not object?"

Their clasped hands fell apart. The Prince looked his incomprehension. The young man was making him a bow of sorts.

"I am charmed," he answered. "But read your cards? I don't understand."

Dupontel arrested an impulse to step forward, to interrupt, to interfere in some manner. He saw that Carigny smiled.

"Yes," he answered. "Tell me which card is which, you know. You see, Monpavon, for the last five years I have been blind!"

His voice, with its foreign accent rendering strange his precise and old-fashioned French, continued to explain. But Dupontel did not hear what it said. He was looking at the Prince. Save for an astonished knitting of the brows, he had not moved; he preserved, under those watching eyes, his attitude. The worst had come to pass the thing he feared had ambushed him? and he was facing it. But presently he raised his right hand, the hand that had touched Carigny's, looked at it thoughtfully, and brushed it with his left. If he had any virtue, he was exhibiting it now. One could defeat him but not discountenance him.

"Certainly," he was saying presently. "The right of choice is yours, Carigny. Ecarte, since you wish it, by all means."

Dupontel, to whom he had explained himself, knew what that handshake had meant. In the move toward the card-table, he caught his eye. The Prince smiled at him. "You see how useless it is to strive," he seemed to say.

The pretence that the onlookers were present by chance was gone when the Prince and his adversary sat down opposite to each other at the little green table. The onlookers thronged about them, frankly curious. The young man, Carigny's son, stood leaning over his father's shoulder. Dupontel was at the back of his friend. He saw the green table across the Prince's white head. The deal fell to the Prince.

He had the pack in his hand when he spoke across to Carigny.

"Carigny," he said. The blind man lifted his face to listen. "The last game was a short one."

The other nodded. "Make it as short as you like," he said. "Make it one hand, if it pleases you, Monpavon. I shall be satisfied."

"One hand!"

"Certainly; if that is short enough for you," said Carigny. "But the stakes you remember them?"

He asked the question as if he would warn his adversary, and as if he himself were certain of the issue. He had the demeanor of a man who undertakes a problem of which he knows the answer.

"Be careful," breathed Dupontel at the Prince's back.

"You lost, let me see!" replied the Prince, unheeding Dupontel's whisper. "It was four hundred thousand francs, I think."

The bearded face opposite him smiled. "You have not forgotten, I see!"

The Prince nodded. "One hand, then!"

He proceeded to deal. He was certain of losing, or he would not have consented to such an outrage upon the game's refinements. And yet, he had hopes; the spirit that presides over cards is capricious.

The young man had sorted the cards and placed them in his father's hands, and was whispering in his ear. Then he stood upright. The Prince waited.

"You propose?" he inquired.

"No," said the other; "I play."

There was a movement among the spectators as some shifted in an endeavor to see the cards. Dupontel was edged from his post for a moment. When he had shouldered his way back to it, the play had already begun. It seemed to him almost indecent that such an affair should rest on a single hand of cards; it was making free with matters of importance. As he gained a sight of the table again, Carigny scored his second trick and the third card fell. The Prince trumped it. The young man smiled and whispered. Another card was played, and the Prince won again, He laid his last card face down on the table.

"Carigny," he said.

"Have you played?" asked the other.

"No," said the Prince. "Listen! I will make you a proposal. I do not know what your last card is; you do not know mine. It rests on that card, our four hundred thousand francs. I may win, in spite of everything. But I offer you half the stakes now, if you like; two hundred thousand instead of four and we will not play that last card."

"Eh?" The blind man hid his card with his hand. His son bent over him, whispering. A man next to Dupontel nudged him. "What is Monpavon's card?" he murmured. Dupontel did not know. The cards had been the least part of the affair to him. The Prince sat still, waiting.

"Very well," said Carigny, at last. "I am willing, Monpavon. Two hundred thousand, eh?"

"Two hundred thousand," corroborated the Prince.

He reached for the pack. Before anyone could protest, he had slipped his card into it and mingled it with the others beyond identification.

"We are quits, then," he was saying to Carigny, and once more the ancient adversaries shook hands.

"But what was the card?" asked a dozen men at once.

The Prince let his hard, serene eye wander over them. He was walking toward the door, guiding Carigny with a hand on his arm. There was a flicker of a smile on his face. Without answering, he passed out. To this day, no man knows what card he held.

Milton Keynes UK
Ingram Content Group UK Ltd.
UKHW010742080324
438959UK00004B/322